PR

THE SINKING OF THE ANGIE PIPER

"Chris Riley's debut novel *The Sinking of the Angie Piper* does everything right: great and complicated characters, shining prose, and a story of emotional and physical conflict that will resonate long after you turn the last page. Both literate and heart-pounding at the same time, it's the perfect pairing of a coming-of-age story and a gripping adventure set amidst the unforgiving seas off the Alaskan coast. Here is the debut of an exciting new voice that you must not miss."
—James Rollins, *#1 New York Times* bestselling author of *The Bone Labyrinth*

"A compelling tale of survival against the odds—highly readable."
—William Napier, international bestselling author of the Attila Trilogy

"Against a richly textured backdrop of Alaskan fishing culture, a crew of mentally and spiritually flawed men clash with each other and the elements in Riley's gripping debut novel. Themes of tenderness and regret play out even amid a desperate struggle for survival. You'll feel the icy spray as *The Sinking of the Angie Piper* sucks you in and doesn't let go."
—Amy Rogers, ScienceThrillers.com

"With eloquent prose, Chris Riley's *The Sinking of the Angie Piper* tells a gripping coming-of-age story about friendship, loss, and the events that forever transform a young man—all

in a setting rendered so perfectly I can practically feel the cold salt water of the Bay of Alaska during tanner crab season. This is a terrific debut by an author well worth watching."
—Chris Culver, *New York Times* bestselling author of the Ash Rashid series

"Whether it's casual details about crabbing the frigid Alaska sea or exploring the boiling maelstrom of the human heart, Chris Riley knows his stuff. The result is entertaining, illuminating and a fine ride."
—Robert Ferrigno, *New York Times* bestselling author

THE SINKING
OF THE
ANGIE PIPER

THE SINKING
OF THE
ANGIE PIPER

Chris Riley

coffeetownpress
Seattle, WA

coffeetownpress

Coffeetown Press
PO Box 70515
Seattle, WA 98127

For more information go to: www.coffeetownpress.com
www.chrisrileyauthor.com

Cover design by Sabrina Sun

THE SINKING OF THE ANGIE PIPER
Copyright © 2017 by Chris Riley

ISBN: 978-1-60381-389-1 (Trade Paper)
ISBN: 978-1-60381-390-7 (eBook)

Library of Congress Control Number: 2017932365

Printed in the United States of America

For Danny

ACKNOWLEDGMENTS

———•———

I'T'S AMAZING WHAT happens when you write a novel. The concept behind this story hit me one morning, while swimming laps. It was a lonely idea yet to find a voice. And before it did, I would come to discover just how generous people can be.

First and foremost, I must acknowledge the members of my critique group, my first readers, and editors: Chris Crowe, Sally Ann Barnes, Tod Todd, Lee Garrett, Denny Grayson, Jane O'Riva, Leonard Little, Chris Smith, Amy Rogers, Caroline Williams, Jesse Cox, James Czajkowski, and Steve and Judy Prey. A warm thanks goes to my Samoan cousin, Robert Netzler, for giving me "Loni." I'd like to thank my writing colleague, Michael Wehunt, for showing me a few things about the craft. Special recognition goes to Leslie Edwards, for his knowledge of Coast Guard operations and protocols … and to Patrick Sherman, for teaching me much about the commercial crabbing industry.

Of course, I am in great debt to everyone at Coffeetown Press—Catherine Treadgold, Jennifer McCord, and feature editor Scott Driscoll, whose combined efforts helped bring this story to life. An undying gratitude goes to my agent, Mark Gottlieb. Without him, you wouldn't be reading this right now.

Last but not least, I must thank my family—Sherry, Jackson, and Jessica—whose love and laughter serve as the brightest stars in my universe.

Finally ... I have yet to step foot on a crabbing vessel, let alone work its deck. But I've been to Alaska, and I have met my share of Danny Wilsons. I hope these merits are brought to mind and I am forgiven should any errors of fact or detail be discovered within these pages.

CHAPTER 1

———•———

THE FRONT DOOR to McCrawley's—made of solid oak, wrapped with wrought iron, and as heavy as a seven-by-seven-foot crab pot—swings open toward the harbor to reveal a stunning view of Kodiak's main attraction: fishing. An array of seiners, trollers, crabbers, and other commercial vessels are moored fifty yards away. If not for the fishing industry, Kodiak would be nothing more than a muddy village. Open during the day, the bar supports its town's commercial endeavor by serving an excellent fish and chip basket for lunch, which goes down quite well, I might add, with a pint of McCrawley's Three Sheet Porter, its signature ale. According to several outdoor magazines, nothing gets a person ready to tackle the last frontier better than a night out at Kodiak's finest brewery.

But on those nights prior to the opening of crab season, unless a person is well known in the fishing community or just a bona fide idiot, it is prudent to stay the hell away from McCrawley's. On those nights, the joint is ruled by the Alaskan fishermen—some of the world's craziest, and sometimes meanest, individuals.

And so, on our third night in town, I wasn't too sure about bringing Danny along to McCrawley's. We had spent the last several hours of the day preparing the *Angie Piper* to set sail the next morning, and even though I was anxious to let off steam that night, I still had my doubts about dragging my life-long buddy into one of the roughest places on earth.

"But what about Danny?" I asked, after Loni hollered for us to go get in the truck.

"What about him?" Loni replied.

"Well, he doesn't even drink. He'll probably get bored."

In response, Loni gave me a shocked stare, as if I had just asked him how many crab were in the sea. "You think Danny would get bored in McCrawley's?" he said, sliding into his coat and zipping it up. "And sitting alone on a ship he gonna live on for the next couple of months will be good?"

Even so, I returned Loni's bewildered gaze with a concerned one of my own.

"You know, Ed, I'm betting that boy can arm wrestle something good now, eh?" Loni added.

And then it hit me: of course. Even though Danny's presence would most likely get us into trouble, as it often did back in high school, it was just as likely that he would end up winning us a shitload of money arm wrestling.

"Go get in the truck, Danny," I said.

McCrawley's is located along Rezanof Drive, west of the general store. Every fisherman, processor, and local yokel has made his or her way through the door of this establishment at one time or another. No one would argue that McCrawley's doesn't carry with it a certain "homey" atmosphere, one that is punctuated by a floor littered with peanut shells. All those salted peanuts make a person thirsty—and the broken shells do one hell of a job at soaking up spills—but people appreciate the hospitality found in free food, especially here in Alaska, where the winter nights are so cold and so lonesome that sometimes the only thing that will get a person through to the next light of day is the warm familiarity of food and drink.

Danny and I were born and raised in Anchorage, a place that gifted us with its own sense of familiarity. Life was much different in that city than in Kodiak. In Anchorage, we had comfort and stability. Our routines were common to the average person. But we were adults now, so our priorities had changed. At least mine had, which was why I got into commercial fishing—a career with routines like none other. Dangerous and difficult as this job was, the prospect of earning more money than I knew what to do with was tempting, to say the least. Danny simply didn't think this way. He was here because of me. This had something to do with the guilt I'd been harboring for much of my life. That I'd failed to defend Danny against his many bullies was only the half of it. At one time, my friend had seen the worst in me, and I had yet to reconcile with that. I owed Danny. Bringing him on board the *Angie Piper* was my attempt at redemption. The job offered good pay and an adventure on the high seas. He'd never come any closer to becoming what he desired most in the world—a Navy SEAL.

When we got to the bar, I had second thoughts about bringing Danny. "I don't know, Loni," I said, once we'd pulled into the parking lot. A sea of rugged vehicles surrounded us— stout four-by-fours with flared fenders caked in mud, shotgun racks, and bulky tool chests mounted high in their beds. Above, the sky was a nameless shade of black and gray. Flashbacks from our high school days hit me, and when I stepped out of the truck I thought about those times when Danny had been thrown into trashcans or had his head dunked into a toilet.

"Maybe this isn't such a good idea after all." But before I could say another word, we were walking through the front door of McCrawley's, into a smoke-filled room containing a fifty-foot-long mahogany bar. A hundred glassy stares greeted us from the dead animals mounted on the walls. Another hundred or so lively (albeit watery) stares from the fishermen and regulars tracked our entrance.

"Just find us a booth," Loni said, motioning to Dave and Salazar sitting at the farthest end of the bar. "I'll be right back." Our crewmates had a head start on us. They were already a few drinks into the night. Though I still worried about whether Dave welcomed Danny as one of our crewmen, the situation with him had calmed over the past few days. As the *Angie Piper*'s engineer, he had spent the majority of those days below deck, making sure the engines were running nice and tight. He stayed out of our way while Danny and I prepped the boat, and we were happy to stay out of his. But here we were in McCrawley's, confronted by Dave's glowering face. I couldn't help but wonder how the night would end. And how tomorrow would begin. Once we started fishing, we would all be on deck working in tight quarters for what would seem like an endless stretch of time. It was going to be hell, even without this trouble. Alaska's winter seas could be ruthless in their own right.

"You let me know when you want to leave, Danny," I said. We sat down at a nearby table. Loni had told us to get a booth, but we were lucky to find what seats we did. Although still early, the bar was near capacity. "Just let me know," I repeated. But Danny's Grand-Canyon-wide smile and lively blue eyes told me he was nowhere near ready.

"This place is like where SEALs hang out," he said, looking around.

"Yeah," I replied, halfheartedly, "I suppose you're right." Danny had seen every Special Forces movie ever made. And since the vast majority of those movies seemed to have a bar scene in them, I had little doubt as to what my friend was thinking about at that moment. "Always living the dream, isn't that right, buddy?"

Danny looked at me, nodded, and shouted, "Hooyah!"

A few minutes later, Loni walked up with a beer in his hand. "You tell Jill to put your drinks on my tab. I'll be buying for you, brothers."

I looked around the bar and spotted Jill standing near the back, loading a tray of drinks. Her long black hair trailed past a checkered blouse, a slim waist, and curvy hips, ending at a pair of smooth legs. Jill often wore shorts, no matter what the time of year, and she was a dream to look at, especially at the end of a long fishing season. A true Alaskan beauty queen—picturesque, but with a temperament as formidable as a grizzly's. Jill took shit from no one.

"Thanks, Loni," I replied, "I'll let her know." Then I motioned to a tall rectangular table in the middle of the room. Absent of any chairs or a stool, this table was McCrawley's designated wrestling booth. "So hey," I said, "when should we get Danny over there at the table?" My anxiety was still turning screws inside my gut.

"Let 'em get a few down, Ed," Loni replied, with his customary smile. "Let 'em get stupid drunk, then we'll see."

I cracked my knuckles and looked around, wondering just how drunk people were, until my stare once again settled on Dave. He was sitting on a stool behind the bar, a shot of whiskey touching his lips. He looked like an overfed transient, with his boxlike head, unkempt, dishwater hair, and scraggly beard. There was a certain ugliness below his surface as well, and I had seen it only days before. Danny had seen it too. Dave made sure of that. He was hell-bent on keeping my friend from working on board the *Angie Piper*. But it wasn't clear why.

"Anyone know when the captain'll be here?" I asked. I figured that if Danny was going to wrestle, it would be a good thing for Fred to witness—further proof to my claim of how abnormally strong my friend was. Even though many arm wrestling enthusiasts would argue vehemently that "technique" was more important than sheer muscle, I doubted many of them had ever witnessed the inhuman strength and mental tenacity of a kid like Danny.

"Yeah," Loni replied. "Be here soon. Could be now, could be later. Could be much later. You know the captain."

Jill strutted over to our table just then through the sea of grimy peanut shells, pen and tablet in hand, her full smile and curvy figure commanding the attention of every leering fisherman in the place. "What'll it be, boys?" She turned and gave Danny a double take. "And who's your friend, Loni?" she asked rather hesitantly.

"You know Ed." Loni raised his beer in my direction. "But this here is our greenhorn—Danny-boy. And he's gonna be our wrestling champion tonight."

"Oh, really?" Jill replied. She gave Danny an affectionate smile, but I could tell she believed Loni's claim as much as she would've believed Danny was a Navy SEAL.

"Okay," Jill said. "Well, good luck with that, 'cause he'll certainly need it. No offense to you, Danny, but Sleet Wellens is here tonight. He's a former state champ." And with that, Jill took our order and returned to the bar.

I watched her leave, thinking about her skepticism. If she only knew …. Briefly, I thought back to the time I'd seen Danny unload eighty-pound bags of concrete out of his dad's truck or the times we'd wrestled and he'd pinned my face to the ground. When we were sixteen, he dead-lifted the rear-end of my first car—a '79 VW Bug—so I could change the tire. People underestimated Danny, probably because of his size, certainly because of his looks. It always felt good when he proved them wrong, though.

Thirty minutes later, the captain came in and sat down at our table. He was looking relaxed, his eyelids drooping, a permanent grin spread across his face. We were ready to get on with the season, and no one showed it more than Fred. As wonderful as Alaska is—with its untamed wilderness and sea, its bounty of wildlife roaming heedlessly, and its charming pockets of humanity found in the many rustic villages and cozy fishing towns—Alaska was still plagued with "Rumor's Disease." And the rumor on that night, in McCrawley's, was that the following tanner crab season was sure to be one of the best in years. Nothing could make a captain smile more than a rumor like that—nothing other than running into port with a ship full of crab.

"We don't need no season, Captain," said Loni. "Danny-boy gonna make us rich tonight."

"You don't say?" replied Fred.

"No, I do say. Danny's gonna take the bar, own it for sure." Loni smiled and nudged his beer toward the wrestling booth. Two men were there getting ready, hands clasped together, their faces ugly and grim.

"Well, shit," Fred said, with a smirk. "What the hell do I know?" He looked around, spotted Dave standing at the bar, and waved. Dave nodded in return, and I was reminded of the tension I'd been feeling for the past couple of days.

"Keep your eye on those guys, Danny," I said, wiping a bead of sweat from my brow. "See how they do it." Danny didn't seem too interested in the wrestling match, however. He was still eyeballing the surroundings, a stupid smile on his face, guzzling 7UP like it was on its way out.

He sat like that for a solid hour, happy as a clam three feet in the mud. And after a while, I too began to relax, mollified by the dim yellow lights, the smell of peanuts and stale beer, and the ubiquitous cackling of excited fishermen. It seemed that with each gulp of ale and each passing minute, my concerns drained away, one by one. I even let go of Dave and his grumpy attitude.

But then, out of nowhere, Loni stood on the table and yelled across the bar, "Hey! You fat boys wanna see muscle? I got it for you!" He held his beer mug high. "We gonna kick your asses now, you see." Then he stumbled and fell down into Fred's arms. The captain laughed, swore, and then laughed some more.

"Captain, I think Loni might be drunk," I said.

"Oh, this ain't nothing, Ed. He's just getting started." Fred hoisted Loni from under the shoulders, settling him back into his chair. "Ain't that right, you crazy Poly?"

"We gonna kick some asses now—right here," Loni shouted in return. "Give 'em hell, Danny-boy!"

Danny stood, raised his glass, and hollered, "Hooyah,

master chief!" He gulped down the last swallow of his 7UP and walked over to the wrestling booth.

During this briefest of moments, I sat in my chair, slightly befuddled. I don't think I had ever seen Danny act like this— almost as if he were drunk. There was something about that bar, about Loni, maybe even Kodiak, or perhaps the anticipation of getting on with the crab season. Something had brought out a side to Danny that I had never witnessed before. Sometime later, it occurred to me that he might have been in his element that night, standing smack-dab in the middle of the bar scene in a Special Forces movie, loving every minute of it.

"Let's go, Danny-boy," cried Loni. "Make us some money!" Even before me, Loni was up and out of his seat, trailing Danny to the booth, cheering him on.

It came to my attention that I was a nervous wreck. My hands felt clammy, my knees weak, and my breathing was shallow. Why was I feeling this anxious? After all, the worst that could happen would be that Danny would lose. Then I'd be back in my chair drinking beer. Of course, I'd hear about it from Dave, but that wasn't the main source of my anxiety. I had made claims regarding Danny's strength, and I wanted them to prove true.

Behind Loni, several fishermen were laughing hysterically. In their cups, these men could be cruel. They pointed at Danny, spit beer from their mouths, heckled and mocked my friend. Even Jill, leaning against a corner of the bar, shook her head and rolled her eyes. It all seemed so familiar.

Standing next to her was Dave. He wasn't laughing like the others. His face was a mask of disgust and his eyes were as cold as the Bering Sea. He stared right at Danny, and then right at me. There was something else there, on that face of his—something in his stare that established a surprising, yet ugly understanding between us. An "aha" moment of sorts, but one that did not sit well with me. It was as if Dave had suddenly recognized a darker shade to my character. Perhaps he suspected a certain history with Danny. Whatever the case, the man was obviously bragging with his eyes, gloating. He could have been just another schoolyard bully, at that moment, shoving me against the wall while he took a cruel swing at Danny. But more distressing was the heavy, sinking feeling his stare left me with—as if I was somehow looking into a mirror. I'd felt this way before, in the past, more than once … when I'd let my friend down. Back in high school, a bully named Robbie used to give me that same look, whenever he gave Danny a wedgie. With one glance, he dared me to do something about it, adding that if I didn't, I was condoning his actions.

Danny stepped up and tapped the current victor on the shoulder. "Hey," he said, in a voice both innocent and non-threatening. "Can I have a turn now?"

The man's name was Brandon and I knew him. He was a middle-aged fisherman with a barrel chest. His forearms looked like sacks stuffed with rocks. He laughed in Danny's face, laughed real hard, from the gut, and then said, "What … you?" That's when I put my money down. Next to mine came Loni's, the captain's, and then, to my great astonishment, Dave's.

Two minutes later, Brandon stared in disbelief, rubbing the pain out of his elbow, cursing his luck. Danny had dethroned the current lord of the booth.

Howling with delight, Loni jumped up and down, spilt his beer and shouted obscenities at the whole bar. "Danny-boy kicked your fucking asses!" It's a good thing Loni was so well-known and well-liked here in Kodiak. That boisterous attitude of his could have easily been the death of him.

There was nothing I could do at this point but continue to place bets, sit back, and watch. I knew how strong Danny was. I figured there was a chance he'd win every arm wrestling match the bar could serve up. For the first hour, that's exactly what happened. Danny wrestled four times in that hour, making the two of us over five hundred dollars apiece.

"You see that, Captain?" shouted Loni. "Danny gonna take the bar!"

The mood had changed. Those lingering, scowling fishermen turned serious when they realized that Danny was the real deal. Or perhaps in their minds, he was the real "something." They stood around, scratching their heads, pondering my friend. They questioned his slanted eyes, his enormous grin with those exposed, crooked teeth, his slurred speech and innocent demeanor. They even began to call him names, such as, "The Alaskan Monster," "The Kodiak Troll," and, "Danny the Bear." Just like in high school, yet in good humor for once. And by Danny's third victory, many of those fishermen had been placing bets on him. By his third victory, those same fishermen were cheering him on, slapping him high fives, bringing him 7UP and peanuts, and nearly pissing themselves from the fun of it all. Even Dave seemed impressed, judging by the look that crossed his face every time Danny won a match.

"What'd I tell you, Captain?" I said, grinning, after Danny defeated two more challengers.

Fred raised his beer in response. "Well, shit, Ed. You know I never doubted your boy."

Sleet Wellens lingered around the booth. I could tell he had been studying my friend. His brown face, native to the wild lands of Alaska—a true Athabaskan, Eyak, Tlingit, or full-blooded Aleut, perhaps—looked on with a perplexed yet admiring fixation. Was he going to pass on wrestling for the night, dumbfounded as he might have been over the current "creature in the booth"? I didn't think so. He was just going to wait awhile, let Danny tire out, if that were ever possible. And Sleet got in another hour of waiting before the whole bar began to call his name.

It was well into the evening, close to midnight. The sun had long since dipped below the blue horizon of Alaska. In less than seven hours the next day would be here, with its promise of a killer tanner season. But nobody, nobody at all, was leaving

McCrawley's. After winning eight consecutive wrestling matches, Danny Wilson was due to square off with Sleet Wellens. I had made over a thousand dollars on my friend, and I bet all of it on this match, the last match. Beside me, Loni was a train wreck of excitement, drunk but functional, screaming profanities at Sleet, throwing money onto the table. Our captain was now over by Salazar and Dave, drinking, talking, laughing. Even Dave seemed happy, smiling and joking with the others, which left me in the dark, wondering.

Amid a great cheer from the patrons of the bar, Sleet shouldered his way to the booth. He took a position opposite Danny, looking like a bear himself. With a grim smile, he shook Danny's hand. I guess Sleet had much more than money to lose that night.

They grasped hands and got ready. Sleet was twice the size of Danny, his arms like solid branches of oak after years of hauling pots, or pulling nets, or cutting trees, or whatever that man did to earn a living. He stared at Danny's face, his eyes deadly serious now. Danny stared at the ground and chewed on a peanut. *Ready, set, go.*

They grunted. They strained. Sleet cursed. Danny sniffed and blew air through tight lips, making a whistling sound, as the two of them fought for the crown. Men huddled silently around the table, as silent as a gathering of drunks could be during a legendary arm-wrestling match. And then, just like that, to everybody's jubilation or heartache, it was over.

The longest, most anticipated battle that night ended after two grueling minutes of muscular tension between two men: a trueborn, proud native, tough-as-nails state arm-wrestling champion and a freak of nature who had not once looked up as he tore his opponent down.

As soon as Danny defeated Sleet Wellens, he reached for his glass of 7UP and sipped delicately through the straw, like a child savoring his first root beer float. I almost died from laughter. After all, Danny had broken a sweat and needed his refreshment.

"Just who the hell are you, kid?" asked an exhausted Sleet.

Loni ended that night with a triumphant howl, "He's our fucking greenhorn, that's who!"

CHAPTER 2

———•———

ALASKA IS A bitch. She is rotten and spoiled, vindictive, harsh in every sense of the word, and quite eager to prove her ruthlessness as often as she can. She is a spiteful bitch, who regards human life as mere fodder for her insatiable hunger, and a meager and temporary sustenance at that. The rest of the world knows her as "The Last Frontier." Yet every person who breathes, walks, and works within this bounteous expanse of land and sea will agree that such a nickname is misleading. A "frontier" by definition can be conquered. The belief that one day this ferocious beast of unrelenting wilderness and grim seas will become a slave to the will of man is absolute folly.

Every year, hundreds of people die in Alaska, in ways the Lower 48 couldn't begin to understand. This land's vast and lonely topography, teeming with frigid glaciers, yawning lakes, and lush blankets of green forests, has a morbid taste for airplanes, considering the astounding number that have vanished over the last hundred years. And untold adventure seekers and hunters have gone into the backwoods of Alaska, never to be seen or heard from again. We even have a term for this phenomenon: "Gone Missing."

"Yo, Henry! Whatever happened to that fish processor out of Naknek?"

"You mean Sam? Gone missing."

No one knows this cruel reality of disappearing forever into the Last Frontier more concretely than I do—that is, myself and every fisherman who works the seas of this miserable bitch.

Days before we left our home in Anchorage, I reminded my friend Danny Wilson about the risk of losing his life. As always, he had nothing to say on the matter, expressing a casual complacency in the form of silence. Danny was rather simple in nature, so his inner thoughts—for as long as I had known him—were "sparse" to begin with. I figured this uncomplicated aspect of Danny's character had to do with the way he was born. An average person might have reminded me that it was my idea to get him a job on board the crabbing vessel where I worked. Not Danny. Danny just kept his mouth shut. And when it was time to leave, he simply picked up his backpack and stared at me with those narrow eyes and goofy smile.

In just over an hour, our small plane had touched down on the tarmac of Kodiak Municipal Airport. The weather was calm, yet a warm gust of wind blew in from the south. Although it was the last week of October—and the tanner crab season (along with Alaska's nasty winter) loomed on the horizon—that morning was nothing but bright and beautiful. Coming in from the north, just before we landed, I pointed out to Danny some of the island's features that made it such an unforgettable place to visit. Tall stands of dark green Sitka spruce intermingled with the city and shrouded the lowlands like a forest veil. Mountain alder were scattered along hillsides, their leaves now faded to a rusty brown. Pacific red elder, fireweed, wild geranium—they all variegated the land, adding a fine aroma and color to a late fall. And cold alpine lakes, those divine destinations for countless anglers, peered up at us like deep blue eyes staring into the heavens.

My crewmate, Sean Salazar, had been waiting for us when we arrived. Built like a scarecrow, a forever-thin man, Salazar could eat as much as he wanted yet never gain an ounce. His demeanor was also perpetually stoic. He kept his thinning dark hair hidden under a ball cap every waking minute. He always wore the same dull outfit—denim jeans, a black t-shirt, a brown Carhartt jacket always in dire need of a good washing, and wrinkled leather boots. In social circles everywhere, Salazar was the forgettable person hovering in the background, or standing in some corner of the room, hiding behind a mug of ale. And even though he spoke tactfully on those rare occasions when he did say more than three words, his quiet personality kept a person wondering what the hell he was thinking.

Not surprisingly, Salazar didn't say much when I introduced him to Danny. He only nodded his head, asked if our flight was good, then turned and headed for the parking lot. I couldn't help myself; I wondered what he was thinking just then. Danny was about to become a "first" in the world of crabbing. I knew from the very beginning when I proposed my idea to our captain, Fred Mooney, that Danny and I would get grief from a whole lot of people. At the very least, there would be weird looks, whispers behind our backs, and probably some boisterous taunts from a few drunken fishermen. I had also known that each of these incidents would serve as a cruel reminder of Danny's childhood, and mine, growing up in Anchorage.

But I had high hopes. First, that my co-workers would accept Danny from the get-go. And if not right away, then once they saw how relentless a worker Danny could be, or how strong he was, or how easy it was to get along with him. I figured they'd all turn the corner eventually.

At that moment, our first hour in Kodiak, Salazar wasn't giving any clues as to how he felt about having Danny as our greenhorn on board the *Angie Piper*. We followed him out to the truck—the captain's battered, 1980 Ford F-150. After throwing our duffel bags in the bed, Danny and I squeezed into the cab. Feeling a surge of familiarity, I was reminded of the continuous battle that played out between us and her—the wicked witch of the west known as Alaska. Our captain's F-150 always looked like it had just rolled out of a junkyard. But when Salazar started that engine, it roared as if it had just been tuned up—as it undoubtedly had. I chuckled under my breath, thinking about that battle and how this wild frontier of Alaska has worked, seemingly without effort, to impose her will onto humanity.

My first lesson was shortly after my eighteenth birthday. I had gotten a job as a salmon processor during the summer months at a plant near the isolated town of Naknek. The place reminded me of the movie, *The Road Warrior*. Each of the vehicles the locals drove across muddy roads or rocky beaches penciled along the vast stretches of tundra was customized against the weather and terrain. And then there were the fishing vessels: massive tenders trudging through murky waters, an assortment of blemished colors masking their hulls, the effects of salt and sea ever present upon every corroded surface. Kodiak was no different than Naknek, with its continuous struggle and upkeep against Mother Nature. You could see the same vehicles, the same fishing vessels. And you could see the effects throughout the city, along the broken pavements and the tired, dull buildings. You could see it in the eyes of the locals. The entire landscape of human endeavor was pockmarked from its battle against the elements.

Salazar drove us southwest along Mill Bay Road, and I took in the mid-morning sights, smells, and sounds of the streets before we reached the docks. He told us where our boat was moored but stayed in the truck while Danny and I grabbed our gear. Apparently he still had more errands to run for the captain, which came as no surprise. I had learned from working on a commercial crabbing vessel for the last four years that even during those months when there were no crabs to deal with, there was always something needing to get done.

Always something to fix, clean, mend, paint, oil, pick up in town. And the list of chores seemed to grow longer with each task we completed. Danny and I had our own list of errands to run that morning, but first I wanted to introduce him to the captain, and to our boat.

When we found the *Angie Piper*, she was looking as good as ever. One hundred and ten feet long, a black hull with a blue superstructure, she had a white trim that reminded me of eyeliner. Her wheelhouse was located in the bow, followed by a long wooden deck that could accommodate one hundred and eighty crab pots. Built in the late seventies, she had been a reliable vessel for more than twenty years. Fred lived in Seattle, and he kept the boat anchored at the Ballard Locks in those few months of the year when we weren't fishing. During that time, I was usually down there with him, working on the *Angie Piper* to repair her wounds from the previous season or getting her ready for the upcoming one.

Danny and I crossed over onto the deck and headed straight for the wheelhouse. I thought I'd seen Fred's shaggy white head through the window when we came up from the dock. But apparently we had just missed him, and he'd headed back down into the engine room. So I showed Danny to our staterooms. It was his first time inside a commercial vessel. I could see the excitement animating his face.

"So, Danny, this is where we'll get nothing but a few hours of sleep in the coming months," I told him, as I pointed to the claustrophobic space, with its confining bunk beds known simply as "racks."

Danny and I stowed our gear in the stateroom, then I gave him the tour of the rest of the boat. It was during this time that his eyes widened, big and bright, like spotlights. I wasn't surprised one bit. In fact, I expected it. Ever since we were teenagers, Danny had been fascinated by those elite warriors, the Navy SEALs. He had never been on a boat the size of the *Angie Piper*, and I'd suspected that stepping on board would evoke those wild dreams he had harbored for all those years, since we were kids, of becoming a Navy SEAL.

I led him through the galley, which was the crew's hideout from the murderous conditions on deck. The galley had a four-range burner, oven, microwave, small refrigerator, and a green-cushioned booth surrounding a square table. A television with a built-in VHS player hung on the opposite side of the booth—an unreliable piece of equipment at best. The player ate more tapes than it played.

The galley served as both the dining and recreation room when we were at sea. But after working more than thirty straight hours hauling gear, those of us who were too tired to peel off our rain suits and make it down the hall to one of the racks often made that room our sleeping quarters as well.

"So, what's the rubber for?" Danny asked, slapping the tabletop, though it emerged as "S'was rubbah for?" Most of the time, Danny's speech was comprehensible, but whenever he got excited—as he was at this moment—he tended to slur his words or even chunk his sentences down into enigmatic fragments. I'd grown up with Danny, so I could usually figure out what he was saying.

"The rubber helps to keep things from sliding onto the floor," I replied. Danny gave me a smiling nod, but I could see it on his face—he was perplexed. "Don't worry, buddy. You'll get it all figured out soon enough."

Everything on the boat could be strapped down, in one fashion or another, to accommodate rough seas. The rubber mats on the table and counter space in the galley worked great at keeping plates, cups, and utensils from sliding onto the floor during normal sailing conditions. When things got particularly rough, we could lock all the dinnerware tight inside the cabinets.

Thinking about rough weather reminded me of a particular worry: would Danny be prone to seasickness? Most fishermen get sick as dogs out there on the ocean at one time or another.

But some of them get so bad, they can't do anything but lie in a rack for days. I wondered how Danny would cope, particularly when things got rough. I'd have my answer soon enough. Crabbing in the Gulf of Alaska during the dead of winter would test the constitution of the most seasoned deckhand.

"All right, buddy," I said, walking out toward the deck, "you'll get the hang of this room soon enough."

On our way outside, we passed the ready-room—the hall where we stored our raingear and suited up for working on deck.

"This is where our pre-game huddles take place," I said, pointing to the hooks on the wall, the various electrical switches, cubbies housing miscellaneous tools, and the narrow hallway leading out to the deck. "When the captain gives us the cue, we have about five minutes to dress up and get out there. It gets real tight in here, as you can see."

Danny nodded, still beaming with excitement. I wondered again if inviting him to work for us had been a mistake. It certainly wouldn't be the first time that I'd exercised poor judgment on Danny's behalf. It seemed my past youthful blunders would never fail to eclipse my present good intentions. Would the blistering cold and horribly rough seas wear a hole right through my friend? Would the incessant drudgery of working in the Gulf of Alaska for hours, days, and weeks at a time eventually grind Danny down? I didn't think so, yet I wasn't one hundred percent sure. What I did know—or figure, at least—was that the romance and excitement Danny had been experiencing at that moment would soon get washed right off the deck. Working as a crabber is a miserable nightmare for just about everyone.

"It usually takes a few days to get your sea legs," I said, as we walked out onto the deck. "Just be wary when you come out here for the first couple of times. When the boat is pitching from side to side, you could easily stumble right over into the sea if you're not careful." I pointed to the portside railing, opposite the pot launcher. "And quit smiling, Danny. It's been known to happen."

A tower of crab pots covered most of the *Angie Piper*'s deck. We had one hundred and eighty of them, stacked five high, from mid-ship all down the length of her stern. Weighing in at nearly a thousand pounds each, these rectangular pots were also called "seven-bys," since they were seven feet long by seven feet wide. And they were by far the most harrowing pieces of equipment on the boat.

All crabbers have a love/hate relationship with the pots. Most of the severe injuries incurred by fishermen come from dealing with those damn things. A thousand pounds of steel swinging carelessly on the end of a boom-crane wakes everyone up real quick. But they are also the one thing that can lift a crew's spirits after weeks of turning gear. Once those pots come up on deck brimming with crab, and you know you're in the money, that hatred for the pots disappears in a flash.

"One of your jobs, Danny, will be to help push those bastards across the deck," I said, watching for his reaction. That first day on the boat with Danny, I couldn't be sure he understood what was expected of him. Re-stacking the first layer of pots on deck took a unique set of skills, such as timing. You had to be alert. It worked best if you used the pitch of the boat as an aid in moving the heavy cages. But it also helped to have real muscle. That was my friend's secret weapon.

I had read somewhere that people like him are known for their tremendous physical strength. When we were kids, we used to wrestle all the time, and try as I might, I never could overpower the guy. It was while pushing one of those crab pots across the deck, in fact, that I got the idea Danny would make a perfect deckhand. I knew that strength of his would come in handy—not to mention his work ethic. But I wasn't so sure how his mind would hold up. Or his spirit, for that matter.

For the next half-hour, I gave Danny a brief tour of the rest of the boat. I showed him how the pot launcher worked, explaining that it operated from hydraulic power to tilt a crab pot over the rail and into the sea. Then I pointed out all the buoys and the coiled rope, carefully describing how dangerous these things were when being pulled by a thousand-pound cage of steel that was plummeting to the bottom of the ocean. Death loitered on the decks of every commercial crabbing vessel.

"Always remember to keep your feet planted firmly on the deck, Danny," I told him, as we walked over to the large aluminum table we used for sorting crab. "You could be standing here for hours on end, picking out crab, and all that line's gonna be snaking around you, just waiting to grab at your ankles."

Danny simply nodded and smiled, seemingly unconcerned. He placed his hands on the sorting table and smacked away at an imaginary crab.

"But don't worry yourself too much, Danny," I added, sarcastically. "Most of the time you'll be over here."

I walked him over to the other side of the deck, where we kept the baiting station. Danny's primary job would be to prepare bait for the crab pots—a task that entailed a small list of mind-numbing duties. I showed him the freezer down below, where we stored the twenty-five pound boxes of herring he would have to carry topside, open up, and dump into the meat grinder. After making "fish pâté," Danny would need to fill hundreds of bait jars. Then there was the rigging of whole cod and other bottom fish onto bait hooks. It was a miserable, full-time job getting the bait ready for crabbing. But as the greenhorn, Danny would be assigned that duty. And for him, it would be the best test to see how well he would do on board the *Angie Piper*, working as a crabber.

After the tour, Danny and I at last met up with our captain, Fred Mooney, who was in the wheelhouse again. He greeted us with his customary jovial attitude and full-bearded smile. Fred reminded me of a Santa Claus reject, cast out of the North Pole for stinking of liquor and brine, despite his jolly demeanor.

"I've heard a lot about you, Danny Wilson," the captain said, holding a cup of coffee to his lips.

"Yes, sir," replied Danny.

"Ed tells me you're one heck of a strong man. Is that true?"

"Yes, sir. I'm a strong man."

"Well, good! 'Cause we could certainly use some strength around here." Fred winked at me. "How was your summer, Ed? We missed you down in Seattle."

"Damn good, Captain." I had taken the last several weeks of the summer off to enjoy some sightseeing throughout Alaska. Normally, I would have stayed in Seattle to help work on the boat, but I justified my trip by saying I had never taken a personal vacation. In truth, I wanted to see how Danny had been doing with his first real job. Earlier in the year, I had secured him a summer position at the processing plant up in Naknek, where I used to work. It was a grueling job, to say the least, but nothing like crabbing. Danny was given the task of separating salmon roe from salmon guts, sixteen hours a day, every day for six weeks. That's what Danny did for the better part of his summer. As it turned out, he managed the job exactly how I'd hoped he would.

I flew up there in July, just before the end of the fishing season, and found Danny happy as ever. When the season was over, the plant manager just smiled and asked if he could keep my friend for the winter. I took that as a passing grade for the test I'd originally planned for Danny.

"So how'd he do up in Naknek?" the captain asked.

I smiled. "Shit, they wouldn't let him go. Had to fight to get him back!"

The captain chuckled, and then walked over to his seat where some maps had been laid out. "Well, that's good to hear." He turned and looked at Danny. "But cleaning fish ain't nothing like hauling crab, son."

"Yes, sir," Danny replied.

"Things get real dangerous out there on the open seas," Fred said, sobering. His face fell, and his eyes and mouth drooped as well. He gave me a brief look before staring out the window. "I suppose you heard about what happened last week, Ed. The accident?"

"No, sir. What accident?"

"The *Polar Betty* ... she went down somewhere outside Chignik Bay. They were fishing for cod." Fred caught my stare. Though he endeavored to keep his face cool and composed, his lips were unsteady. "No survivors," he muttered, as he took another sip from his cup.

I swallowed hard at the words, "No survivors." I felt my pulse quicken and my eyes well with tears. I knew everyone aboard the *Polar Betty*—the entire crew. We used to hang out together at McCrawley's, and then down in Seattle, sharing our fishing tales of woe and grandeur. The captain was a giant man named Molly McDowell, and he and Fred seemed thick as thieves whenever they got together. There was a ton of history between those two men, as well as our crews, and so Fred's news—that the boat had gone down and taken everybody with it—broke my heart.

I stared out the portside window then, observing the lonely ocean in the distant horizon, its gray body a cold grave for so many men. I shook my head and sighed.

Alaska .... She is a bitch. And she seemed inclined to stay that way.

Chapter 3

———◆———

O N THAT SAD note, Danny and I left Fred and the *Angie Piper* and headed back into town to buy gear. We had agreed to meet Salazar at the general store in two hours, which gave us plenty of time to sightsee and get lunch. It was our first day in town. Already I was feeling a stab of regret. It was the old wound, I would later realize—the scar from my past scratching below the surface of my everyday life. I felt its burning as I stepped off the *Angie Piper* and thrust my hand out, making sure Danny got across safely. Maybe this was my subconscious trying to speak to Danny, reaching out to let him know he could trust me. That this time, yes, he really could.

As we walked along the pier, I didn't say anything for quite a while. I observed the dozens of moored boats, thinking about the *Polar Betty* and the poor deckhands who went down with her. Was it just rotten luck that had crossed her planks and boarded the boat? Or was it an act of fate? Had her time, as well as that of the entire crew, simply come to an end? Another cruel play from God's hand.

I stared at the fishing vessels we passed, picking out particular details—details that would have likely escaped my attention on any other day. Flecks of paint chipped off hulls now lay somewhere at the bottom of the Gulf of Alaska. Frayed hawser lines were on the verge of snapping. Hundreds of thousands of gull droppings were scattered across the entire fleet of crabbers, dinghies, tugboats, and trawlers, all tied up there in Kodiak's harbor. I was reminded of how insignificant a single boat—and its entire crew—were to the oceans of Alaska. And a particular memory rang in my head like a fire alarm at three in the morning: something my dad had said long ago that sprang to mind at that moment.

Mr. Edward Thurman Senior, otherwise known as Big Ed, once told me that children were like vessels waiting in a harbor: not yet ready to sail, but most eager to do so. Ironically enough, he told me this after I had witnessed something deathly eerie in our own backyard.

I grew up on the outskirts of Anchorage, in a three-story house with four bedrooms and an attached, two-car garage. I knew I was a lucky kid. Our house was quite large by the standards of my youth. Except that my mother ran a daycare, so most days there never seemed to be enough room to breathe.

Before I was born, my dad had painted our house eggshell white with teal trim, and in the dead of winter, it glowed amid the layers of snow, a ghostly presence. But in the springtime, when the last ton of snow had finally melted off the roof and through the gutters, our house gleamed like a piece of lost jewelry found on the forest floor. And this was the time of year when that eerie event occurred.

"Get in the house!" my mother had screamed, in a voice that was both loud and horrifying, driven by panic. I was maybe five or six years old at the time, and knew by her tone that she was deadly serious.

My mother's name was Cynthia Thurman. She was short and plump, and kept her baby face and red hair for life. Unlike any other redhead I've come to know, she had a calm disposition; however, under certain conditions, or under pressure, the woman could explode, like she did on that morning. The catalyst? An eight-hundred-pound grizzly bear was standing thirty feet away from me and the rest of the kids out in the yard.

We later learned that the grizzly was a full-grown male fresh out of hibernation and looking to put on weight. He was munching on the berries strewn across the chain-link fence that ran along the perimeter of our house. This wasn't a particularly uncommon sight in the streets and neighborhoods of Anchorage; bears frequently raided trash cans or created havoc in the occasional open garage, in search of pet food. The bears are as familiar in that city as the moose are, standing in the drive-thru of a fast-food restaurant. But to be so close to a bunch of children ....

She busted through the metal storm door, broom swinging over her head, yelling for us kids to get into the house. This was one of those moments when everything went by as fast as a terrified heartbeat—but also in slow motion. I remember my mother's foot stomping down on the head of a toy army man I had planted behind a coil of gray, plastic barbed wire. I also remember, in vivid detail, catching a whiff of the distinct odor that clung to her as she breezed past on her way down the steps: cinnamon and spice with hints of sage, stale grease, and dish soap. That was my mother.

"Everybody, get in the house!" Once I realized she wasn't after me, I stood up the rest of the way and looked around the yard. A dozen kids scattered across the lawn like overgrown rats, some screaming and waving their hands, others silent, expressions stony. They were determined toddlers running from the madwoman swinging a broom—that was what I thought, up until the moment I spotted Danny.

Danny Wilson: the little blond-haired kid with almond-shaped eyes. Sporting a winning smile, he stood by the fence with his hands cupped together through the chain-linked gaps. He was holding clumps of green grass for the bear on the other side.

Calm, almost couth, the bear seemed to wear an inquisitive

expression as it stared down into Danny's hands. It was as if the creature were considering the various culinary components offered. *Hmm ... "Nugget" bluegrass, with a bit of clover.*

The bear came unglued when it spotted my mother, though. It let out a loud grunt, then stood on its hind legs, towering over the fence ... and Danny.

Danny pulled his hands away, but aside from that he didn't move a muscle. I saw the side of his face from where I stood on the steps. He was staring up at the grizzly with a smile that never once faltered. Even when the bear slapped his front paws onto the top of the fence—as if to say to my mother, *Bring it on, Little Red Riding Hood*—Danny hardly blinked.

My mother threw the broom at the grizzly, grabbed Danny by the arm, and yanked the boy across the lawn and into the house. Seconds later, all of us kids watched from behind the kitchen window as the bear made a few swipes at a blackberry bush then ambled back into the forest. While my mother was on the phone with the police department, she patted a few of us on the shoulders. Five minutes hadn't gone by before a couple of officers were roaming our backyard, shotguns in hand. They didn't find the bear, and shortly after they left, it was as if nothing had happened. The entire incident slipped away from the majority of those kids, as most events do, once they re-engaged themselves in the world of play. For Danny, this was certainly the case.

As for myself, I couldn't take my eyes off the kid. I sat on the couch in our living room and stared at Danny for quite a while as he played on the floor with his Legos. This was a long time ago, and even though I was comparatively the same age as Danny, I'll never forget what I thought about him at that moment. I'll never forget what I felt.

I looked at his face, and for the first time I contemplated just how different it was from other children's: the weird angle of his eyelids, the overly large mouth fixed in a perpetual, dumb grin. I thought about his "stocky" build and wondered if he was strong, or just fat. And I wondered what kind of dimwitted fool would walk up to a grizzly bear and offer it a handful of grass to eat. These were my shameful thoughts at that moment, and unbeknownst to me, they would cultivate harsh feelings of disparity from then on.

Over the years, fate would take Danny and me far beyond the confines of my childhood backyard. It took us together through grade school and high school and then onto that dock in Kodiak. Fate waltzed us into McCrawley's, where Danny showed off his awesome strength to some of the strongest men and women in the world. And finally, fate swept me and Danny into the tragic events that would unfold a few days later. In light of all that, those mean-spirited thoughts I had as a child are nothing when you consider what would come to pass between Danny and me.

When my dad came home later that day—the day of the grizzly—and we were all sitting at the dinner table, my mom told him all about the bear and Danny. He laughed aloud. Then, with a smile, he made the comment that kids were vessels in the harbor—ships just waiting to set sail.

Now, as I recalled those words, Danny and I stood quietly on the dock, taking in the cold, salty air, staring at all those boats. Danny remained silent while he waited for me to snap out of my reverie, even after I heard his stomach growl.

"Come on, buddy," I finally said with a laugh. "Let's go find you something to eat."

CHAPTER 4

———◆———

OUR STROLL UP Shelikof Avenue took us north of the docks to a favorite diner of mine in town. Just like the whole of Kodiak, the restaurant was packed with busy fishermen, processors, otherwise known as "cannery rats," and locals feeding off the energy generated from an impending season of crab fishing. Danny and I had to wait thirty minutes just to get a seat, so I took the time to explain to him some of the unwritten rules of crabbing, such as how fishermen rarely associated with cannery rats. Or how there were always certain "totem poles" one had to climb to secure a well-paying job in the fishing community. Danny was our incoming greenhorn, and on board the *Angie Piper*, as with most all other crabbing vessels, he would have to earn his full share. That meant he wouldn't be paid the same as the other crewmen. Some captains had their greenhorns work an entire season without pay, just to prove their worth. But I knew that if Danny worked hard and got his job done without screwing things up, Fred would give him half a share. Not bad, when you consider that amount could easily add up to several thousand dollars.

"What would I do with all that money?" Danny had asked, weeks before, after I proposed he work with me on the boat. His curiosity was genuine, and testified to the simplicity of his character. Danny had never been in want. All he needed was the basics. I told him not to worry about the money. His father would help him spend it—in a good way, of course.

I had known Stephen Wilson, one hell of a man, my whole life. He had raised Danny in the house next door to where I lived. Of average height, with thin white hair kept military short, Mr. Wilson had an odd characteristic: despite his normal size, he had humongous hands. He worked as a firefighter for the city of Anchorage, and on his days off, he worked around his house doing a variety of jobs. I don't think I ever saw him sitting around. I only remember him chopping wood, or cutting away berries along the fence out back, or tending to his garden. Mr. Wilson also dabbled in woodworking, and sometimes Danny and I were fortunate enough to help him with these projects. Mostly we found ourselves cleaning up the garage—which earned us an ice cream cone from the local drug store. It wasn't until I got older that I began to earn money from Mr. Wilson, doing specific jobs such as organizing his tool shed or stacking wood out back.

I had been stacking wood for Mr. Wilson on a Sunday afternoon, as I recall, when I had an emotional epiphany, and I started to wonder about certain things. How had Danny's father done it all those years? How had he managed his household without a wife? Danny's mother, Marlene Wilson, died from breast cancer when I was in the first grade. I'll never forget the night Mr. Wilson came over to tell my parents his wife had passed. Staring out from the crack in my bedroom door, I saw my mother in tears. My dad seemed confused, not knowing how to react. But Mr. Wilson never cried, not so much as a single tear. He just sat on our couch like a cold, somber statue.

As I stacked the cord of wood on that Sunday afternoon, asking myself those questions, I realized that I had been shedding tears myself. I felt true empathy—pitying the man, and Danny, and even Danny's sister Mary, all having to grow up without a mother in the house. Later, when Mr. Wilson came out to pay me for the work I had done, I just shook my head and told him not to worry about it. I told him it was the least I could do. Then I quickly turned around and walked home.

Presently, Danny and I got a table next to a window overlooking the busy street. Men and women wandered the sidewalks, carrying duffel bags or backpacks, making gossip, laughing with one another. These were people from all across the globe. Drifters, college students, locals, and even a few tourists. Most of them had jobs lined up with the fishing community, but others might have been on their way down to the docks in search of work. All of them, however, would likely be busy once the crab season hit.

I looked up at the pale blue sky with its banners of orange fire tearing across the horizon and was reminded of another set of rules all fishermen abided by.

"Red sky at morning, sailors take warning," I said, over the rim of my coffee cup.

"What's that?" Danny asked.

"Superstition," I replied. Danny looked at me and blinked. "That's the other thing you'll learn, buddy. We've got hundreds of them—hundreds of superstitions." And that was the truth. Working a boat on the deadly seas of Alaska, a person discovers real quick how fragile life can be. A person will begin to observe every ill omen, imaginary or otherwise. He will curse the presence of a woman on board a vessel. And he'll salute a passing seagull, paying homage to the lost fisherman whose soul now resides in the feathered creature.

"What's a super-tition?" Danny asked. It was a tough word for my friend to pronounce, and an even tougher one for me to explain.

"Ghosts and things," I said. Danny blinked again. "Black cats crossing the road ... you know—bad luck."

My friend at last nodded his head, but he still seemed confused. He might have been wondering what a black cat crossing a road had to do with fishing for crab. I dropped the subject once the waiter came over and took our order. But in the back of my mind, I wondered if there were any superstitions that accounted for having a person like Danny on board a fishing vessel.

It wasn't the first time I had pondered this possibility. I had even joked with Fred over coffee, on the morning he told me to give Danny a call. "I guess we'll find out, won't we?" Fred had said. I had convinced myself that Danny would be nothing but good luck, considering how much he reminded me of his father. Like a mule, Danny could work straight into his grave without so much as asking for a break, let alone complaining. In fact, Danny never complained, not ever. And when it came to hard work, my friend was like a machine, tireless and showing no emotion.

The waiter swooped in and delivered each of us a cheeseburger and chili fries, with a small bowl of canned fruit.

"Eat up, Danny," I said. "We've got a long, hard day of work ahead of us."

Seconds later, Danny smiled, then mumbled through a mouthful of food, "Sailor take warning."

CHAPTER 5

———◆———

For all his simple, easygoing attitude toward life, Danny had a legendary stubborn streak. As a little boy, he was nicknamed Sitting Bull by his dad, in that when Danny got angry he would drop to the ground, sit criss-cross applesauce, fold his arms tightly over his chest, and remain like that for hours on end. One time, when he was about five years old, Danny sat in that position all through the night, exhausting both his dad and his sister. Apparently, their jaws dropped in speechless wonder when they found Danny still sitting there in the hallway the next morning. In all my life, I've never met a person who could be as stubborn as Danny Wilson.

But I don't mean to paint my friend in such a bratty light. In many ways, Danny was a typical five-year-old boy. And he wasn't all that unusual at age twenty-four, the year I got him his job aboard the *Angie Piper*. Danny, in fact, was basically an average young man, despite not being the sharpest tack on the wall.

If compared to others with his condition, Danny's IQ would have measured favorably, in that he had always been regarded as "high-functioning." Many times, I had seen him demonstrate sound common sense. And he seemed to learn skills that required physical coordination with surprising speed. Danny did learn how to read, and could perform basic mathematical computations. In fact, he was damned proficient at taking care of himself. So much so, I believe, that given the opportunity, Danny could have been successful living on his own.

But people like Danny can never escape their DNA. And for anyone who's known a person like him, the way that I have, it goes without saying that the condition carries with it a whole mess of symptoms not listed in any medical guide.

I pondered these symptoms as Danny and I sat in the diner and ate our lunch. Even while seated, I couldn't help but notice the occasional glance from a fisherman, or baffled stare from a processor. This was nothing new, and hardly surprising to either Danny or me. We both had years of experience tolerating this type of public gaping. But thirty minutes later, after we'd left the diner and were standing in the general store, Danny and I received what I call the "googly-eyed stares."

What the hell? Are you kidding me? These were some of the thoughts I'd imagined running through the heads of the people in that store, once they spotted Danny trying on gear. At that time of year, most of the shoppers were people who planned to work in town or the seas beyond. They bought up all the raingear, boots, gloves, knives, jackets, beanies, and every other sort of gear needed to prepare for the harsh winter jobs. Whether they planned on catching the crab or canning it, these people knew that the coming days would be nothing but long, cold, and miserable. So what in the hell was a kid like that doing here?

I knew the confrontation would come at some point. I'd even prepared a few words for when I might need to defend Danny's right to work there on the outskirts of Alaska. But also, for myself. I had a lot of emotional baggage to cope with.

As Danny struggled to pull on a rain boot in the middle of an aisle, a burly man passed by. At his odd glance, my thoughts flew back to our years in high school.

I would love to say that the kids at our high school had taken Danny under their wings and nurtured him like a mascot, the way teenagers do with their "special" peers these days. I would love to say that, but I'd be lying.

Poor Danny had a hell of time. The kids at our school picked on him relentlessly and seemingly without shame. They played tricks on him, poked fun at the way he looked, bullied him in the bathroom, and called him every kind of name a person can imagine. I couldn't believe how Danny persevered through all that crap, for all those years. And he did this without once losing his temper. Nor did I ever see him break down. He just took their abuse like a faithful, longsuffering dog, until it was over.

As for me ... I never once stood up for my friend. I was too much of a coward. I was too afraid of getting picked on myself. Or, more precisely, too afraid of having my reputation damaged.

Out of all the names those kids used to call him, their favorite was Beluga Boy, or something along that line. They'd call him the Beluga Monster, the Beluga Freak, or sometimes just plain old Beluga, all because the shape of Danny's face resembled a beluga whale. At least that's what the high school kids decided one year when Danny showed up for swim tryouts. Our school's swim coach, Mr. Elmsworth, had taken quite a liking to Danny. I think he recognized Danny's spirit and ambition. But no way in hell could Mr. Elmsworth let my friend onto the team. Simply stated, Danny couldn't swim, not like the other kids. But those kids certainly had a field day when they saw him try.

Startled out of my bad trip down memory lane, I reached out and grabbed Danny, preventing his fall in the middle of the aisle of the general store; he had lost his balance attempting to get a rain boot on.

"That one's too small, buddy," I said, handing him a larger pair. "Trust me. For comfort, you've got to wear these things a size or two bigger."

"Thanks, Ed." Danny took the boots and plopped his feet into them. "These are big," he said, his face screwed up in concentration.

"Working on a boat is a lot colder than on a dock, Danny." I took a guess at what he might be thinking at that moment. Because of Danny's work as a fish processor up in Naknek the previous salmon season, he was accustomed to wearing rain boots and raingear. But that was in July, in a warehouse, away from the ice-cold seas and rasping winds of Alaska's ocean. Danny had never been doused by a ten-foot wave while standing on a slick deck in freezing temperatures.

"When you're wearing two pairs of wool socks, they'll fit just fine," I said. "Now let's go find you some gloves."

Thirty minutes later our shopping cart was piled high with Gore-Tex, rubber, and wool. Although I already had my gear stored on board the *Angie Piper* (save for a new pair of boots in the cart), I spotted Danny the money he needed so that we could buy him an extra pair of everything. It was a dumb fisherman who headed out to sea without more than one of every essential item. And every item of clothing is essential when you're a deckhand on a commercial fishing vessel. One season of crabbing could wipe out an entire wardrobe.

"So when do we go?" Danny asked, as we walked toward the checkout counter. "When do we catch the crab?" His voice vibrated with excitement, as if we were simply heading for our favorite fishing hole. I had already told him it might be a few days before we left Kodiak. A lot of preparation still needed doing on the boat before we could pull anchor. But I thought I understood how Danny felt. Everyone in that town shared a certain excitement, which struck me as rather odd and contradictive, since we all knew what awaited us beyond the horizon: cold, miserable days spent in everlasting winter darkness. There would be brutal snowstorms, cast down from the north, bringing with them hundred-knot williwaw winds. Fishermen would clock countless hours of tedious work out upon a sea consisting of nothing but gray—a maddening color if there ever was one. And beyond the numerous concussions, lacerations, broken bones, bruised ribs, and predictable bouts with pneumonia, there would also be death. During every season, the undeniable truth that that grim fate could await us lingered in the air, waiting, biding its time.

But the stakes were always high in Alaska. The probability of earning thousands of dollars in a few short weeks was incentive enough to accept the constant presence of the Grim Reaper. The money attracted all sorts of people to fish these waters, many of them desperate and tough as nails. There were the young fools like me, eager to capture a full share of life from the bountiful seas of the last frontier. And then there were the broken wrecks of humanity: chain-smokers who'd spent their happiest days on board a golem of steel, riding the boundless sea. For these people, the Harry Hallers of the world, no other place in life—be it a secure job, a loving family, or the blessed sanctuary of land—could provide the sense of belonging they hungered for.

At the checkout counter, I looked at Danny and realized I was wrong. He might be the only person in Kodiak who thought the way he did about fishing. My friend couldn't care less about making money, and he certainly wasn't running away from anything. Hell, Danny might have been the only person in the town eager to catch crab for no other reason than to do it. This simple outlook might be another symptom not listed in any medical guide: a trouble-free personality prone to innocence and beautiful naivety.

"Don't worry, Danny," I said, "we'll be out there soon enough. I promise."

The guy who rang us up was named Dewey. He was a wiry kid with a brown mullet and crooked teeth, and he smiled as if nothing on earth mattered more than the customer. I had seen him often enough in the bars, cackling and drinking, having fun, never too popular with the women.

"You guys find everything?" Dewey asked, giving us his biggest smile yet, although failing miserably to keep from staring at Danny. He might have been wondering about my friend, and perhaps dying to ask us a few questions, but he refrained.

"Yeah, we sure did," I replied.

"Hear about the *Polar Betty*?" Dewey continued, still smiling, as if this nugget of gossip was the highlight of his day. "Your captain, Mooney, was in here earlier, talking with another guy. They both seemed pretty upset."

"Well, we were good friends with the crew," I replied.

"It's a damn shame, ain't it?" Dewey added, bagging our supplies. "Seems like every year, more and more boats go down."

"Yeah, I suppose so," I said, my tone deliberately casual. But in reality, I was feeling anything but casual. Dewey had hit the nail on the head in one respect. Not so much that more and more boats were going down—that might or might not be true—but that this job was beyond dangerous. One mistake could easily cost the lives of an entire crew.

As I stepped outside, the first thing I did was inhale a lungful of wild Alaskan air. My neck and shoulders were cramped and tight, like they'd been welded together. I was glad that the first part of our day was almost over. Looking down Shelikof Avenue toward the docks, I realized that I had been anxious all afternoon. Just like in high school, I was nervous that Danny would draw unwanted attention, there in the streets of Kodiak. I guess I had been looking forward to pulling anchor myself, getting on with the crabbing season and heading out into a massive ocean where no one could possibly taunt Danny—or me, for hanging out with him. I'd been pushed around and barraged with insults more times than I could count just for being friends with Danny.

From half a block away, I spotted Salazar leaning against Fred's truck, lighting a cigarette.

"Come on, Danny," I said. "It's time we get back to the boat."

I took a step, and then from behind I heard, "What's going on, Ed?" I turned and saw our engineer Dave Jenkins walking toward me, from across the street. "Do anything crazy with all that money you earned last season?"

"Oh, you know me, Dave," I replied, "blew it all on meth and booze—the usual."

Dave gave a dutiful chuckle, then said, "What did you really do?"

"Just some traveling, that's all. A few weeks here and there, nothing too spectacular. What about you? What'd you spend your fortune on?"

"Oh, you know," Dave said, "the usual—meth and booze. So who's this?" he asked, his gaze landing now on Danny.

"This is Danny Wilson, the new greenhorn."

"This is your friend—the one the captain hired?" Dave sounded incredulous. His face flushed, and his eyes widened in alarm.

"Y-yeah ..." I stuttered and squirmed at the awkwardness of the situation. "Danny's tough as nails. Wait and see—he'll work out."

Dave exploded into a fit of anger. "Fred Mooney up and lost his fucking mind!" He threw his hands in the air and began pacing the sidewalk, side to side. Then his eyes went cold and dark, and he looked at me, scowling. "This was your fucking idea, wasn't it?"

This was Danny's first meeting with our fellow crewmember. Dave was known to be ill-tempered. He often appeared sullen and irritable and was given to sudden shifts of mood, but he knew how to run crab gear as well as most deckhands. He was also our ship's main engineer, and could keep a vessel running better than the best mechanics. His instincts about machines made him invaluable. Dave had been with the boat for over ten years and was a trusted friend of the captain. I had learned how to get along with the man, how to tolerate him and his irascible nature. I had also learned when to stay out of his way. But because of our captain, I never thought Dave would have much of a problem with Danny. Fred had told me that if Danny worked as hard as I had claimed he would, Dave would give him a decent enough chance. And that made sense to me, because underneath the bluster, Dave seemed to be a reasonable fellow.

"That son of a bitch!" Dave shouted. "What the hell was he thinking taking on a gimp like him?" He jerked a thumb toward Danny but kept his eyes on me.

Oh yeah … I'd planned on what I would say, knowing that sooner or later it would come to this. I'd mentally rehearsed my lines several times: *Danny has a right to be here! He worked up in Bristol Bay, and kicked ass so much they didn't want him to leave! He's as strong as you are, fool!* But just like when we were back in high school, once the brutal words surfaced, I sank back into my weakness, a broken vessel headed for the bottom of the sea.

Salazar suddenly appeared next to us. "Cool it, Dave," he said.

"Cool it? You want me to fucking *cool it*?" Dave turned a shoulder and spat on the ground. "Fred's hired us a goddamned idiot! As if greenhorns aren't stupid enough … and now we've got this guy?" His head looked like an overripe strawberry about to burst, pushing out through his full and scraggly beard. He lowered his voice into the black depths of a threat, pointed a finger at Danny, and said, "You've got no business being on the *Angie Piper*, kid. No business at all."

"Hey, come on." Salazar raised his hands in a gesture of exasperation.

"Don't 'come on' me! Last year we had a hell of a time with that fruit loop from Nebraska. Who knows how much money we lost on account of him?" Dave paused for a second, staring hard at Danny. I wanted to think that maybe, in that brief moment, he was beginning to recognize how much of an asshole he was being. And that maybe Dave had caught a glimpse of Danny's talents buried beneath his goofy, innocent exterior.

But then Dave turned and headed toward the store. "This is total bullshit!" he hollered, shaking his head as he yanked the door open. "We'll fucking see about this!"

CHAPTER 6

———•———

W E PULLED UP to the docks and parked the truck. I stepped outside and a salty breeze rushed past my face, stirring up a flurry of emotions. I felt vaguely depressed, knowing that we would be leaving soon. This feeling came as a surprise, though it is not uncommon for fishermen to get a bit down prior to the start of a season. Leaving the safety of land often means leaving the ones you love—perhaps forever. It's a dreadful thought for sure, but it's mitigated by excitement. Within every crab pot pulled up from the bottom of the sea lies the prospect of a hefty paycheck.

At present, I felt more than depression and excitement. I felt anxiety. My hands trembled from fear. My whole body tingled with dread—all because of Dave. I had felt this way many times before, back in high school, when I watched one bully after another taunt the hell out of Danny. The fear of becoming yet another of their victims held me back from making even a slightly courageous gesture to defend my friend's honor.

Up on the ridge north of us, I spotted a brown bear leaning against a tree, scratching its rump on the bark. I saw this as a good excuse to break the tension among the three of us. No one had spoken a word since Dave had lost his temper on the street corner. Not while Danny and I had loaded our gear into the back of the pickup. Or in the ten minutes it took us to drive through town and to the docks.

"Look up there, guys," I said, pointing. "Isn't that a grizzly on the hill?" Neither Salazar nor Danny replied. They both looked at the bear, but only Danny stared at it for more than a few seconds.

Salazar was quick to get back to work. He pulled a dolly from the truck and began to load it with boxes of supplies. He seemed morose, obviously upset in his own way over how Dave had talked to us. Salazar was a solid man, classy. Although still young, in his mid-thirties, he always reminded me of an old cowboy in a Western movie: a man of few words who minds his own business but is a crack shot when the bullets start to fly. That said, Dave Jenkins wasn't his fight, and unless he was pushed into a corner, that wasn't about to change.

A flock of seagulls passed over our heads, squawking. I heard a couple of guys laughing from a boat off in the distance, breaking the lull of the midday harbor swell. And again, the smell of the ocean air assailed my senses. Thick with brine, the odor was a curious reminder that Alaska is teeming with life, and that brought me back into the moment.

"Let's go, Danny," I said. "Let's get your gear stowed down below." I picked up a bag and slung it over my shoulder. "We'll be back to help," I said to Salazar, who just nodded in return, never taking his eyes off his work.

Once on the boat, we tossed Danny's gear onto his bunk in the stateroom and then headed back to the truck. "You can sort your stuff out later," I said, "after we help Salazar."

"Okey-dokey," Danny replied. His voice seemed calm and steady, not shaky like I'd expected, considering our confrontation with Dave. Not shaky like my own. But I reminded myself that Danny had a lifetime's worth of confrontations behind him. I assumed he was just used to guys like Dave.

As on all crab vessels, it was absolutely necessary for the crew to have several weeks' worth of supplies on board before we headed out. Just about anything a person can think of is a mandatory item on a fishing boat, ranging from food and first aid kits to movies, books, and pictures of home. Salazar still had a few more trips to make into town.

"It's gonna be a long day, Danny," I said, an hour later, standing in the galley. We were unpacking the boxes we had brought down from the truck, placing a variety of items onto the dining table for sorting. "I want you to put all the canned food over here," I said, pointing to one side of the table, "and everything else on the other. Oh, and keep an eye out for tools, Danny—they go over there on the counter."

"Ed ... are they going to kick me off the boat?" Danny said without warning.

The comment caught me off guard. "Are they going to what?" I replied.

"That man in town—he's mad at me. Will I have to leave the boat, Ed?"

"No, Danny, don't you worry about that. Nobody's going to kick you off the boat."

"But who was he, Ed? Who was that man who was yelling at me?"

"Well ... he's with our crew. He's with our boat, and he's been here for a while, but he can't kick you off." Suddenly, I felt like a fool. Tangled up by my own concerns, I hadn't even bothered to tell Danny who Dave was. More importantly, I'd misjudged my friend, how much the incident with Dave had affected him. "He used to be the deck boss, actually," I continued. "Now, he's just a deckhand, and the ship's engineer. But don't you go and worry about him, okay?"

"What's the deck boss?" Danny asked.

I had already taught Danny some of the different terminologies, titles, and specifics about being a crabber. But I knew how things were for my friend. He had trouble learning new things through an exchange of words. I knew it would be difficult for him to retain information unless he stepped right in and got his hands dirty. His dad was the one who explained this to me, actually, years ago. Mr. Wilson had said that Danny had a limited short-term memory. When he needed to teach Danny something complicated, he would practice with him repeatedly, day after day. Things like the alphabet, reading, using a calculator.

That said, for any skill that required muscle memory, Danny couldn't be beat. I had considered this when I first pictured him on our boat. Much of the day in and around a crabber's life was dedicated to physical labor, requiring little thinking and lots of doing. And for Danny's position—as our bait-boy—I didn't think he would have too much difficulty learning his job. In fact, I knew he wouldn't.

"The deck boss is the guy responsible for running the deck," I replied, "and that's Salazar. Dave used to have the job, but he's too much of an asshole. The crew kept complaining about it, which pissed the captain off, so he gave the job to Salazar."

"So, is Salazar our boss, then?" Danny asked.

"That's right," I said. "When we're running gear on deck, Salazar's our boss. But remember, the captain is the boss of everyone, all the time."

"But then why was that man yelling at him? Salazar is the boss. You can't yell at the boss."

I scratched my head and looked up. "Well, it's kind of complicated, Danny." I wondered how many times my friend had heard that phrase in his life. How many times from me alone? "Just don't worry about it, okay?" I slapped him on the shoulder and moved on.

Danny kept quiet for the next few hours while we stowed away all the gear. It's a big job getting everything organized on a boat, but this was good exercise for Danny. It helped him to learn his way around, which is a necessary skill in the event of an emergency. There's certainly more than one tale of a fisherman who has crawled through the inside of a sinking vessel, in the deepest blackness and a rough sea, to escape his impending tomb. Only his time spent on board, unconsciously mapping out the lay of the boat, with its corridors and recessed rooms, had saved such a man. Knowing the ins and outs of the vessel was what guided him to the proper exit—be it the ready-room, wheelhouse, or whatever existed for him at the time.

"Get to know the boat, Danny," I said, gesturing to the various corridors. At present, we were in a stateroom putting away canned goods. "Get to know the *Angie Piper*, 'cause you never know when you'll need to bail out of here in the darkness."

"What do you mean?" Danny asked, his eyebrows scrunching up tight.

"If this boat ever flips on us and the lights go out, you'll need to know where to escape from." I saw the look on my friend's face and the way his body responded: frozen, both hands holding a can of pork and beans in midair. "I'm just kidding with you, Danny. Don't you worry, this boat is solid."

And that was no lie. By the time I was hired on as a greenhorn, the *Angie Piper* had an excellent sailing record. She had kept a crew of six men busy fishing for close to two decades. Millions of pounds of crab had passed in and out of her hold, earning her crew millions of dollars over the years. And all that time, she'd never had so much as a "close call" on the open seas.

As the story goes, Fred had bought the *Angie Piper* from an old Tlingit captain named Henry Fall. The boat had only been on the water for five years, so she was still considered rather new for a fishing vessel. According to Fred, he had also gotten her at quite the steal.

We were anchored down in a small bay, waiting out a ferocious storm, when I first heard the captain's tale. It started out as a bet—an arm-wrestling match in one of the bars of Unalaska. Fred got his "ass handed to him," as he would say, by a man who looked like he had been dead for fifty years. Feeling sorry for Fred, Henry bought a round of drinks, and before the end of the night, they were talking business. One thing led to another, and a few months later, Fred became the new owner of the boat, which Henry had been trying desperately to get out from underneath. However—and here's the irony—two years later, Fred ran across Henry in Kenai. He said the man looked like he had gotten twenty years of his life back. His face had lost a few wrinkles, and his eyes looked "young again." Fred commented as much to the old man, who just laughed and replied, "That's funny. I was thinking you looked twenty years older, yourself."

It was common for our captain to exaggerate his stories, particularly when he was in a good mood. All that mattered was that the *Angie Piper* had not been a ship plagued with bad luck. Some boats broke down just days prior to the beginning of a season, costing their owners thousands of dollars before they caught a single crab. And of course, others never made it back home, breaking down in the middle of a winter storm, loaded with ice-covered pots, their crab tanks brimming over, and with three-story waves crashing over the decks. The *Angie Piper* had her expenses, like any other boat, but when the crabbing was hot, she never failed to run her gear, or make the cash. Until we took Danny out there for his first season, she'd never broken down.

Danny and I were almost finished unpacking a box of canned goods when we heard Dave hollering up in the wheelhouse. "You're making a big mistake, Fred!" It surprised me, as I hadn't known he was on the boat yet. "Mark my words: this is a huge, fucking mistake! Having someone like him on board is just ridiculous. Not to mention bad luck."

"I need you to shut up, already!" replied the captain.

"Think about it, Fred. That kid will be nothing but a liability—for all of us. You know how easy it is to get killed out here."

"I'm done talking to you. We're done. Get to work already, or get off my boat."

Danny looked me square in the eye. His face was pallid, ghost-like, marked by a fear I'd never seen in him. It sickened me to see him that way, but the truth was, I felt the same. Dave could be a bastard when he was unhappy, and he obviously had no intention of letting go of his first impression of my friend.

"Don't worry, Danny," I said, rather unconvincingly, as I reached out and touched his arm. "Once Dave sees how hard you work, he'll cool off."

"Are you sure they won't make me leave?"

"No way, buddy. Fred is a good guy. And he's tough—a lot tougher than Dave. He's the captain, and what he says around here, and when we're out to sea, is like ... well, it's what goes." I gestured to another box of canned goods, and Danny opened it. "Forget about Dave. He'll come around."

Just then, I heard Dave leave the wheelhouse and stomp down the stairs. At the bottom, he glanced up and spotted Danny and me in the hall. Under the glow of yellow lamplight, I saw his face turn the color of a lobster. Then his lips twisted a bit, revealing an inner struggle, as if he wanted to speak but was battling with his rage.

Dave walked down the hall but then turned to direct his piercing stare on me for a long moment. He shifted his gaze to Danny, then back at me. "You know, Ed," he said, casual-like, "you really disappoint me. I suppose ... well, I guess I used to think you were something special, Ed. Hardworking kid and all. Level-headed." He glanced again at Danny and I saw it in Dave's eyes, the sheer magnitude of his resentment. I thought I even saw a touch of fear. "But now this," he added. "Really?"

"Look, Dave, we don't want any trouble with you. Can't you just give him a chance?"

"You'd like that, wouldn't you, Ed?" Dave paused, almost on the verge of a grin. "Well, you can forget about it. By the end of this season, you'll both be off the *Angie Piper*. I'll make sure of it." Then he turned and walked down the hall, through the ready-room, and slammed his way out onto the deck—an ugly storm of hate and fury and menace. I wondered what had happened to the man that he should react this way. What was it, exactly, that bothered him about Danny's presence? There was something about my friend that tapped into the absolute worst of Dave.

"They're going to make me leave, Ed," Danny said, handing me a can of creamed corn. But then, he delivered a classic Danny line. With a laugh, he pointed at my face and said out loud, "Special-Ed. That's funny."

CHAPTER 7

———•———

MINUTES AFTER DAVE left, the door from the ready-room leading out onto the deck opened again. The short, brown-skinned man, who would later egg Danny into arm wrestling, stepped inside, carrying an olive duffel bag. Eloni Popo Winston, otherwise known as Loni, was our sixth and final crewmember. He threw me his trademark no-holds-barred grin before he turned to shut the door.

As a senior deckhand, Loni had been crabbing with Fred for almost ten years. He was well known and well liked throughout the fishing community, mostly because of his upbeat personality.

Loni hailed from Samoa's large island of Upolu. This was a man who had been steeped in a rich culture—a culture that also took nothing for granted. Loni hadn't started out with much, in terms of material possessions. But that Polynesian had much more of what really counted in life—an enormous family who defined love—and the rest of us secretly envied him. His dozens of relatives—cousins, aunts, uncles, brothers and sisters, and of course, his parents—would drop everything to help one another. How many possessions does anyone really need to make the best of things, when they have a family like that on their side?

Since the day we met, I'd liked Loni. I couldn't help it. He'd spent the first half of his life collecting a treasure trove of experiences and memories on the island of Upolu. As a result, he was a radiant person who promised entertainment at every turn. I admired the man. Upon Loni's face I could see children running on a beach, laughing in the waves, tossing seashells into the surf. Reflected in his eyes was a warm, orange sunset. Even in the way Loni shifted his duffel bag to his other shoulder and walked down the hall toward Danny and me, I could discern that sharp sense of confidence that poured out of him. Little things like that made me think that Loni had life figured out. And that's what I envied most. Nothing was more important than a good laugh with those he cared about, and Loni was hell-bent on keeping things that way. It was his mission in life. And that meant cutting through all the bullshit.

"What's gone up his ass, now?" Loni said, in his thick accent. He rubbed his hands together then gave a short whistle. "Daveman, he's all fired up."

"What's going on, Loni!" I shouted back. I was excited to see my Poly friend, "Poly" being the slang term he preferred when referring to people from the Polynesian islands. I knew that his presence would help dispel the negativity Dave had brought on board.

"How ya doing, Ed?" Loni replied, glancing from me to Danny. "You ready to catch us some crab?"

"You're damn right I am." I jerked a thumb toward Danny. "And this is our new greenhorn who's gonna make it happen."

"Hmm ...." Loni scratched his chin, sizing Danny up. "This brother's got a look to him, Ed. Looks like he might have him some muscle." Loni placed a hand on Danny's bicep and squeezed. "Oh, yeah. I can tell. This brother's nothing but muscle."

Danny's face broke into a goofy smile, his crooked teeth gleaming in the yellow light of the overhead lamp. He shifted his feet, then looked down at them, obviously embarrassed by the sudden attention.

"You've no idea, Loni," I said. "Danny is stronger than anybody you've ever known."

"Oh, is that so?" Loni replied. "Well, we'll see about that. Got us some real strong boys back on the island." He looked Danny up and down once again, then said, "Kinda short—like me. Might be good on deck …. Might be bad."

Loni had a point. It took all kinds of physical talents to be successful on a crab boat. Tall people like Dave were naturally strong, but often clumsy. They had trouble controlling their center of gravity, especially when the boat swayed violently in rough seas. Smaller people fared better on deck, but they were also prone to exhaustion after pushing thousand-pound crab pots around for days on end.

That said, we were talking about Danny Wilson.

"He got him some big hands, that's for sure," Loni said. He scratched the black whiskers on his chin, and then looked at me. "This the same boy you told me about—the one who worked in Bristol Bay?"

"He sure is," I replied, with a smile. Months ago, I had told Loni all about Danny's processing job up north, just to ease the worry that he wouldn't be ready for working the long hours. And because Loni was such a friendly guy, so easy to talk to, I went ahead and told him a lot more about Danny.

"And this means we've got us a future SEAL-man on board?"

Danny looked up, beaming.

"Yep. The one and only," I replied.

"Well … guess the *Angie Piper* might be in for some good fishing this year, eh?" Loni said, punching Danny on the arm.

"Hooyah, master chief!" Danny replied.

"My cousin, Lenny," continued Loni, "he's a Ranger with the Army. Says them SEALs are real bad-asses. Says they the toughest men alive."

"SEALs are the best!" Danny replied, his words slurring together once again. When he got excited—usually while discussing anything that had to do with Navy SEALs—even I had to listen hard to catch everything he said.

I've mentioned Danny's obsession with SEALs before. The excitement he felt over those elite warriors, and his dream of one day becoming one, went all the way back to our adolescence. We used to go to the movies a lot, which was a hoot in and of itself, all because of Danny. He would sit in the theater with a giant tub of popcorn and a giant soda and make a ruckus, crunching and slurping away. Not only that, but Danny would giggle, laugh, and cackle all throughout the movie. Even during times when there was nothing worth laughing at, Danny would laugh. He drove everyone in the theater crazy. But for me, listening to him was often more entertaining than the movie itself.

Things were a bit different though, when Danny and I were in the eighth grade and went to see *Navy SEALs*, staring Charlie Sheen. Danny didn't laugh much during that film, but he still managed to disturb everyone in the theater with his oohs and aahs, pointing, even jumping up and out of his seat. He thought the world of that movie. He went to see it five more times, checked out some books at the library on the subject of Special Forces, and asked a million and one questions of our neighbor, Ted, a marine veteran of the Vietnam War. Before long, Danny was telling everyone he met that one day he would become a Navy SEAL.

It was funny to hear my friend go on like that. He even adopted his own phrase from that elite community: *Hooyah, master chief!* Except with Danny, of course, it was never quite that clear. Eventually you figured out what he was saying, because he used the phrase every chance he got.

People would just smile and nod when Danny talked about becoming a SEAL. They did it in such an awkward fashion, knowing that the boy they encouraged would never see the fruition of his dream. But whether he was aware of it or not, Danny didn't seem to mind. He knew in his heart that one day he would be required to report for duty out on some blacktop, gear in hand. For Danny, it was as if he was any other guy.

"You got that right, Danny," said Loni. "They the best." Interestingly enough, Loni had no trouble understanding Danny. But then again, he was a great listener. "So how long you boys been here?"

"Only a few hours," I replied. "We flew in this morning."

"You eat yet? Might get me some lunch in town."

"And why am I not surprised?" I asked. "Here, have some pork and beans, then you can help us with all this shit."

"Oh man!" Loni said, laughing. "You a cruel man, Ed. A cruel man." Loni was one of those guys who would eat anything on his plate. He had the appetite of a grizzly bear, and would likely eat a bowl of rubber if it came with a bottle of Tabasco sauce.

"The diner has good food," Danny said, giving it a thumbs-up.

"Oh yeah, it does," replied Loni. "Real good food, in fact. Think I might go there right now." He threw his duffel bag into the stateroom and then headed back toward the door. Hesitating, he asked, "So why's Dave all mad like that?"

"Oh," I replied, "just bugging on shit, as always."

"Yeah, well, we gonna see about that. I don't know, Ed. Don't know if I can take any more of his talk."

The comment sounded more menacing than what I would have expected, coming from Loni. I was taken aback, speechless for a second. "That sounds almost like a threat, Loni," I replied.

"Might be that it is, Ed," Loni said. "Might be Dave's gonna get him a big surprise this season."

I wondered what Loni meant by that. And even more, I wondered what he would have done had he been with us earlier, on the street corner outside the general store. It was a thought that once again brought a small sense of relief. Loni was the greatest ally a person could have.

He smiled then, as he stepped out onto the deck. It was a curious smile with a hint of mischievousness. And from it, I observed the twinkling eyes of Maui, the hero-trickster of Polynesian mythology, and this brought an answering smile to my face. "Hey, Loni," I said, just before he closed the door, "we doing McCrawley's later?"

"Damn right, brother!" he said. "Can't sail without watering up."

I laughed. "See you when you get back, then. And don't worry, we'll save some work for you."

CHAPTER 8

———•———

THREE DAYS LATER, I was recovering from our famous night at McCrawley's, feeling like my head had been crushed between two crab pots. When I finally crawled out of the rack from inside my stateroom and into the dark belly of the *Angie Piper*, I realized the captain must have been screaming at me, and Loni, and the entire crew for quite some time. He was mad as a hornet, calling off orders, anxious to get us up and running.

Staggering over to the bathroom to wash my face, I noticed Danny was nowhere in sight. But I found Loni curled into a tight ball, his head over the toilet, hands grasping the rim of the bowl.

"Shit, Loni," I said, "we haven't even left the harbor yet."

Loni had his sea legs, there was no question about that. He was just working his way through a terrible hangover. I was wondering how Danny would get along out there on the open sea. I wasn't sure if there were any precluding conditions about someone like him being on a boat. Maybe Danny would get sick as a dog once we got running, endlessly puking his guts out, left completely dysfunctional and useless. It had happened often enough, causing dire situations. But when we were kids out on the playground, Danny would ride that little rusty merry-go-round for what seemed like hours, never once getting sick. I guess I was relying on that memory and hoping things hadn't changed much since then.

Fifteen minutes later, I stumbled into the galley in search of coffee. Salazar was there, standing next to the stove, cooking eggs, sausage, toast, and pancakes—the whole enchilada. A cigarette dangled from his lips as if he were a short-order cook out in the field with a bunch of Marines.

"Captain ain't gonna let us eat breakfast in town, is he?" It was a dumb question, but I asked it anyway.

In his usual taciturn way, Salazar simply shook his head and grunted.

"Well, have you seen Danny? Smells good, by the way."

Salazar pulled his cigarette from his lips, as if to speak, but then jerked a thumb toward the deck.

"Be right back, then," I replied. I left the galley, walked through the ready-room, opened the door, and stepped outside onto the deck. Like another smash in the head from a crab pot, the brightness of the day stunned me. Yet it was hardly bright. The morning might have been cast in silver, embodied by heavy cloudbanks. They were immense, like gray whales rising from the ocean to greet our world with their stories of the deep Alaskan waterways.

After rubbing knuckles into my eyes, I noticed Danny standing by the door. His hands were stuffed into his coat pockets, a beanie on his head. His pants were tucked into rubber boots, and gloves dangled from his back pocket. A Leatherman Multi-Tool was clipped on his belt, and his face …. Well, his face reflected uncertainty, a bit like the bright yet foggy day. Danny Wilson was ready to work.

"Morning, buddy," I said, still blinking away the sudden brightness. Danny nodded in return. He was staring out across the deck, his eyes fixed on nothing in particular. I studied the boat anyways. The *Angie Piper* looked good, ready to sail. The stacks of crab pots towered before us, a host of webbed rigging and steel ribs. The deck looked tight and clean, devoid of clutter and extra supplies. A thick brine clung to the morning mist, and was heavy to breathe. You could taste the ocean in the air.

"Eat anything yet?" I asked.

"Nope," he replied, his tone short and decisive.

"Well, come on, then. Let's get some breakfast."

"I'm okay." *Okay, shit.* Danny could eat three cows for lunch before coming up for air. He was a bottomless pit, and his dad was always going on about how much it cost to feed "that boy." I had observed this enormous appetite of Danny's for as long as I could remember. Furthermore, unlike Little Mikey from the Life Cereal commercial, Danny would eat damn near anything. He didn't have any issues about food, dislikes or favorites I'd noted with most other people. Danny was easy when it came to eating. He was an easy, bottomless pit. And naturally, breakfast was his favorite meal.

I took a guess as to why he was standing out in the cold. "Come on, Danny. Don't worry about the captain. He's just eager to get us going." Opening the door wider, I motioned for him to come in. "Smell that? Bacon and eggs. Sausage. Pancakes."

"Captain wants us to work," Danny replied.

"Danny. If you don't get in here, the captain's gonna eat your damn breakfast!" He hesitated, looked at the door, the deck, the crab pots, not knowing at all what to do even if I did tell him to get to work. "Would you get the hell in here already?"

Danny finally came in from the cold, causing an uproar of laughter amongst Loni and Salazar when I told them he was standing on deck, ready to work. Fred seemed pleased with Danny's enthusiasm as well. He seemed less rigid, more casual. This was, after all, the last relaxing meal we would likely have until our tanks were full of crab and we were running back into port. As we lumbered into the galley, I explained as much to Danny and told him to eat up. As soon as we started turning gear—working twenty, thirty, even forty hours straight—he'd be lucky to get a candy bar down his gullet for breakfast.

"Whatcha want on your plate, Danny-boy?" Being a true fisherman, Loni was completely unfazed by his episode in the bathroom minutes before. He was at the stove piling scrambled eggs onto a piece of toast, smiling, chipper as ever. "I'm gonna serve our greenhorn," Loni said. "Boy made me a shitload of money last night."

"Pancakes, please," said Danny, sliding into the booth.

"Pancakes?" replied Loni. His eyebrows twisted in apparent confusion. "You gotta eat more than that out here, Danny."

"Don't listen to him, Loni," I said, pouring myself a cup of coffee and leaning back against a pantry door. "He'll eat anything you give him, and lots of it—so just pile it on."

"I like sausage too," Danny said.

"Again, don't listen to him, Loni," I repeated. "Like I said, he'll eat anything. So load him up."

Changing the subject, Loni chuckled and asked, "How much did everyone make last night?"

"Danny and I made two thousand dollars each," I said, lifting my cup into the air, offering a toast to nobody in particular.

Loni squealed with laughter, but Salazar just shook his head, cursing softly to himself. Being overly conservative, he found betting on an arm-wrestling competition way too risky for the likes of him. And man did Salazar regret it just then.

The captain, who had been standing next to me, slid into the booth beside Danny. "What about you, Loni?" he asked. "How much did you take in?"

Loni placed a heaping plate of food and tall glass of orange juice in front of Danny. "This boy made me three-thousand dollars. And when this season's over, I'm gonna buy him a real good steak. Fat and juicy, huh, Danny?"

"Yes sir!" Danny said, grinning. He drove his fork into the steaming plate of food.

Just then, Dave walked in from down the hall, dressed and ready, hat on, a smear of grease across his cheek.

"How 'bout you, Dave?" Loni asked.

"How 'bout me, what?" Dave replied. Once again, his mood was black as coal. He walked straight to the stove and served himself a plate of food.

"What'd you make last night?" Loni continued. "I saw you smiling when Danny-boy beat that state champ."

"I don't know what you're talking about," replied Dave. He turned around and walked toward the hall, stopping briefly to give the captain a status report. All was well—except for his attitude, which he then took outside, along with his breakfast.

Obviously, Dave had been up for a while. But that didn't surprise me. For all his asshole-ness, he was a dedicated employee. He'd been down in the engine room, likely tinkering with nuts and bolts, belts and gauges, and whatever else we didn't want breaking down on us once we were out on the open sea. There were plenty of stories about boats going down all because of a ten-dollar part, such as a gasket or a washer. And each of us on board—except for Danny—knew those stories damn well. Briefly, my mind went back to Molly McDowell and the *Polar Betty*. What were the circumstances surrounding their tragic end? Just what exactly sent that boat and her crew into the abysmal depths of the Gulf of Alaska? Was it a leaky gasket? A failed pump? A ten-dollar part? Was it something more unpredictable and violent—a rogue wave? In the end, we'd never know. Molly hadn't been able to get a clear transmission to the Coast Guard, explaining the details of their trouble. And nothing from the boat was ever recovered. In the blink of an eye, The *Polar Betty* and her entire crew was lost forever.

"That man got too much darkness in him, captain," Loni said. He turned and sat next to Danny at the table. "Too much evil darkness. Too much anger."

"Don't stress about Dave, Loni," the captain replied. "You know him. He'll drop some of that evil darkness once we get on the crab."

There was a brief roll of laughter amongst us, but then Fred looked up and stared at me. His face was pale and serious. I'd been standing against the pantry door once again, plate now in hand, fork in mouth, yet my body froze at that stare.

"Ed, when you boys are done eating, I want you to take Danny down the hall and fit him with a survival suit. Show him the routine—how to get in quickly and zip it up. And make sure he can beat the time." The captain looked away then and reached for his coffee. I observed his eyes, his hands, the way he held his cup …. He looked sad and distant. It was as if he had been right there with me, in my own mind, thinking about Molly and his crew.

"Sure thing, Captain," I replied.

"And when you're done with that, take a good stroll on deck. We're throwing lines in an hour, so let's be ready." He put his cup down and continued eating. "But take your time with them suits."

That's exactly what Danny and I did, once we finished breakfast. The route to the survival suits led us down the hall and into the stateroom adjacent to ours. I reminded Danny about the importance of learning every nook and cranny of the ship. About knowing the location of every exit and having these egresses mapped into his brain not just as they were, but how they could be: in absolute darkness, twisted, rotated, flipped, and cockeyed because the damn boat had just lost all power and took three rolls from a giant wave. How it could be.

Danny nodded gravely as we pulled out a survival suit from the large wooden chest mounted against the stateroom wall. I guided him on how to get into the suit properly: feet first, body next, weak arm straight in while your strong arm waited so that you could use it to affix the hood. Then you slip that arm into the suit and zip yourself up. It was slow going, but Danny managed to get the suit on.

"Last but not least," I said, "blow into this tube. It'll inflate the suit, keep you from sinking."

"We don't want that to happen," Danny replied. My friend

looked like a giant orange marshmallow puffing on that bladder hose.

"That's good," I said, looking over his suit. "That's how you do it. Now take it off and put it back on. You've got one minute, Danny. Gotta be able to get this suit on in less than a minute, so make it fast. And remember, you might be in the dark, so go ahead and close your eyes."

Thirty minutes later, Danny was still practicing getting his suit on. I told him not to overdo it, that he could work on it another time. Nevertheless, he kept sliding into that damn thing, stubborn as always. But that's how Danny had always been. Whenever he got something into his head, he stuck with it until the end.

Ironically, this aspect of Danny's character always conjured up a sad fantasy. I often wondered what his life would have been like if he'd been gifted with normal intelligence. What was his true potential? What could he have done? He would have made one hell of a Navy SEAL, that's for sure. Just like his dad, Danny knew the value of hard work. And just like his dad had told me, Danny always learned best by practicing something, over and over again.

I remember the day Danny had showed up for swim tryouts at our school, and Mr. Elmsworth lowered his head and told him he couldn't be on the team. Danny didn't sulk or whine. He didn't even argue. He just smiled, and then had his dad sign him up at the YMCA the following day. And on that day, and every day forward, that's where I found my buddy after school: swimming laps as awkward as hell, one after the other. Practicing to be a Navy SEAL.

It shames me now to think of what Danny's true potential might have been. I'll never forget what happened to my friend—what happened to us. It seemed as if the struggles we faced growing up—the challenges Danny and I both had, especially *his* challenges—were simply meant to prepare us for the biggest battle ever.

"What's that right there?" Danny asked, pointing to a roll of yellow reflective tape sitting on a shelf.

After I told him, Danny took that tape and constructed a crude bull's-eye on the back of the suit he'd been practicing with.

"What the hell are you doing?" I asked.

"In case they need to find me," he replied.

"In case they need to find you?" I teased.

Even as a kid, Danny never knew how funny he could be. "What are they going to do—shoot you?" I burst into laughter and told him he had five more minutes before he really saw the captain get angry. "I'll meet you on deck," I said. Then I walked away.

CHAPTER 9

———◆———

TWO HOURS LATER, Danny threw out our last hawser line and the *Angie Piper* chugged away from the dock. I stood on the deck, starboard side, and watched as we motored away from the safety of Kodiak's beautiful landscape. Her shaggy green hills, rocky shorelines, and pine-laden outcrops stretched like fingers out into the sea. People were hustling up and down the wharf, sorting boxes and gear, preparing boats, unloading trucks, running cranes, laughing and cursing, waving goodbye. Most crabbers are not actually from Alaska. Like birds, they migrate to this land from distant places such as northern Oregon or Seattle—like Fred, whose boat was moored there during the off-seasons. Friendly waves from fellow fishermen or complete strangers on the shores of Kodiak were expected when we headed out to sea. In their own way, the people who work in Alaska—local or not—can be kind and understanding. They know the dangers of fishing for crab in the dead of winter, with the dreaded williwaws, the fifty-foot waves, the deadly icing-over of vessels, and any number of other possible tragic outcomes.

"This boat here," I said to Danny, "she's nothing but good luck, buddy. She's gonna get us onto the crab soon, and then we'll be working our asses off."

The gray sky and thick fog of the morning thinned out as we headed southeast, toward the Gulf of Alaska. But the smell of brine still sat heavy in the air and grew thicker once we passed the sheltered inlets south of Kodiak. Teeming with life, these miniature bays serve as excellent catchalls for kelp and the various critters of the ocean. Over the rail, I spotted three sea lions crossing our bow as we rounded the point near Chiniak Head. We were now heading into the rougher waters of the Gulf.

"Ride's gonna be different soon, Danny," I said, sliding on my gloves. "Now we'll see if you've got any sea legs."

Danny smiled in return. "What do we do, master chief?" He slid on a pair of gloves and adjusted his hat.

"We're gonna double-check the gear, make sure everything's good and secure. Then we'll get you started on making bait." I crossed the deck to the stack of seven-bys, all one hundred and eighty of them, and began looking over their chains. Regular procedure on our boat was to make sure no slack had built up on the pots or anything else we needed secured on deck before we got ourselves into rougher waters. Although the present conditions were nice and smooth, the weather in Alaska could flip-flop at a moment's notice. Best practice was to be prepared.

Long before we left Anchorage, I taught Danny some of the basics of such preparation. First, though, was how to tie knots. The most common knots used on our ship were the bowline, clove hitch, and carrick bend. I even taught Danny how to splice together two lengths of rope. Splicing was simple enough on its own, as were the knots, and Danny had picked up both these skills without much trouble. However, there is a common problem with learning various knots that I call the "phenomenon of application." Most people have little difficulty learning how to tie a knot while sitting at a table—that's easy. But when they have to tie that same knot in different settings, onto different parts of a structure, and particularly during a nasty storm—with ten-foot waves crashing over the deck and onto their heads—it is a different story entirely. Suddenly, you don't have the faintest idea where to begin. Danny had quickly learned the basics of knot-tying, at a table, but it actually took him quite a while before he could apply them effectively. So while on deck, I made sure he got plenty of practice.

Once we finished checking tie downs, chains, floorboards, and everything else on deck, I gave Danny instructions to start bringing up the boxes of herring from the freezers below. As he continued to work, I went up to the wheelhouse to consult with the captain. I passed both Salazar and Loni in the galley, stacking things away, preparing for rougher seas themselves. They were talking about their families back home, and it made me smile; the two of them were so different in just about every way.

Loni had a large family—a wife of fifteen years, along with four kids—and lived in Puyallup, Washington. He had three brothers and two sisters, each with families of their own living in and around Seattle. On Saturday nights, it was virtually impossible to find a place to sit at that man's house. Either because of the warmth of Samoan culture, or his open personality, or perhaps a combination of both, family gatherings were simply the way it was for Loni. I don't think he would have known what to do with himself without a big family at home.

Salazar, on the other hand, lived alone in a one-bedroom studio in Bellingham, Washington. I had seen Salazar's home. It matched his simple character: a single room with a single window overlooking the side of an apartment complex. He had one plant and a calico named Georgina. That was about it, aside from his toys, which were an electronic drum set and a five-thousand-dollar stereo system. Salazar was big on music. This usually quiet guy would talk your ear off if you asked him a question about jazz, rock, reggae, or even calypso. Music was his life, eternal bachelor that he was. As for family, his closest relative was a brother living in San Diego, California, whom he hadn't seen since their mother's funeral, years past.

I know that Salazar entertained the idea of getting married and having kids. On more than one occasion, he'd mentioned how nice it would be. But Salazar was so damn shy around women, it seemed unlikely that he'd ever meet one to settle down with. Again, he was so different from Loni. But there they were, making sense of their lives in the galley. Finding commonalities through conversation, as any crabber knows, is a cherished pastime after spending days, weeks, even months away from home. Smiling, I headed up the stairs past the galley.

When I entered the wheelhouse, I found Fred and Dave hovering over a map.

"I'm thinking we'll try this spot right here," the captain said, pointing to an area roughly thirty miles southeast of Tugidak Island. "There's a shelf that yielded some good crab a few years back. I'd like to check it out again."

Dave nodded and puffed on a cigar. That was Dave's tradition: a stogie on the way out, and one on the way in. He had family too—three boys, each about the age of Danny and me. I always assumed they didn't have much of a relationship with their dad. Dave's life, from what I knew of it, wasn't particularly unique and far from glamorous. During the off-season, he was known to be a chronic drunk. His wife had left him years before— maybe she finally got fed up with him smacking her around. His only sober periods, in fact, were when he was fishing. Dave wouldn't drink a drop of liquor while on board the *Angie Piper*. I suppose that might have been what was unique about the guy. Nevertheless, I had known Dave for four years, and during that time I concluded that he'd turned out the way I'd imagined every bully encountered in high school would. However, he wasn't always so one-dimensional. Despite his abrasive nature, there were times when he was good to be around—even borderline pleasant. That was usually when we were on the crab. And in those four years, the man had taught me a lot about fishing. He was a good instructor, for all his "evil darkness," as Loni had said. One could safely say, in the spirit of fairness, that Dave was a complicated man.

"If we fish here," continued the captain, "we'll still have the bays to anchor up in when the storms hit. The forecast …. It's already looking bad."

Fishing in these parts was different from fishing for king crab in the vast Bering Sea, where hundreds of lonely, bleak miles kept a boat and her crew in constant threat from the onslaughts of wicked storms or meandering ice packs. For us, many of the hotspots for tanner crab were near and around the various bays of Kodiak Island. A common strategy was to drop gear at a preferred location, and then head back into the safety of a bay when a storm came in. Your pots stayed out and soaked. Even without the storms, many boats ran their gear using this strategy. It offered a reprieve from the dangers of the Gulf of Alaska, not to mention rest and hot meals for the crew. This tactic broke the monotonous drudgery of endlessly turning gear: picking up pots, sorting the catch, re-baiting and dropping pots—over and over again, out upon the abhorrent dullness of a frigid sea—until a man was ready to slip into the realms of insanity.

But then again, that was crabbing.

"Excuse me, Captain," I interrupted. "Danny and I just double-checked the gear and the deck. All is good. I'm gonna show him how to make bait now, if that's okay."

"Go to it, Ed. Get him chopping and filling them jars." Fred sat back into his captain's chair and took a drink from a large coffee mug. "I expect we'll be dropping gear tomorrow morning, early. So let's be ready."

"Sure thing, Captain."

"Hey, Ed?" Fred said, stopping me just after I turned to walk away. "I'm excited to see how well Danny's gonna do. That boy sure is strong."

"You haven't seen anything yet," I replied. "Not only is

Danny strong as a horse, but he's a working machine." That was the honest-to-god truth. Danny was a Clydesdale, equipped for hard labor, built for the long run. And the best thing about him was that he was just like his father. He loved to work. Whenever he stayed with us, Danny always liked helping my mother clean the house. As he got older, he would often get after the younger kids when they made a mess. It cracked me up watching him scold those kids, pointing his finger at them and mumbling. Half the time they didn't understand what the hell he was saying.

I smiled and walked downstairs into the hall, past the galley where Salazar and Loni were now discussing the nuances of classical music—Loni could talk to anyone about anything. Then I went out on deck, where Danny stood next to several cardboard boxes. I could see that he was ready to get busy again.

"Okay, Danny, let's chop this stuff up already." I opened the first box—twenty-five pounds of frozen herring—and dumped its contents into the grinder. The grinder itself was essentially a miniature wood chipper. You'd push the fish through the funnel on top and a mush of meat and bones would get deposited into a large metal box—instant cat food. From there, you simply scooped the mush into small plastic jars—each perforated with tiny holes to allow for "seeping," or chumming of the crab—and hang them on a bar above the table.

"Think you can handle this, buddy?" I asked.

"No problem, Ed," Danny replied, with a smile. "I can chop fish now."

"Yep. You sure can, Danny. You can chop fish." Making bait is a tedious, mind-numbing, hand-aching process—so naturally, Danny took right to it.

After a few minutes, I left my friend there at the table and went inside to use the head. Down the hall again, toward the staterooms, I encountered Dave standing near the steps below the wheelhouse. He stood in the shadows, staring at me as I approached, the cigar in his mouth burning brightly like a distant sun hovering in the blackness of space.

"Hey, Ed?" he said, mimicking the captain's voice.

I turned and looked at him, waiting. I knew from the look on his sallow face and in his cold eyes—from my own experience with him, and with guys just like him back in high school—that what he was about to say would be sheer ugliness.

"You think you're pretty cute, don't you?" he continued.

"What do you mean?" My voice rattled with nervous laughter. Adrenaline was running in my veins like a school of salmon up a river. Was this what it was like to be one of his sons? Did he bully them like he was bullying me?

"You know what I mean." He took a drag from his cigar, and then blew smoke into my face. "You really think that boy of yours—that 'Danny-boy,' as Loni likes to call him—is gonna survive out here?"

"Yeah, I think he will." I thrust my hands into my coat pockets, aware of how much they were shaking. I'd been in this position before, many times, and always, it was so damn tiring, so exhausting facing a bully: looking him in the eye, standing under him, being bombarded with threats and insults. It zapped the energy right out of me.

"You haven't seen anything, yet, Captain." Now he was mimicking my voice, mocking my conversation with Fred. My response was to stand in silence, there in the hall, the dark shadows of the *Angie Piper* enveloping me. "Well, we'll see about that," he added. "Don't forget what I said about this being your last season. Start counting your days on this boat, Ed."

He brushed past me, his shoulder knocking me like a linebacker's, jolting me against the wall as he barreled down the hall and outside. What was up with that guy? Again, I wondered why he hated Danny so much. Or why he apparently hated me now, as well. But also, why had he bet on that arm-wrestling match back in the bar? I'd seen Dave angered many times before, but he always seemed rather tolerant of me, even when I was the greenhorn. Something about Danny really got the man's goat.

After my encounter with Dave, I went straight to the head, where I contemplated my predicament. I could talk to the captain, who knew about Dave's dislike but maybe not the extent of it. Then again, that might only make things worse. Or could it get any worse? I was confused, and scared, and worried. And as I sat there, trying to take a shit in a bathroom that rocked back and forth—a situation I never could get comfortable with—I thought about Danny. My friend had been picked on his whole life. But unlike me, he never seemed to care. Danny had this resilience to the pressure about him; things just rolled off his back like melted butter. And it wasn't that he was too stupid to understand what was happening when people were being mean to him, either. Nor was he immune to fear. No, my friend wasn't fearless. It's just that, for Danny, most of the time his fear existed only in the present, the moment at hand. He didn't hold on to anxiety—about anything—like the rest of us "normal folks" did.

On the way back from the bathroom, I grabbed more bait jars from below and then met Danny at the grinder. He was already halfway through his fourth box of herring and had a good pile of fish pâté built up in the steel container. A dozen seagulls circled above us, attracted to the strong odor. Within the hour, twice as many of those creatures would be trailing us, perching on the rails, scrounging for the first scraps of the season.

"How's it going over here?" I asked. Since we had been riding through the rougher seas of the Gulf for a few hours now, I expected that if Danny would have a problem with being sick, he would start to show signs. Making piles of bloody chum with foul-smelling herring would certainly contribute, as one would expect.

"Chopping fish, Ed."

"I can see that, buddy." I dumped the bait jars into a large tote next to him. "So are you feeling sick yet?"

"Nope. Why would I feel sick?"

"Oh, I don't know. Maybe because we're on a swaying boat, and you're working with a pile of bloody chum."

"You mean seasick?" he replied. Sarcasm was often lost on my friend.

"Yeah, I mean seasick. Are you seasick? Right now? Do you feel like you need to hurl?"

"Nope." He picked up another chunk of iced herring and shoved it into the grinder. "I don't think Navy SEALs get seasick, Ed. So I won't get sick either."

And like that, Danny had his sea legs. Not once did he get sick, and he stayed in balance with the listing of the boat, only stumbling once or twice. Perhaps my initial assumptions were correct, that a kid like him was immune to vertigo. Or maybe it was because Danny never worried about it.

CHAPTER 10

———◆———

"**N**OW WE GONNA see what kind of man you are, Danny-boy!" The entire crew was full of excitement, and Loni was freely expressing it. Roughly twenty hours since we had left Kodiak, we were ready to drop gear. As planned, the captain had picked a spot a few hours south of Tugidak Island, and was toiling with the decision to either test the area with a single line of pots, known as prospecting, or to simply dump our entire load. He told us we'd drop forty of the steel cages at a minimum.

"We gonna see you work real hard, that's for sure." Loni laughed with sheer glee as he unfolded a brand-new set of raingear. "Time to catch us some crab, boys."

Crammed together in the ready-room, we struggled to don our clothing and essential gear for working on deck. Using Duct Tape, we sealed our jacket sleeves tightly against our wrists. Our thick rubber boots covered wool socks, doubled for added cushion and warmth. And bulky raingear sealed us from head to toe. Last came the gloves—the first of many pairs we would wear out during the season. Handling tanner crab, with their spiny legs and prickly carapaces, often tore right through a well-worn glove, if you happened to be careless. And after working eighteen hours straight, bent over at the waist, you grew more careless with each passing minute. I can't count how many gloves we've gone through on the *Angie Piper*.

After suiting up, we bustled through the door and out onto the deck—a parade of orange and yellow raingear taking the first steps of dropping crab pots into the mighty Gulf of Alaska. The seas were rough, with icy swells pushing high across our bow. A few enormous waves known as "poop sweepers" had already poured over the rail prior to us walking outside. How did we know this? Streams of foam rushed to our starboard scuppers as the *Angie Piper* swayed forward—a clear enough sign for everyone. Except Danny, of course.

I really did wonder how my friend was going to handle being out there. It crossed my mind that it might terrify him to realize what was expected of a crab fisherman. Once he comprehended the full, potential threat of working the most dangerous job in the world, would he freeze with fear like so many other men and women? Would he quit on the spot, and then hole up in his bunk, waiting to get dropped off at the nearest port? Of course not. Who the hell was I kidding? Danny was the first one out the door, his childlike grin spread across his face.

"From here on out, you're gonna be our deck ape, Danny." I had to shout to be heard. The noise surrounding our boat—the clank of support chains, the bang of boom cables clinging to metal rigging, the growl of the diesel engine running half open, the roar of the ocean, the howl of a thirty-plus knot wind—these sounds all took center stage in a concert of chaos. Damn, it felt good to be fishing again. Pausing briefly, I took a huge breath of ocean air, savoring the raw taste of a salty mist sweeping around me.

"Deck ape?" Danny asked, walking straight to the bait table. Snapped out of my moment of elation, I followed my friend. The "bait table" was all that Danny knew about fishing right now. The chopping and scooping of herring was his comfort zone, and until I told him otherwise, he would just hang out there at that table, processing bait. For sure, this was Danny's one observable weakness. He wasn't ambitious, a go-getter who required little or no hand-holding or instruction. Danny was not the type to figure out how to run a deck on his own, simply by watching the other crewmembers. But I had long ago prepared myself for this reality. I knew how to teach Danny. What he did have over most other people was that once he started working, he wouldn't stop until you told him to. Danny would work himself to death if you let him. That made him the perfect deck ape.

"Yeah! You're gonna be our deck ape—the guy with the muscle. So listen up, Danny." I stood between the bait table and the large totes of whole cod we used to complete the bait setup and pointed to the jars hanging off the rail. "Listen for Salazar. When he gives the call, I want you to bring one of those jars, and two of those fish—don't forget to hook them. I want you to bring them over to the pot with the rest of us. We're gonna clip all that shit on the inside." Confusion mingled with excitement on Danny's face. "Here, I'll show you."

I grabbed a filleting knife off the table and sliced through the bellies of the cod—heavy, fat fish, the size of small dogs. Baiting crab required a setup that included at least one of these fish, along with a bait jar of crushed herring. The entire rig would get clipped on the inside of the crab pot. The task was easy enough, but you could get clumsy if you hadn't mastered it. Or you were beyond tired.

"Just start cutting through these guys, like this," I said, slicing open one fish after another. "We're gonna be using them real soon now."

Leaving Danny, I jogged across the deck over to Salazar, who stood behind the hydraulic controls, a cigarette dangling from his mouth. Referred to as the "hydros," these controls are mounted on a small table about three feet high, near the ship's superstructure. They control the various machinery we run on deck, including the picking crane used for transporting the crab pots. The hydros are the heart of a crabbing operation—without them, we'd be screwed. As our deck boss, Salazar ran the hydros and had the privilege of staying out of harm's way. But this privilege also came with the responsibility of keeping the crew safe. One miscalculation with the picking crane, and a thousand-pound steel cage could suddenly become a swinging menace for everyone on deck. It could easily crush a deckhand, or send him over the rail to an icy death.

"Are we still dropping forty?" I asked Salazar.

"Yep!" Pulling his cigarette from his lips, Salazar flung it over the side and tested the controls to the crane. On a smooth day with a solid crew, forty pots meant roughly forty minutes of labor. We could drop one pot a minute and be back inside the galley sipping coffee within the hour—not a bad way to start a season. Yet the waves were crashing hard against our ship, causing our entire world to sway up and down, making it a challenge just to stand in one place.

"Gonna be rough!" Salazar shouted, casting a glance at Danny.

"Yeah! I know," I replied, with a nod. "I'm gonna help him out some."

Just then, over the loudspeaker, the captain announced that we should start dropping. Loni gave a cheer while he and Dave took positions near the pot launcher—the hydraulic ramp used to load and off-load crab pots, as well as dump them into the ocean. With a squelching sound, Salazar navigated the picking crane over to our stacked gear—the tower of seven-bys—and I followed along, mentally preparing myself to climb on up.

A very tricky and dangerous job was climbing up and down the anchored pots (known as the main-stack) in order to secure or unsecure them, as needed. One slip and you fell over the rail and into the freezing sea, or straight onto the deck with a broken neck. Nothing about the task was easy; the pots were wet or icy or both. In any case, they were slick under a rubber boot. And the swaying seas were a constant threat, as you fought to keep a tight grip and firm balance along the gear. It was the one feature of my job that both scared the shit out of me and filled me with exhilaration. I had done it many times before, so I knew what to expect. And what I expected was that Danny would want to do the job also. Although not necessarily a daredevil, Danny was caught up in the thrill of working on the *Angie Piper*. He showed it the minute we had stepped on board. I assumed that he was living his Navy SEAL dream, and I feared that because of this, he might also get a little too careless.

"You just stay right there," I told Danny, as I grabbed hold of the steel framework of the lowest crab pot. "Get a jar and some fish. Make sure you're ready."

"I'm ready," Danny replied.

From the corner of my eye, I saw him pull a jar then look back to watch me scramble up the tower of steel cages. Seconds later, I was at the top, securing the crane cable to a pot. Then, unsecuring the chains of that particular pot, I released it from the main-stack. Down again I climbed. Salazar skillfully hoisted and transported the pot over to the pot launcher, where Loni and Dave grabbed it and positioned it in place. Suddenly, there we were on deck, our first launch seconds away. Danny's first real test was about to begin.

"Bait boy!" Dave shouted, a clear note of contempt in his voice.

"Let's go, Danny!" I ran up to help him, but Danny was two steps ahead of me. Carrying two fish and a bait jar, he led the way to the pot launcher, not really knowing what to do but willing to try all the same.

"Watch this, Danny," I said, relieving him of the bait setup. I climbed inside the pot—an eerie task if there ever was one—clipped the bait jar and bloody cod onto the steel rigging, and then climbed out. "That's it, buddy. It's that easy."

"Now we gonna see," Loni said, as he swung a crab-pot line onto the cage. Roughly six hundred feet of coiled rope that sat nearly three feet high, the line weighed almost a hundred pounds and required a certain finesse and swing of the hips of a man in order to toss it anywhere. Loni was a master of the maneuver, and could toss one line after another for hours at a time. "We gonna see a whole lot, for sure!" Loni repeated, as I stepped back and watched him and Dave tie shut the cage's door. "Gonna see that boy work. Gonna see this pot come up full. We gonna see money in our hands, yes sir!"

A blast of wind slapped me broadside, ripping down the hood of my raincoat. This was our first pot over the rail for the season. It was a symbolic moment, one familiar to every crewmember who had ever fished the seas of this world.

"Let her go!" Dave shouted. Seconds later, with another hydraulic squeal, our first pot went over the rail and into the frigid seas of Alaska. What followed was a quick dance between Dave and Loni as they both worked together to hurtle shots of line and buoys attached to the thousand-pound cage. One false move—a lift of the foot at the wrong time, for example—and a person could find himself attached to the descending pot, following it into the icy waters and pulled to the bottom of the ocean in a matter of seconds.

"Remember what I said about your feet, Danny." I pointed to Dave and Loni. "See how they keep their feet always on the deck?" Danny stared, scratching the whiskers of his chin. "It's important, Danny. Always, always, keep your feet planted on the deck. Keep 'em there, and you'll stay there."

"Hooyah, master chief!" he replied.

Dave hollered, "Next!" which was the cue for our second launch. Loni raced across the deck to retrieve another coil of crab-pot line, a job that would quickly become one of Danny's. Salazar maneuvered the picking crane toward the main-stack once again, while I crawled up it. Danny gathered another bait setup over at the table. And Fred jogged the *Angie Piper* against the trough of the waves. We chugged along roughly thirty miles south of Tugidak Island: a fully operating fishing vessel, prospecting for the elusive snow crab some five hundred feet below us.

Loni was right: over the next few days, the crew of the *Angie Piper* would see a whole lot of things. Many things. Things that looked gray, such as the belly of the ocean churning up and down in her endless roil of anger. Or the leering face of a cruel sky, lifeless in its own hoary shade, yet mocking all the same the insanity in which every fisherman conceives at one point or another. We were going to see things that would drive a man wild with hate and sullen with fear. And things that no person should ever have to endure, regardless of their sins. Finally, I was going to see something much more than any of this, something that would forever change who I was, or what I thought, what I believed in, and ultimately, what I would do for the rest of my life. I would see my true character—my strengths and my weaknesses. And I would see these things within Danny Wilson, as well.

"Is it time to bring the bait now, Ed?" Danny was standing by the table, a fistful of bleeding fish in one hand, a swinging bait-jar in the other. His barrel chest and rigid shoulders, in all their mighty strength and bulk, pushed against the inside of his raingear. And his almond-shaped eyes, dripping with candor, lit a fire of enthusiasm straight into my soul.

"You're damn right it is, sailor!" I shouted. And with a crashing bellow, Salazar landed our second crab pot onto the launcher, while Dave and Loni manhandled it into position. "Bring on the bait, Danny-boy!"

CHAPTER 11

———•———

FORTY POTS LATER became another forty after a two-hour ride west of our first string of gear. Six hours after that, we dropped twenty more pots north of Tugidak Island, and the day was yet bright, and half over. The rough seas calmed down considerably, allowing for easy going as the captain acted on a "hunch" and steered the *Angie Piper* west for another thirty miles. Awake now for over fifteen hours, Fred told us to get ready to drop the last of them. Sixty more pots, and then we would break for the northern end of Tugidak Island to anchor down and get some rest.

By this time, Danny was proficient at doing his job as bait-boy, which pleased the hell out of me. I noticed that he watched and listened to the sounds of the operations on deck. And, uncharacteristically, he began to take the initiative in retrieving the crab-pot lines for Loni. But above all, Danny swiftly showed signs of becoming a true fisherman—which I think pissed Dave off more than anything else. Just as I predicted, Danny had proved that he was exactly what every fishing crew looked for in a greenhorn: someone who would work constantly, ask few questions, not once complain, and simply do their damn job until told otherwise. Like his dad, Stephen Wilson, Danny demonstrated that he understood the value of hard work as he slit open fish after fish, pulled jars, secured bait setups, and dragged pot lines across the deck.

Furthermore, despite the chaos inherent in working on a crabbing vessel, Danny quickly established a routine. It was easy enough to do, and quite expected considering the repetitive and limited nature of his tasks. And although it probably wasn't a conscious decision on his part, more of a natural reflex to the stresses of the job, it worked in Danny's favor all the same. Our first day of fishing would soon be over, with sixty more pots to drop, and looking at my friend, you might conclude it had just begun.

But then he tripped over a coil of rope and fell flat on his face.

"Ha!" shouted Dave. "You guys all see that? That's what happens when you let a gimp on board."

I grimaced as I went over to help Danny up, Dave's words still echoing in my head. It dawned on me that Danny's greatest strength might also be his greatest weakness. The fact that Danny would work himself to death if you let him made him a potential liability. He might become injured and unable to do his job. I wondered if there was some truth to Dave's words, after all. It was an ugly fall, caused likely from fatigue, and I feared Danny might have broken something.

"Don't be starting on like that, Dave," Loni said. I glanced over and saw his scowl. Loni's brows drew together, anger mixed with Samoan pride, as he stood up for Danny—something I could never seem to do for my friend.

"Oh, come on, Popo," Dave replied sarcastically, referencing the nickname Loni used among his relatives. "You really think that guy's gonna work out? Do you? You think he'll be able to rough it out here for a month? Shit, I bet he couldn't count the money he'd earned even if he did make it through a season."

"You be careful, or he might go and work you out of your job. I'm thinking that's what scares you now, huh?"

"Go fuck yourself, Loni!" Dave shouted.

Dave's face grew redder with each word Loni spat back at him. We had just worked some long hours with a few more left to go, and fatigue was beginning to set in, the limits of mutual respect tested by Dave's natural response to stress. We had all seen his grumpy side many times. Unlike Loni, I chose to ignore the big man when he blew off steam at the end of the day. Shit, what am I saying? I was a coward; I didn't choose much of anything.

But this time was different. Danny made it different. I was nothing like Loni. He grew up in a culture that valued the ways of the warrior, with Mother Nature being their toughest adversary. Loni "Popo" Winston wasn't the least bit afraid of using the big stick he kept hidden under his ostensibly jovial character.

"Cool it, guys." Salazar's reasonable voice rang out between the two arguing men, carrying as much authority as his position of deck boss allowed. At times I wondered if he just hated it. Running hydros on deck was a risky enough job that took hours of practice, precise timing, and careful observation of everything around you. Salazar was excellent at it, maybe because of his experience as a drummer. But the added responsibility of being a deck boss—having to come between two cranky pit bulls—was something no man liked to do.

"You all right, Danny-boy?" Loni asked, effectively changing the subject, breaking off his argument with Dave. He crossed the deck to inspect Danny. It turned out the fall wasn't bad. I had worried about him snapping a bone in his ankle or falling overboard, but he just picked himself up and was fine. "Don't go working too hard now," Loni said, "you gonna make us look bad." He smiled, but I caught the sidelong look of triumph he threw at Dave.

"I'm not hurt," Danny replied. And he wasn't. The fall had scarcely fazed him. "Just a war wound, master chief. It's just a war wound."

"That's right." Loni patted Danny on the shoulder and laughed. "A war wound here ... for our Navy SEAL."

I remember thinking that Loni must have been one hell of a dad. His kids probably loved him to death, as I bet he played with them every minute of the day when he got home from fishing. Loni wasn't stuck at a certain "level" like many other fathers—unable to relate to the fantasy world children play in, let alone that of a person like Danny. That Samoan had Danny's number the minute we stepped on deck, and was fearless in his way of demonstrating as much. I felt warm inside as I thought about this aspect of Loni's character. It was great to have such a strong person in my corner, ready to throw punches on Danny's behalf. But also, I felt envious of the man. Why couldn't I be so fearless? What was Loni's secret?

"All right boys, let's get dropping." Fred's voice broke in over the loudspeaker, and everybody sprang into action. Shifting mental gears, we began the process of dropping those last sixty pots. Daylight was waning. The bitter sky was a blanket of gray ash. It was anybody's guess as to what the impending weather would be like, but I figured a storm was on the horizon.

We hustled for two hours to get our gear off the deck. The routine was the same for the whole crew: retrieve a pot with the crane, load it on the rack, insert the bait setup, tie the door, add crab-pot line, drop the pot, and finally, throw out the trailing shots of line and buoys. But it still hurt like hell.

After our last pot went over the rail, I inhaled deeply. My body was stiff, sore from the relentless labor, and the prospect of sitting down in the galley for a hot meal was all that kept me going. Yet Danny and I had more work to do. While the rest of the crew went inside to change clothes and take a break, I showed Danny how to secure the deck, getting it prepared for "running."

First, we dealt with the hydraulic block. It was a pulley system the size of a basketball, and looked like a stout arm hanging over the rail when operated. We pulled it in and secured it. Next, we battened down all the hatches and cleared the deck, making sure nothing was out of place or unsecure. Anything left loose would be gone after a few big waves crossed us.

Although securing the deck wasn't a job that took a whole lot of time to complete, it felt like forever to me—a cold wall barring my path to the wonderful serenity of the galley. I understand how ridiculous this sounds, but while fishing the seas of Alaska, a person learns new definitions for words such as dullness, drudgery, and tedium. They also learn what it means to hate every long second of a day that has no apparent end to it. Isolated from friends and family for months at a time, exposed to nothing but an endless gray sea and the everlasting prospect of death, a person also learns very quickly how brittle and limited the human mind really is.

And yet, there were some days I couldn't get enough of it.

Alas, we were only a few days into the season. Danny seemed only slightly fatigued when I gave him the nod indicating our job was done, and we left the growing cold of an early dusk, entering into the ready-room of the boat. We stripped off wet raingear, gloves, and boots, and I told Danny to go change into something warm. "Make sure you're dry. Wet clothes will kill you quicker than a heart attack out here." I did the same, and before long, Danny and I were sitting in the galley, our eyes heavy as anchors, as we dug our forks into a plate full of food cooked by none other than grumpy old Dave.

Our dinner was a healthy portion of reconstituted mashed potatoes and gravy, chicken-fried steak, mixed vegetables, sourdough rolls stuffed with butter, fruit cocktail, and last but not least, our choice of several varieties of soda. For dessert, I ate a bowl of vanilla pudding and three candy bars. Content, I was ready for bed, and just about to slide out from the dining booth when Loni boldly spoke up.

"So why you always busting Danny's balls, Dave?"

Dave didn't miss a beat. "He's the fucking greenhorn," he replied. "Why shouldn't I?"

Most of us were crowded together in the dining booth, but Dave sat on a barstool near the kitchen. There was a television and VCR mounted on the ceiling above him, but nobody had the energy or mental wherewithal to put on a movie. We all simply wanted to eat and go to sleep.

"But he's a strong greenhorn," Loni smiled, pointing his fork at Danny.

"He's strong right now ... I guess. But ..." Dave took a big bite and chewed slowly, letting his words hang dramatically in the air, "give him a few days, then you'll see."

"See what?" asked Loni. "He got all I need to see. This boy here is solid. Nothing but strong muscle, a strong mind. Gonna make a fine fisherman."

Dave's features screwed up and the tension in the galley was close to the snapping point. I expected a full-blown argument to ensue, but surprisingly, the man kept his cool. Salazar was half asleep in the booth, and I, like Danny, just sat there waiting as Loni confronted Dave. I knew I should have said something at that point—something noble and in defense of my friend. But my mind kept racing back to my previous encounters with Dave. He was a cruel bully at heart. He knew how to scare the shit out of a coward like me.

"Yeah, well ... we'll see." Dave finished eating. Before he left the room, he added, "Don't forget to clean up the fucking mess, greenhorn."

I let out a sigh of relief. "Damn," I said aloud, "several more weeks of this shit? I don't know, Loni."

"He'll cool off, once we're on the crab," stuttered Salazar.

"He better," Loni added. "Or captain gonna get a piece of my mind soon enough. Danny's a greenhorn, but he don't deserve none of that."

Typically, greenhorns took a bunch of crap from their fellow crewmembers. Sort of a rite of passage. Newbies had all kinds of extraneous duties thrown upon them. And oftentimes, they weren't treated with the same respect as the other crewmen. But Loni was right. Dave's attitude had been downright hostile the minute he laid eyes on Danny. Worst of all, he hadn't let up for a second. Not even after Danny won him that money back in the bar. Or recently, when my friend proved how competent he could be on deck. I really hoped that Salazar was correct. I prayed, in fact, that once we found the crab, Dave would lighten up.

A few minutes later, Danny and I left the galley for our staterooms. It felt like heaven to crawl under my blankets and curl up for some much-needed rest. The steady, up and down motion of the boat was like the gentle swing of a baby's cradle. And the persistent hum of the diesel engine down below was sweet music to my ears. I closed my eyes and thought about the day. I could've counted crab pots, had I needed help falling asleep. The notion seemed ridiculous and made me chuckle. I felt the warm blanket of sleep drifting over me.

Then Danny's words jolted me wide awake. "Hey Ed," he said, sounding alert and impulsive. "You think there's another storm coming?"

I waited a minute before answering. "Maybe so, Danny. Maybe so." And then I drifted off to sleep once more, to the sway of the boat, the sound of the engine, my friend's last words from our first day of crabbing echoing in my ears.

CHAPTER 12

———◆———

THE STORM HIT a few hours into our course toward Tugidak Island. With light drifts of snow, and frigid, fifty-mile-an-hour gusts, it was pathetic compared to what we all knew loomed on the winter's horizon. And it did little in terms of slowing us down toward our destination point, north of the island. We'd arrived and dropped anchor there while I slept.

Despite my overwhelming exhaustion, I left Danny snoring after six hours in the bunk and headed above deck. At the top of the stairs I opened the door and stepped into a pungent plume of smoke and the smell of oiled leather. From a mile out, the wheelhouse was an aged lantern, cozy and bright, swaying freely in the black hollows of a midnight ocean. This was where I found Fred, drinking decaffeinated coffee and puffing on a cigar stub. His feet were stretched out on the bridge. He sat in his captain's chair, gazing out into the gloomy darkness. With the *Angie Piper* now securely anchored, the captain was ready to get some much-needed shut-eye himself. And since I had the first watch duty, I was there to make it happen.

For six hours, it would be my job to make sure our boat didn't drift. Staying awake was usually the most difficult part of watch duty. But on occasion, huge problems could arise. Problems such as rough currents and storms.

"Hey there, Ed." The captain greeted me in his usual jovial manner—broad smile, red cheeks, and twinkling eyes. "You want one of these to keep you company up here?" He lifted his cigar.

"Sure," I replied, "why the hell not?" I took a seat on the bench next to his chair.

Pulling a cigar from a humidifier, Fred clipped the end before handing it to me. He then lit it. Although I can't recall which brand of cigar it was, I remember observing the motions Fred completed in that short task of retrieving and preparing the stogie. They were methodical, almost like in a Japanese tea ceremony. He moved his hands slowly, deliberately, with careful precision. It got me thinking about what other interesting character traits Fred kept hidden behind that broad smile of his.

"So how long does it take to become a captain, anyways?" I asked.

Fred waited to answer the question, keeping his eyes closed, dragging on his cigar. "As long as a person lets it, I suppose." He exhaled a pillow of bitter vapor, and then looked at me sideways. "Why do you ask, Ed?"

"Oh, I don't know." But I did. I had entertained the idea of getting my own boat someday, and this was the first time I'd brought up the idea with Fred. The natural path to becoming a captain of your own fishing vessel was to learn the ropes from the one you worked under. I knew that Fred would make an excellent mentor. In due time, I expected he would teach me all that was needed to run a crab boat and her crew. The latter part was by far the job's toughest requirement.

"Are you thinking you'd like to have your own boat someday, son?" he asked.

"Yeah," I admitted, choking on my stogie, "I guess so. Seems like it could be a good enough job."

Fred's belly shook from his laughter. "A 'good enough job,' you say," he replied, after composing himself. "Well, I'm not so sure about that." He sat up, pulled his feet from the bridge, and grew serious. "Let me tell you something, Ed: being a captain is a fucking bitch of a job. It comes with lots and lots of stress. More stress than you could possibly imagine."

"Yeah, but you get used to all that stress, don't you?"

"Hell no," he replied, matter-of-factly. He gazed out the window, focusing on something in the distance. "At least not me. Think about what's at stake, boy. Being a captain is much more than fishing, that's for sure. If I don't do my job right, then that's six families who'll go without. And if I fuck my job up, then there's six lives that could easily be lost." Fred slowly stood and stretched his arms to the ceiling. I heard vertebrae snap like peanut brittle. "That's a lot of stress for one man, Ed, believe you me. That's more stress than any sane person can handle."

"So why do you do it, then?" I asked. "Why run a boat if it's not worth it?"

"Oh, I didn't say it wasn't worth it, now did I?"

I fell silent and stared at the floor, thinking about Fred's words. I wanted to be so much more than who I was. I admired the notion of becoming what I considered a "noble man"—a man with guts of steel, ready to shrug off any pain brought on by Mother Nature. And I wanted to be a strong man who could smash down bullies like Dave, without so much as a taste of concern, that forever nagging and exhausting fear.

Looking up at Fred, I changed the subject. "So what's up with Dave? Why is he such an asshole to Danny?"

"Yeah …." Fred hesitated, scratching at his chin. "Dave's got him a certain … history, Ed."

"What do you mean by that? What kind of history?"

Fred's reluctance to continue this conversation seemed a bit too obvious to me. His eyes kept darting about the wheelhouse, avoiding mine. "I don't really have any business getting into it, son." He stepped past me, heading for below, then paused at the door. "You're gonna have to talk to Dave about that. Or …

maybe just let it go. But don't worry. I'll tell him to back off with our greenhorn." Fred smiled. "That boy's got some muscle in him, that's for sure. Who would've thought, huh? A kid like that working on a crab boat." He turned and walked down the stairs. "Give a holler if she gets off course."

After Fred left, I dropped into the captain's chair and looked out the window into the pitch black of night. The storm had retreated, and the first light of dawn burned at a corner of the horizon like a distant forest fire. Orange and red beams cut through a thick purple sky, bearing down on the grassy shores of Tugidak Island, lying not far across the *Angie Piper*'s bow. I sat back in the chair, put my feet up on the bridge just like Fred had done, and reflected on my audacious surroundings: the beauty of the Alaskan waters and the foreboding solitude of a desolate island. And then the possibility of one day becoming captain of it all. Fred's words lingered in my skull, and truth be told, I found in them more of an inspiration than the warning they were meant to be.

Outside the window, I observed three gulls flying in lazy circles around our boat, and my mind took a turn back to Dave. Dragging on my stogie, I pondered what Fred had meant about Dave having a history. What kind of history? I didn't dare ask the man, as the captain had suggested. But I was damn curious. I thought I had a basic understanding of Dave, with his drinking, his presumed tendencies toward being an abusive husband and father. But there was something there, in Fred's words. In his voice, I suppose. Something unique about "Dave's history" that might explain his recent hostile attitude.

Oh well. I gave up thinking about it, satisfied that the captain would talk to Dave about cutting some slack for Danny. He and Dave were good friends, and had been for many years, which never failed to strike me as ludicrous, given their differences. Fred was a good man, always true to his word. He treated his crew fairly and was generous with everything he had. Like his expensive Cuban cigars ... or his advice about how to run a fishing vessel. Fred had a wife back in Seattle who had stayed with him for over thirty years. His three kids were all grown up and had families of their own, living in Washington and Oregon. The captain was fond of talking our ears off about his family vacations, visits, and holidays with the grandchildren. He and Dave were nothing alike. They were completely different, in fact. And as I sat in that chair, smoking my cigar, I wondered how it was that they'd managed to remain close friends for so long.

Four hours passed with nothing but a calm sway on the anchor. The *Angie Piper* casually rode the passing swells of seawater. Periodically, I entertained myself with the prospect of running my own boat as I observed the various controls, knobs, monitors, and indicator lights scattered about the wheelhouse. These were tools of the trade, such as the steering controls and jog stick. Radar and Loran machines. Heading selectors, fathom meters, single-side band radios, and of course, the only thing I knew how to operate proficiently: the watch alarm. Every fifteen minutes, that alarm made sure that I stayed awake. If I happened to fall asleep, failing to turn the alarm off when it beeped, it would trigger a loud horn down below, alerting the entire crew that I'd screwed up—a surefire path to a shitty morning.

The watch alarm happened to "beep" just as I broke away from a car and truck magazine to stare out the window and observe the lonesome beaches of Tugidak Island, now bathed in morning light. A gray fog hung above the ocean surface off our starboard side; it reminded me of a thick woolen blanket. But the sun fought its way through onto the sand and grass, the beach foam and pebbles, and painted the near horizon pastel gray.

"What a sight. It has its own kind of beauty." I said this out loud, to myself. I had just turned off the watch alarm buzzer when suddenly the *Angie Piper* swung hard and fast to the north.

I sat up and peered out the starboard window, my eyes wide. Our boat was being pulled by a massive surge with an outgoing tide. The anchor was dragging hard on the ocean floor. I felt a violent jolt, heard the rattle of glass and metal, the strain against the hull, the sounds of things loosening up around me. Something fell to my left. Absently, I chucked my stogie out the side window and dropped the magazine. My mind clouded over—I couldn't remember what to do. Fire up the engines, pull anchor, readjust, call down for the captain .... Each of these thoughts ran through my mind. Sure as shit, I froze and watched the *Angie Piper* tug along a grim course, winding her way out to sea into the deeper waters. Would our anchor catch on a rock? Could the momentum of our vessel riding the outgoing current snap the anchor chain like thin twine? We'd lose our anchor and be forced to head back to Kodiak. A lost anchor would cost the captain several thousand dollars to replace, not including the time and money we'd lose waiting for a new one. And it would likely cost me my job.

That was not okay. Close to a panic, I lunged over to the stairwell and called for Fred. To my relief, he was already halfway up the stairs. A dedicated captain, he'd felt the abrupt change in position of the *Angie Piper* even while he slept. And since his quarters were right below the wheelhouse, it took him no time at all to push past me and take over the helm.

"She just started heading out!" I hollered.

Fred didn't say anything at first. He just fired up the engines and began steering the boat against the tide, keeping her steady, mindful of the anchor's position.

"I just froze, Captain." I felt ashamed at my reaction, or lack thereof. And to top it off, a groggy Dave came rushing up the stairs, face twisted in apparent crankiness after being awoken so suddenly. Like Fred, Dave knew the *Angie Piper* like the back of his hand. He had spent countless hours tinkering down below, learning the sounds and hums of a healthy engine. Or a sick one. He knew the feel of a secured boat, with the gentle glide over passing waves, and he knew danger in the sudden pull of a dragging anchor.

I was screwed. I'd messed up, and now Dave was there to point it all out. I figured he would never let me forget this mistake. Yet much to my relief, that's not how it played out.

"How long has she been drifting?" Dave asked.

"Only a few minutes," I replied. "Fred got here damn quick."

"We're good, Dave," said the captain, working the controls to bring the *Angie Piper* back into shallower waters. "Might have to keep running against this tide a bit, but we're good."

"Here," said Dave, brushing past me, "I got this." He offered to relieve Fred at the helm, but waited a few minutes until the captain stepped away. "It's about my turn for watch duty anyways." Dave looked at me then and grinned. "What'd she do, get away from you?"

"It was the current," I replied, defensively. "It just came out of nowhere."

"Mother Nature is a scary bitch," Dave said. "It's a good thing you called down, Ed. At least you didn't try to be a fucking hero, then end up losing our anchor."

"Just keep her steady against the current, then," repeated the captain. "We'll be here for at least another twelve hours, so let's get comfortable."

I realized the entire incident was no big deal for either the captain or Dave, who had been in this situation more times than they could count. They both reacted to the emergency with an ease that spoke to their unlimited experience of sailing the seas of Alaska. There was a bond between the two of them, despite their differences, and that bond made itself known right then and there, in that wheelhouse. It likely showed itself more often than I knew, but obviously I had not yet been of a mind to observe it. With a mere four seasons of crab fishing under my belt, I was still a damn greenhorn compared to the mighty Fred Mooney and grumpy Dave Jenkins.

The captain must have read it in my eyes. On his way toward

the stairs leading back down to his quarters, he slapped me on the shoulder and laughed. "So was that fun enough, or what? Don't let it eat a hole in you, kid. It happens to the best of us. Now go get some food and some rest. With any luck, we'll be turning gear this time tomorrow."

Ten minutes later, I sat alone in the galley, eating a ham sandwich, nursing my pride. On a listless morning, I couldn't even keep the boat secured at anchor. How then could I possibly tackle the worst weather? And I'd thought I might be captain of it all ....

CHAPTER 13

———————

IT WAS MUCH more than twenty-four hours before we got around to our first pot of the season. Shortly after the *Angie Piper* had dragged anchor, another storm came in, much stronger and longer lasting than the first. We were forced to hole up near Tugidak Island for forty hours and alter our anchor point more than once due to the strenuous currents and wicked winds.

The meager excitement of readjusting our position helped us to wait out the storm. Mostly, our time spent on board the *Angie Piper* during that wait was an exercise in defeating boredom. We were all restless, tired of reading books and magazines, tired of eating, tired of watching movies, and sick and tired of staring at one another. We were sick of wondering how long it would take before we could get moving again.

Of course, Danny was the exception. He seemed to have no problem waiting out the storm. He occupied much of his time wandering the boat, learning this or that, trying to figure out what things were and how they worked. Once, while Dave was taking a nap, he even explored the engine room below.

"Just don't touch anything," I told Danny. "That guy doesn't need any more excuses to bitch us out."

Danny even spent time with both the captain and me while

each of us took turns with watch-duty in the wheelhouse. Fred never trusted greenhorns to watch the helm. But for a time, he seemed more than happy to let Danny keep him company and ask questions, of which Danny had several. Despite his simplicity of character and manner—not uncommon for a person of his ability—he gave the captain quite a surprise with the types of questions he asked. His general interest in life on the sea led to specific inquiries regarding various mechanisms around the boat.

"So what's up with all these damn questions, Danny?" the captain eventually asked. "You plan on running this boat when I'm dead?"

Danny was lucky. Some captains wouldn't let greenhorns spend more than five minutes in the wheelhouse. Fred indulged Danny. And in those hours of waiting, I was reminded of our youth, watching Danny stand there, listening, nodding his head, asking all sorts of questions. He'd acted this way after we saw that movie, *Navy SEALs*. Poor old Ted, our former-Marine neighbor. The man couldn't walk outside his house without Danny hounding him. *What was it like? Tell me all about it.* The intrigue of being a warrior, and the excitement of the battle; the camaraderie found within a team of soldiers who had spent numerous hours crawling through mud and jungle, through blood and sweat. And the years of training. I knew Danny would never experience the Navy SEAL life, but he didn't know that, and so the dream persisted.

Standing in the wheelhouse, listening to Fred and Danny talk, Fred reminiscing, I felt sorry for my friend. I'd never told Danny that I pitied him, of course, and I'm not sure he would have understood even if I tried to explain. After his mother had passed, my own parents jumped right in and helped Danny's father in whatever way they could. Because of my mother's daycare business, it wasn't long before Danny was right there among the rest of us, playing, shouting, making a mess—your typical kid. Sure, he was difficult at times, considering his stubborn nature. But for the most part, Danny was fun to be around. He'd laugh at just about anything, which made me feel like a true comedian. And unlike most kids, he never complained much. He was a good sport, when it came right down to it.

But ever since we were kids, the part of Danny that had me so twisted up with emotion, so distraught and sorry for him, was the pure sorrow my friend conveyed whenever he was upset. Danny didn't cry much, but when he did, it was so damn genuine and heartbreaking that I figured he must be crying for his mother.

I felt sorry for Danny when I thought of him missing his mom. I felt sorry when I imagined him finally understanding that his dream of one day becoming a Navy SEAL was outright ridiculous. And I felt sorry for Danny when he got picked on at school, beaten up, thrown into trash cans—while I just stood there like a fool, watching, not doing a damn thing about it.

Those forty hours had passed, and now the *Angie Piper* was riding through a bleak surface under a grim horizon. We pushed onward toward the first pot, its orange buoys staggering against the tide and the wind. The night loomed high above our stern, bringing with it the shadows of a cold winter. And with the flip of a switch, the yellow deck lights shone down on our anxious faces. At last, we were ready to bring aboard the crab—or so we hoped.

Loni stood at the rail with the grappling hook in his hand. Our first toss of the season was just minutes away. Each of us prayed that the Polynesian didn't miss. *Make sure you're quick on the hook, Loni*, I thought, *or we'll have us a bad omen.* Dave stood next to him, and Salazar waited at the hydro controls. The moment stretched out until finally Loni let loose, sending the hook line a good thirty feet past the buoys. There could be no better throw.

"Yeah!" we all yelled in unison. Danny and I pushed forward the sorting table—a metal platform on wheels that we used to receive and sort the catch. Loni's arms swung in quick motions as he pulled the buoys in and then ran the pot line through the hydraulic winch. Seconds later, the squeal of the winch sang across the deck as the seven-foot wide, seven-foot high steel cage ascended through the bitter sea at three hundred feet per minute.

The straining winch squealed like a teakettle, a welcome sound to the veterans on the boat. Although Danny had no idea what it meant, he would learn soon enough. That sound indicated a heavy pot. And heavy pots usually meant pots stuffed with crab. I caught Loni's grin as he began to coil the retracting rope into the barrel at his side.

"Sounds like money, boys!" Fred said over the loudspeaker. He had been listening also, his head poking out the starboard window just above us.

And then it was on. The pot rose from the ocean with a dramatic pause, almost in slow motion, as thin foam and seawater fell away as if a dozen faucets had been cranked open. The cage was bulging with crab. Thousands of spiny legs, the colors of orange, brown, and white, delivered an awesome contrast to the boat, the creatures flexing en masse against their collective bulk. The sight drew a scream of joy from Loni as he and Dave manhandled the pot over the rail and into position against the pot launcher.

"There's a sight to see!" the captain shouted. And then he laughed.

What followed was a graceful dance between Loni and Dave, including Salazar at the controls. With a heavy clang that reverberated across the deck, the pot was forced onto the rack, lowered, and then clamped down by two hydraulic hooks known as "dogs." Loni and Dave unhooked the pot bridle from the crane and then untied the door while Salazar worked the controls, lifting the rack. Gravity took over at that point. Exactly six hundred and thirty-one legal tanners, snow crab destined for hungry markets, plunged down onto the sorting table.

"Get in there, boys!" Loni shouted. "That's money on that table! That's a fucking treasure, I'm telling you!"

A feast of crawling legs and carapaces undulating before us, I motioned for Danny to follow my lead. I had to teach him how to sort the crab, which is something a person can't really learn until they are waist deep in it. Danny needed to figure out how to find the winners and spot the losers—the dirty ones, the dead ones. He had to learn how to measure a crab using a ruler known as a "stick," and eventually, his naked eye. And most of all, he had to learn how to quickly clear the sorting table before our boat hauled in the next set of buoys.

"You're gonna pitch them in one of two places, Danny," I said, pulling a mound of crab from the middle of the table. "You either slide them down here," I continued, sliding half the mound down an aluminum chute that led to a hole in our deck, dropping the crab deep into our live tanks below, "or chuck them over there." I flung a reject crab over the rail.

After securing the empty pot for re-baiting, Dave and Loni joined in, sorting the crab. Their excitement was obvious, which felt real nice; finally, the entire crew was in good spirits, and it was beautiful not to be waiting off the shores of Tugidak Island any longer. And there was no more uncertainty and anxiety about where to find the crab. No more storms—the weather had cleared, and the sky looked down on us with a pale-blue radiance. Even though Dave still seemed apprehensive about Danny, it was nice to hear him laugh, which he did just after Loni shouted the number of our catch up to the captain.

I laughed. So did Salazar, because hell, we all knew what we were tasting just then. Full pots meant a ton of crab, a ton of cash, and a shorter season. If this kept up, we would all be going home real soon, and we would be going home rich. Even Danny, our greenhorn.

"Get her back in!" Fred suddenly shouted. He knew right away that we were "on the crab," and he ordered us to re-dump the pot once we'd cleared it. As long as a catch was clean—

without too many females or young crab, and not infested with fleas or barnacles, which this one wasn't—it was not uncommon to re-bait the pot and drop it back over the side.

"Go get a bait setup," I told Danny, nearing the last few crab on the table. Time was of the essence. If we wanted to keep Dave off our backs, Danny would have to be quick with his job of re-baiting the pot currently on the rack. Fortunately, he noticed the excitement and gravity of the situation without Dave's yelling. Before long, Danny was at the rail with a bait jar and two bloody cod. In no time at all, he had the bait secured, and we dumped the pot back into the ocean. A communal cheer from the crew was followed by Loni's primordial howl into the sky as he tossed the line buoys far and wide.

The subculture that exists on the deck of a fishing vessel has its own language, which is only ever heard, or seen, or spoken between the steel rails that crown the bulwark of any working ship. That language brims with thrill and chaos, as it witnesses victory over the sea. It is a language of sorrow when it succumbs to absolute dread, and then ultimate dismay. It is an ancient language, a song from the mariners of past, and with it comes the notion that yes, there is something great and mighty at work within our universe, and though it fashions our fates, it does so with neither favoritism nor malice. It has no concern for the individual.

When we cleared that first pot of the season, and Loni's cry—a cry born from the depths of a man who had wrestled with Mother Nature since the day he could walk—rang true and loud, I couldn't help but shed a few tears.

What moved me at that moment was something much deeper than the language of the fisherman. It was the validation of watching my friend Danny succeed. It was that full pot of tanner crab, telling everyone on deck that I was right, and that no, "Danny the Beluga Boy" was not a bad omen to have on board. And it was the knowledge that maybe, just maybe, Justice does have a voice of its own, in this grand universe of ours. A voice that can be heard somewhere between the howling winds of Alaska's breath, the dull crash of untiring waves against steel, and the pinch and growl of a hydraulic winch, pulling Hope and Destiny up from the bottom of a cold and bitter sea.

CHAPTER 14

———◆———

IT WAS A tremendous day—an overwhelming day. Our first pots of the season came with a day that seemed to last forever, made more brutal by an icy wind from the south and an ever-increasing rush of angry waves slapping at the rail, over the rail, and onto the deck. Throughout a cold and wet chill, we turned all our gear, harvesting the crab. The *Angie Piper* careened over the sea surrounding Tugidak Island while we picked up pots, worked the table to sort the crab, stuffed the hold, and set more pots. We worked tirelessly, a joking crew, knowing that we were hot on the crab. Only one of our four pot strings had come up empty. This was a good haul.

Hours stretched into the horizon. One day became two, pushing against three, and reality dimmed and blurred: it was the haze from working over forty straight hours. Our mealtimes were lost at sea. Sleep became a distant memory. And coffee became our best friend. We plowed through our jobs. That timeless fog in the Gulf of Alaska. Finally, for a brief period, it was over.

Those first forty hours of turning gear left me in a shadow, bereft of memories. This was a common side effect of being a deckhand on board a crabbing vessel. Everything seemed to mesh together, like a gill net used for catching salmon. I do remember, however, waking up sometime later, lying in the booth in the galley, my stomach growling fiercely. I still had on my raingear, and the clothes underneath were damp, clinging to my skin. I was cold and shivering, and hungrier than I had ever been in my life.

Danny was lying next to me, on the opposite side of the dining table, snoring like a bear. His raingear was off, so I presumed he had changed his clothes once we all came back inside the boat. After we had finished setting our last string of pots, Fred gave us the signal to secure the deck, and he steered the *Angie Piper* back to our anchor point off Tugidak Island. Back to the land of mind-numbing boredom. Only this time, nobody would complain. Everyone would get much-needed rest while our gear soaked right on the crab.

Climbing out of the booth, I noticed Danny's hands were beat to hell. Quarter-sized bruises blotted his knuckles, and two of his fingernails were black. Dried blood was caked around three of his fingers. Even his face appeared swollen, his forehead and eyebrows bulging like a Neanderthal's.

My body had been punished in its own right, and I noticed it as I hobbled over to the kitchen. My right ankle and both shoulders screamed in their stiffness, and they woke with cold fire. My back protested my efforts to stand erect. I was suffering from the other common side effect of working a crab boat: injuries. No matter how smart, athletic, or downright lucky a person might be, they couldn't escape the damage that came with stepping on board a fishing vessel in Alaska.

I paced the galley until the pain of my injuries faded. Then I realized just how cold I was, shivering at the galley door, looking for the other crewmembers. Everyone seemed to be asleep, so I headed for my stateroom. Before I cooked dinner, I would need to get dry clothes on; the risk of becoming sick while out at sea was simply too great. At the very least, being sick meant enduring a misery you wouldn't wish on your worst enemy. It's not like you can rest in bed and heal while everyone else picks up your slack. Being sick on a fishing vessel means puking over the side between sorting crabs. It means ignoring your migraine while steel pots clang repeatedly, endlessly, against the steel launcher. It means enduring the chills while you rough out hours of laborious work. Becoming sick, even with an initially minor ailment, can also lead to death.

Roughly thirty minutes later, warm and dry, I stood in the kitchen again, and began the challenging task of cooking a multi-dish meal while my entire world bobbed up and down and side to side. After a brief check-in up at the wheelhouse, I learned that everyone was asleep, with Salazar watching the helm. We were about an hour south of Tugidak Island, which meant that I had only slept for a few hours myself. No wonder I was dragging. Nobody had eaten much more than sandwiches, so I sought to remedy that by cooking as much of a hot feast as one man could manage.

I started with a pot of coffee, unconcerned that the caffeine would prevent me from sleeping after I ate. I was that tired. The percolating sounds and sweet aroma were comforting, and they eased my weariness for the time it took me to cook dinner.

I pan-fried the ten-pound halibut we'd found in one of our pots, earlier in the day. It had taken Loni all of three minutes to fillet and bag the fish and then stuff it in the fridge for later. I also fried some chicken legs and stirred up three boxes of scalloped potatoes. Two cans of French-cut green beans mixed with two cans of sliced carrots went into a steamer basket, and then I warmed my hands over the rising heat, smiling, looking over at Danny as my friend began to stir. He would wake soon, the smell of hot food whetting his appetite.

I reached into the pantry and brought out a few cans of creamed corn, because hell, I love creamed corn, and I was the cook that night. Nobody would argue, of course, in light of everything else I'd cooked. If there was one perk every crab boat in Alaska shared, it was the bounty of food available to the crew. Hot meals were an irregular event, especially when we were working the crab. But when we had those meals, they were an all-you-can-eat affair fit for a king. Therefore, I was having creamed corn.

On the *Angie Piper*, the captain usually did most of the cooking. His brother ran the kitchen in a fancy restaurant in Vancouver, and during crabbing's off-season, Fred made at least one trip up north to see him. Back on the boat, the captain would occasionally show off by indulging us with his own versions of fine dining. But mostly, he just cooked us comfort food, knowing that what our bodies needed above all else were good old wholesome calories.

And that's what I was cooking on this night—comfort food. For dessert, I opened a box of Danish rolls and laid them out on a plate, snatching one up and eating it in the process.

"What's for dinner?" Danny finally asked. My friend stood, found his feet, and stumbled toward me, his bruised knuckles rubbing his eyes.

"Oh, a little bit of this, a little bit of that," I replied. From the microwave, I pulled out a cup of hot chocolate and passed it to Danny. I knew he preferred it over coffee, which he rarely drank. He had an unrelenting sweet tooth, and by way of example, he polished off two of those Danish pastries within a minute. But who could blame him? My friend had worked damn hard. I still held on to the hope that Dave would turn the corner and accept Danny as one of us. The captain had said that he would have a talk with Dave, so at least I could count on that.

"Well, the food's pretty much ready. You don't have to keep eating Danishes." I handed Danny a plate and stepped aside as he served himself a small mountain of food. "We're just waiting on the chicken. Don't want anybody getting sick out here."

"But when do we go back to the crab?" Danny asked.

An involuntary chuckle escaped me before I looked at him and said, "What, no break for you?"

Danny kept his eyes on his plate, turned and shuffled back to the table. "I like this job, Ed," he said, matter-of-factly. "I like it a lot. So thank you. I owe you something for this."

Again, I couldn't help but chuckle. This was so much like Danny. Give him a job shoveling shit, and eventually he would find the sweet-smelling side of it.

"Forget about it, buddy." I piled a plate of food for myself and walked to the table, joining him. "You don't owe me anything. Just make sure to get some rest, okay? You need to heal your body, 'cause don't worry, we've got a lot more work ahead of us. A lot more crab."

A few wordless minutes passed as we plowed through our dinners, the droning of a determined diesel engine below keeping us company. It was a peaceful moment in an otherwise chaotic environment. Finally, Danny said, "I think my dad would like this job. What about you, Ed? Do you think he would like it?"

"Yeah, he probably would," I replied. "I bet he would, in fact."

"Except ..." Danny continued, "he might be too old for it." My friend looked at me, his swollen forehead wrinkled in thought. "Do you think it would be too hard for him, Ed?"

"I don't know, Danny. Maybe." Shrugging my shoulders, I forked a wedge of halibut off my plate. "Your dad is pretty tough, though. You know that. He'd probably do fine crabbing."

Danny hesitated, shoveled down more food, and then abruptly asked, "When do you think my dad will die, Ed?"

It hit me with the weight of a fully loaded crab pot. Here was one of the fears that ran through the head of Danny Wilson. I had never truly understood until that moment. Shit, I thought I understood, observing how so many things simply rolled off my friend, as if nothing in this world could ever put the worry on him. We were both mentally tired, physically sore, and when a man gets to that point, certain things tend to boil over and find the surface of a conscious mind. Ever since I was a kid, I had an intimate knowledge of my fears. But as I got older, I guess I never worried about what would become of me once my parents passed away.

I stared at my friend. And I didn't say anything for a while. We consumed our halibut, scalloped potatoes, creamed corn—our meals fit for Poseidon. Danny had lost his mother, and now he worried about losing his dad, because hell, what would he do then? Where would he go, and who would take care of him? His sister, Mary, living in Seattle with her husband and two kids? Maybe … but maybe not. Shit, Danny might have to go into a "home." I think he was aware of that, and it scared him to death.

I could have said it just then, there in that galley. *Don't you worry, Danny. You can always live with me. I'll take care of you.* I could have said that, but I didn't. For my entire life, it seemed I had walked a path of psychological dormancy, of mental retreat, and even now, when I needed desperately to wake the fuck up because my best friend needed me to, I couldn't.

So I ignored Danny's question. "I think that chicken might be ready now," I said, walking over to the stove. The chicken smelled good, and I said as much as I turned off the heat, shoveled a few pieces on a plate, and walked back to the table. Danny wasn't as dumb as most people figured him to be. He dropped the subject about when his dad would die. More accurately, the subject of who would take care of him once he was alone in the world.

We ate our food, then headed for our racks and fell right back to sleep. Seven hours of gorgeous rest passed before I woke to the sound of waves lapping against the sides of our boat, and a heated exchange amongst a flock of seagulls somewhere outside. We were anchored down off the shores of Tugidak Island once again, and I wondered who was awake. Danny was still sleeping below me, snoring as usual, so I climbed down, dressed, and left our stateroom with as much care as possible, hoping not to wake him.

The rocking of the boat was peaceful, almost non-existent. I heard the sounds of a movie from the television in the galley. Proceeding down the dimly lit hall, I almost made it into that room. Loni was in there, watching *Aliens*, eating cold chicken and leftover scalloped potatoes. Curiosity turned me toward the other sounds I had heard—another heated exchange, this one coming from the wheelhouse. I stopped halfway up the stairs and listened.

"At this point, Dave, I don't give a rat's ass anymore!" Fred Mooney was a different breed in the world of boat captains. Unlike most, he kept himself steady and cool, rarely raising his voice to the crew. But now, he was outright pissed. And I presumed it had something to do with that "talking to" he had told me about, the one planned for Dave.

"He's supposed to take shit," Dave said. "He's the fucking greenhorn, for Christ's sake! That's his job." Not surprisingly, Dave had been attempting to disguise his intimidating attitude under the veil that all greenhorns had it coming, and that they were destined to be treated like shit. However, Dave had crossed the line on more than one occasion with both Danny and me. And now Fred was calling him on it.

"This is about way more than him being a greenhorn, Dave. Don't you fucking kid around with me!"

"Oh, give me a break, Fred! It's a matter of common sense, that's all. Speaking of which: what kind of sense puts a fucking retard on a boat where one mistake can get a man killed?"

"Why, you son of a bitch! You let me worry about that!" I heard a dull thud, a fist smashed onto a table perhaps, and then a brief silence, followed by, "You need to let it go, Dave. Just let your past go. It's eating you up inside, and the whole world sees it."

"I don't know what the fuck you're talking about."

"Oh, yes you do. The drinking. The bar fights. You're letting your past tear a hole inside you."

"My life is my business, Fred. So do me a fucking favor and stay out of it."

More silence. Then, with a castigating voice, the captain replied, "All right, Dave. I'll stay out of it. But remember: this is my boat. And every goddamned thing that happens here is my business. So change your fucking tone with our greenhorn, or you'll be finding yourself a new job."

Dave went out through the side door with a slam, most likely to cool off, get some fresh air, and compose himself. And while standing on the steps, slightly alarmed, I heard the captain mutter a few curses under his breath. I remained frozen for a while, wondering, attempting to process all that I had heard. But it was several minutes later, while sitting next to Loni in the galley, watching a man get ripped apart by an alien, that it dawned on me. The captain ... he had something specific in mind when he told Dave to let his past go.

CHAPTER 15

———•———

RELENTLESS ARE THE waters that own our world—from the seas, mountain rivers, and alpine lakes, to every single drop of rain that casually falls on the planet. The force of water is ancient by its own right, timeless, and only temporarily yielding to the other forces of this world, for it is also ravaging with its transient ways, and a master in the art of deception. Water is yielding only long enough for a man to stare at it from the other side of a steel rail. If even for that long.

That's where I was, on this day when the water seemed sparse and dry. A light rain sporadically swept my cheeks and lips. For fourteen hours we sat at anchor, resting away our weariness. And for fourteen hours our pots sat underneath all that ancient water, baiting crab. Or so we hoped.

Looking out across the rail, I spotted the two orange buoys that marked the first pot we'd left since our anchor point near Tugidak Island. The buoys swayed in the tide listlessly as I held hook and rope, took aim. I'd worked long hours hooking pot buoys in the past, but Loni mostly did the honors now, since he almost never missed.

"Be quick on the hook. Don't think about it," was Loni's advice. I stood at the rail, "thinking about it," and tossed that damn hook three times before the captain cursed me over the loudspeaker. The crew burst into laughter, Dave shook his head in disgust, and Fred worked the *Angie Piper* into a wide circle. We had one hundred and sixty pots sitting out there, which meant another forty hours of work ahead of us. Even more if those pots were as full as we expected them to be. But for every pot missed with the hook, that was another ten minutes added to our day. *Just don't think about it,* I told myself.

Danny had been standing next to the sorting table when I failed to retrieve those buoys. He was toying with a measuring stick and seemed amused by my blunder, but mostly, he was eager to sort the crab. Damn if my friend wasn't meant for the sea. This observation stuck in my head for the entire time it took to make our second pass on that first pot. Afterward, I took slipshod aim, tossed the hook, and snagged the buoys dead center—the payoff for not thinking about it.

The hook-man's second responsibility is more crucial than the first. After hooking the buoys, I pulled them onto the deck as quickly as possible, careful not to let them sweep along the side of the boat and catch up in the engine prop—a catastrophic mistake. Once the buoys were over the rail, I tossed them to the side and fed the crab-pot line through the block and the winch, beginning the process of pulling over a thousand pounds of steel, and hopefully crab, up from the bottom of the ocean.

With roughly a minute before that pot broke the surface, there was little to do other than wait. I thought about it now, the entire job of working a crab boat. It was a horrible lot. Always cold, wet, and seasick, your body getting tossed around the deck by waves four stories high—just another day at the office. With this job, a deckhand's life was not unlike bait at the end of a hook, luring grim reapers from the bitter shadows below. Each breath was in constant danger of becoming doused by the coldest death one could imagine. What kind of friend was I to bring Danny into this hell?

The hard truth is that for some people, fishing is the only

occupation that makes any sense. For them, it is the "land" that feels foreign and dangerous. On land, there are too many shark-like forces—human and otherwise—roaming about: scary, callous, harmful in the most unimaginable ways. And on land, ironically, there are few places to run or hide, unlike the vast horizons of the open sea.

The winch squealed madly on this first pot of the run, sending my hopes in flight like gulls to the wind and erasing my reflections. "Money" was on my mind, as I watched that steel cage rise from the depths. Tanner crab, clean and plentiful, twisting in a cage that bulged out from all sides, produced a clamor of cheers from the crew—smiles all around.

Danny pushed the sorting table up to the launcher while Loni snagged the pot bridle with a gaffing hook. Dave and I joined in to manhandle the heavy cage into position. Once we lowered the pot down onto the launcher, Salazar tossed a switch at the hydro station and sent the dogs in. The crab pot now clamped down hard, we opened the door, and out spewed several hundred dollars worth of squirming bounty.

"Might be a short season!" hollered Loni. "Tons of crab. We gonna go home soon!"

For the duration of that first half of the string, that was what most of us believed, even joked about. Twenty pots later, Salazar broke character by dancing on the deck, his asinine grin clamped down on a smoking cigarette. He looked like a leprechaun dancing a jig, and I almost cracked a rib, I laughed so hard. Each of those pots contained on average of four hundred legal crabs. And with twenty more pots to go with just this first string, it was likely that Danny was the only one on the boat not doing the math.

But then, up came crab pot number twenty-two. None of us even realized the first sign of our misfortune, hidden in the vague sound of the winch. It was a dead, hollow sound, unrestrained by a mere thousand pounds. In rapid shift, that pot broke through the olive-colored sea, pronouncing boldly its vacant core, salty rivers sluicing clean through steel and mesh, effectively washing away our current elation. *Goddamn, nothing lasts forever.* Not a single crab in the pot, and it struck each of us as both alarming and peculiar. Our previous pot contained five hundred and ten tanners. Could it be that our string was suddenly "off the crab"?

In the world of crabbing, there are two distinct ways to rob a crew of their catch. The first, and most common form is a practice known as "potting down." Despite the enormity of both the Gulf of Alaska and the Bering Sea—the two greatest fishing grounds the North Pacific Ocean has to offer—it is still entirely possible and likely to create a boat full of enemies when a captain decides to drop his pots within a few hundred yards of another vessel's string. This happens on occasion, mostly perpetrated by rookie captains. Such an incident, more often than not, is "settled" via a distressing confrontation at a bar such as McCrawley's, or even over the radio.

The second form of robbery is not as common and more sinister. It is the simple hauling and taking of crab from another crew's pots. And that's what we encountered halfway through that string, beginning with crab pot number twenty-two.

"Son of a bitch!" shouted Dave, smacking the pot door against the sorting table. Our telltale sign, other than the lack of crab, was that the door ties of that pot had not been wrapped the same way we'd tied them. Dave made a quick reference to Danny, wondering, but then Loni dismissed it by reminding him that our greenhorn hadn't tied any of the doors. "Fucking bandits!" Dave concluded, smacking the door on the sorting table once more.

"Pirates in the Gulf," growled Loni, coiling rope to the side.

"What happened?" Danny asked. He was at the table, sorting the last of the crab from the previous pot.

"Another crew ripped us off, Danny," I said. "Got here before us and took the crab." Danny looked away then, perturbed, at once cautious. He didn't say anything else, just went back to work. I could tell he was thinking about it, though.

The news was unsettling, and Fred came down from the wheelhouse to examine the pot himself. "Well, shit," he said, working his hands over the door, the bait jars, even the pot bridle, presumably searching for clues.

"I'll bet the rest of this string is empty too," replied Dave.

"Yeah, probably is." Fred gave a shrug and ran a hand through his hair. "Not the first time it's happened, that's for sure. Go ahead and set her back down, boys. They're not coming back." Fred said this as if he knew the tactics of crab thievery firsthand. His experience as a captain was speaking. Throughout his years, he had seen just about everything in the world of fishing. Minutes later, he was up in the wheelhouse, sending out a warning to all the other fishing vessels running gear. For now, this was the only way to deal with the culprits, as the thieving captain would most certainly hear Fred's announcement and scoot on out of the area.

From then on, work felt like someone kept driving a finger into my eye. We pulled nineteen more empty pots up from the sea, re-baited them, then sent them right back down again. Danny did his job without complaint, as usual, clipping bait setups and retrieving crab-pot lines. I noticed how fluidly his feet moved about the deck now, and how he stayed clear of the danger spots such as wayward rope, crab-tank holes, or the picking crane used to transport our crab pots. Any one of these components of the vessel would quickly cause a man writhing pain if he were careless around them. To my relief, Danny had a "routine" dialed in, and it was the one small thing during those moments that actually put a smile on my face, as we turned our "pillaged" gear for the next hour.

We finished that string and then took a three-hour break in the galley while the boat motored off toward our last three strings. Fred gave us the option to take a short nap, but we were all too wired from coffee and the agitation born of having our full pots violated. I sat in the galley. Consuming more coffee and more candy bars, I wondered who had stolen our crab, and how they'd done it.

Without a doubt they took our catch during the smallest hours of the day, shrouded in darkness to protect the identity of their boat. Their captain, paranoid over thoughts of being caught, probably never took his eyes off the radar. Or perhaps he didn't care. There were plenty of young skippers out there who thought nothing of stealing another man's livelihood. I imagined this man's crew on deck working the pots, handling crab, the very image of us, excluding the rounds of snickering they must have shared. I even considered that they knew about me, and Danny, and that perhaps their intentions extended further than monetary gain. Maybe they were in cahoots with Dave, and stole our catch to help support his argument against having Danny on board.

That last thought was farfetched, but when a man gets too tired, his mind starts to play tricks on him. He starts to imagine things. I knew that before I became a deckhand, and realized the true meaning of "tired." But shit, it was too early in the season for me to feel that way. It was too early in the day, for that matter. We hadn't been away from Tugidak Island for more than six hours, and even though I might have been imagining things there in the galley, I found the notion unsettling. I guess I expected more from a young man like myself.

"Just the first sign of more bad news to come; that's all it is." Dave's sudden pronouncement prophesying our future shook me out of my dark thoughts. I stared at the man leaning against the fridge, drinking from a can of Mountain Dew. We all knew what he was thinking, who he was referring to, and for a split second, there in the recess of my "tired mind," I thought I might tell Dave to fuck off. It would have come as a complete shock, of course. Not just to Dave, but to the entire crew, including myself. It probably would have resulted in a smack across my face, never mind Fred's strict intolerance for fighting aboard the *Angie Piper*. Probably. But of course, I kept my mouth shut.

I looked over at Danny and Loni, both sitting next to Salazar, all three of them squeezed into the booth of the dining table, drinking an assortment of beverages, and eating chips and salsa. They each had blank, tired stares, and seemed indifferent to Dave's comment, until Loni casually said, "Fuck off, Dave."

In response, Dave simply shrugged. Downing the last of his Mountain Dew, he crushed the can in his hand, tossed it into the sink, and grumbled, "Mark my words ... you will all see." Then he left the room.

Something about those last words, or the way he left, or perhaps the entire short exchange, sent an icy shiver through my body. I wrapped my coat more snugly around my shoulders, gripped my coffee tighter, and tried to close my mind to the foreboding born of Dave's comment.

CHAPTER 16

———•———

"LOOK OUT! LOOK OUT!" Salazar's scream rode the top of the forty-foot wave that slapped over the deck. The seas were high and came up on us almost without notice. Our last string of this run, and we were nothing but shivering men on a steel slab in the darkest of nights. The wind howled down from the north at sixty-plus knots. Rain pelted us like bullets. We were all eager to get inside the boat. But damn if there weren't ten more pots left in the string.

"Look out!" Salazar screamed again.

From the sorting table I'd been clinging to, I swore in disbelief at what was now transpiring before us on deck.

"Everybody, take cover," shouted the captain, over the loudspeaker. Apparently he had seen it too, and it sure as hell wasn't a wave.

Loni pitched his body to the side. Dave tucked under the rail, the swells of a black ocean pouring over him like a waterfall. An errant crab pot swung madly across the *Angie Piper*'s deck. The pot was attached to the picking crane. Salazar was in the process of transferring it to the main-stack for chaining down when our boat abruptly careened portside.

Every deckhand's fear had become a reality. The thousand-pound cage swept past me, nearly clipping my head as it crashed into the stack of pots to my left. With almost all our gear onboard, there was little room to evade the monstrous block of steel. And if it nailed any of us, we'd certainly be dead or messed up beyond repair.

"Drop it!" shouted Dave, from under a curtain of rushing water. He had a point—releasing the pot could possibly help stabilize it. But then the thought occurred to me: who would be in the way once that thing came down? Like the weapon of an angry giant, it smashed haphazardly across the deck. Salazar worked madly at the hydro controls in hopes of ending the chaos, but twice he had been knocked down by the surge of saltwater that had turned our deck into a small pond.

And then it dawned on me: where was Danny?

"Danny!" I hollered. No one seemed to hear me, my voice drowned out by the cacophony of smashing steel, crashing waves, and howling wind. "Where's Danny!?" I repeated.

For a brief moment, the pot wedged itself between the portside rail and main-stack. It was a moment of tense hesitation, allowing just enough time for Salazar to take some slack out of the picking crane's cable. I saw Loni at Salazar's side, holding him steady, keeping the deck boss from falling down once again. I still couldn't find Danny, and I continued to scream out for him.

All eyes scanned the area, and then panic set in. Man overboard? I was about to call it out, fearing that my friend had been swept away by that forty-footer, but then the pot broke loose from the rail, swinging again. I had to get down.

I ducked, and the cage missed my head again—another disturbing attempt at bashing it in. And that's exactly how it felt at that moment—like that crab pot had a mind of its own, was hell-bent on taking one of us out. Fear told me that it already had, that it had knocked Danny clean into the raging waters of the Gulf, and now that steel menace wanted more.

Once the pot cleared the deck again, I stood and looked out into the waters surrounding our boat, hoping and praying not to see a man in yellow raingear bobbing in the sea. I was terrified, for myself and the entire crew. For Danny, not knowing where he was, fearing he was somewhere down there in the deep. I was terrified by the sheer tenacity of the force that had so rapidly taken control of our lives—all in a matter of seconds. The uncertainty was staggering. It seemed the villainous seas of Alaska were wantonly toying with our lives. I loathed everything about being a crabber just then. I felt cold, sick to my stomach. I felt helpless, and errant in my own way.

"Man overboard!" I finally shouted. "Man overboard!" I repeated, and Fred signaled the alarm—a siren that blasted from stem to stern in the riotous night. Everyone moved so fast, all hands on deck, all eyes blinking over the rails. Suddenly, just like that, Danny stood up from the center of the deck.

Danny had been covered by two feet of water, hidden in plain sight. My friend looked at me with a dumb smile only he could have pulled off. *No big deal, it's only water.* Those might have been Danny's thoughts at that moment, and I might have laughed right along with him, but we were hardly in the clear.

"Get down!" This time we all screamed. The rogue crab pot crashed toward him. The pot moved in slow motion, yet too quickly for me to do anything. I was simply too far away to help Danny. He was on his own. The rest of us could only offer our high-pitched warnings.

Danny locked eyes with the incoming pot as if mesmerized. My friend seemed incapable of movement. He was about to get slammed over the portside rail and into an icy graveyard—gone forever.

But Danny surprised us all. Moving like a linebacker, he stepped to his left and the pot brushed past him. Amazingly, he was clear. Relief washed over my shoulders and down my back. My friend had escaped certain death.

Gesturing with my hands, I shouted, "Get off the deck, Danny!" He was three steps away from safety, which would put him next to Loni and Salazar. Yet to my horror, he did something shocking. Still crashing out of control, the crab pot had swung to the starboard side, when Danny reached out and … *grabbed it.*

I'd never doubted Danny's physical strength. Most certainly, he was the strongest person I had ever known.

But Danny was no match for that wild pot, swinging from the sway and list of our fully loaded vessel in the angry Alaskan sea. Danny was no match for the tantrums of Mother Nature.

"What the hell!" Dave bellowed, running along the rail, barely escaping the path of Danny and the pot, as both went sailing out over the rail and above the water.

I rubbed my knuckles into my eyes. I couldn't believe what was happening. I couldn't believe what I was seeing. Here was my friend, hanging on to that pot by his fingers, legs dangling inches above the icy sea, all that strength and stamina now put to the ultimate test. If Danny lost his grip now, he'd be a goner.

"Get him over here!" Our captain was frantic, jumping down the steps near the wheelhouse. Instantly soaked from the heavy rain, Fred shouted repeatedly, waving his arms to get Danny and the pot back over the rail.

"Hold on, Danny!" I screamed, looking around for the gaffing hook, or anything to grab him in case he went into the water. Loni lunged over and grabbed the life ring near the cabin door. Salazar worked the hydros frantically, to no avail. Over the rail and above the sea, Danny and the pot hung like some freakish maritime gibbet. Nothing seemed to be happening, and the entire situation stayed on "pause." The *Angie Piper* leaned far to her starboard side, caught in the trench of the roaring waves.

"Hydros aren't working!" Salazar shouted. "They're stuck. Must be a leak!"

"What are you saying?" Fred didn't wait for an answer. He ran back up to the wheelhouse.

"Hang on, Danny, just hang on!" Dave shouted, standing at the rail, reaching for his leg. "The captain's gonna steer you toward us."

Dave knew exactly what was going on. Somewhere in the hydraulic system that ran the picking crane and launching table, there was a sudden leak that had caused a loss of pressure. Until fixed, that pot, along with Danny, would stay as they were—ten feet from the safety of the deck. The timing of the leak couldn't have been worse, and in order to get Danny back, the captain was going to have to steer the *Angie Piper* a hard left, portside, allowing gravity to bring Danny and the pot closer to us. It was a desperate measure, to say the least, but it was also our only hope to save my friend.

"Hold on tight, Danny-boy!" Loni wedged himself between the rail and the main-stack, the aft-most point of the boat accessible. He had a life ring ready to throw, and his eyes squinted against the barrage of wind and rain. If Danny fell, his body would travel toward Loni, and there would be less than one second to grab that life ring before Danny got sucked down into the engine prop.

"Keep your legs up!" Dave shouted. "Grab on with your heels if you can!" Finding the gaffing hook, I ran up next to Dave and reached out, attempting to grab the pot. "Just hold her steady!" Dave advised. Salazar cursed from behind us, still working at the controls, trying to get the pot moving. Still, nothing happened. We were at the mercy of the infuriating sea, Fred's ability to get our boat to turn quickly, and Danny's extraordinary strength and endurance. How long could my friend hold on?

The *Angie Piper* rode high, cutting into the top of another enormous wave, and we all knew what was coming next: the fall. It was the descent of our boat into the trough, or valley of the waves, and it might actually be our chance to get Danny back on board. Splitting seconds, Fred cranked a hard left and we lunged down between two fifty-foot monstrous walls of water, effectively swinging the errant pot back over the rail.

I threw the gaffing hook to the side and grabbed Danny's waist. Dave had him by the legs. Together we pulled him down onto the deck. In mere seconds, it was over. We had saved Danny from certain death. I sent forth a silent prayer, thanking God.

Inexplicably, I was convulsed with laughter just then, and so were Danny and Loni. The three of us sat for a minute, midship, hugging and laughing hysterically. Even Dave seemed relieved as he looked at Danny. "You okay?" he asked.

Danny nodded in reply, and then gave his most pathetic "Hooyah" ever, which made Loni and me laugh even more.

But the humor was short-lived, as Dave broke into a rant. "That was pretty fucking dumb, you know that? You could've gotten yourself killed, Danny. Or one of us, for that matter."

Dave stood and walked over to Salazar. Back to business as usual, but who was I to complain? Most certainly, Dave had been instrumental in saving Danny's life—an action I would never forget. And for the briefest of moments, I no longer saw Dave as malevolent.

I looked up and saw the captain leaning outside the wheelhouse door. His face was ghostly white, but I thought I spotted a small grin hidden under his beard. Dodging back inside, he slammed the door against the storm and calmly said over the loudspeaker, "Cut her loose, boys. Then get the hell inside already!"

With that, Dave pulled out a pocket knife and sliced rope, sending the dangling crab pot, that menacing beast that started it all, straight to the bottom of the ocean. Business as usual.

CHAPTER 17

———◆———

S HIPPING IN THE Gulf is considered the most dangerous job in the world. How we all managed to escape those fast, short minutes of peril without injury or death is still beyond me. Certainly, a combination of skill, luck, and lots of quick thinking. But aside from the components that allow a man to survive from one season to the next, year after year, in the end, it all comes down to fate. When it's your time to go, then it's your time.

I know that that might sound like a shallow statement, but it's about the only thing a deckhand can hang their raingear onto when they're dead tired, cold, and wet, and simply done for the day. That's how I felt, and how we all looked once we came in from the storm and actually did hang up our raingear. No one said a word for at least fifteen minutes. I suppose each of us had to process the ugly ordeal we had just survived: a massive wave pounding over the deck, a cage of steel swinging madly for us, Danny hanging on for dear life over the water. It was all too much, and that's not counting the fact that we had been working gear for over twenty-four hours without sleep. As for those last ten pots of the string, I don't think any of us would have complained if they just went straight to hell.

But it wasn't like we had a choice in the matter. With the

hydraulic controls now shot, we couldn't retrieve those pots even if we wanted to.

"Captain says we're gonna ride the storm, wait till it breaks," Salazar mumbled, coming down from the wheelhouse. He still had his raingear on, and his body was shivering intensely, making him slur his words. Salazar sounded pretty much like Danny. But he moved quickly and his demeanor was serious. He slid his beanpole frame out of his wet clothes, and then flung water off his hands. Face drawn into a rigid scowl, he fished his pockets for a pack of cigarettes, found them, spirited one out, then lit it with a lighter he produced out of thin air. "And next chance you get, find that leak, Dave," Salazar said, glaring through a vague sheet of smoke. "We're shit out of luck otherwise."

The hydraulic controls were the backbone of our entire operation. If the leak was too difficult to access, or too big to patch, we would be forced to head back to Kodiak for repairs. Even though this would give us time to offload our current catch of crab while in port—a rather thin silver lining, if there was one—the opportunity lost from fishing would cost us thousands of dollars. As it was, our crab tanks were only half full, and the captain wanted to drop all our gear onto a spot that had so far yielded the biggest and cleanest numbers of crab. If his hunch were correct, we would fill our boat in less than two days. That notion appealed to all of us, except for Danny perhaps, who up until a few minutes ago had seemed indifferent on the matter.

For all intents and purposes, Danny appeared to love his job as greenhorn. Even though he still couldn't do the more complicated or dangerous jobs, such as chaining down the gear, he had become a master at all the annoying tasks no one else wanted to do. Making bait setups and clipping them into the pots before launching now seemed trivial for him. Danny had also mastered the routine of preparing gear dialed in, never missing the opportunity to bring pot lines and buoys over to the launcher. When the time came for sorting the crab, I had long since stopped advising Danny. I'd grown comfortable with his skill at measuring clean crab and spotting the "dirty" ones, and his speed with clearing the table in time for subsequent pots was quick enough. But the best thing about Danny Wilson was the fact that he never once complained ... about anything. He never griped over working long hours or moaned about the incessant wear and tear on his body. He never bitched about working with anyone, either. Although Danny only had a few jobs on deck, he was as relentless as a bull shark when it came to getting those jobs done. He stayed on top of them, oblivious to who he was or what others thought of him, and he never once let his inabilities get the better of him. Danny damn near made the rest of us complainers feel as worthless as an empty crab pot.

That said, I wondered how Danny felt after almost losing his life.

Presently, he sat next to me. Shivering on a stack of buoys and coiled rope, he struggled with his rain boots. He was shaking worse than Salazar. I worried that maybe he had been dipped into the ocean after all, while hanging onto that pot.

"Did you go in?" I asked. Danny gave me a blank stare. "Did you get dipped in the water?"

"I don't know," he said. "Maybe I did." Reaching down, Danny pulled off his other boot, tipped it, and then chuckled as a stream of water fell to the ground. "Wow. I'm really cold, Ed."

"I can see that, buddy. Let's get you into some warm clothes and into the rack."

Dave, the only one of us still wearing his raingear, stepped up next to me. "He never went in," he said, flipping the switch to a flashlight, "but he's still soaked. Get him into the rack before he gets too cold. And get him some coffee ... or something hot." He left us then, headed back out onto the deck, but I thought

I heard him mumble, "And keep him there," before slamming the door.

The rest of us headed to our staterooms for dry clothes. Outside, the wind howled ferociously, like two lions battling to the death. Wave after wave slammed into our vessel, rocking us side to side, up and down, as if we were nothing at all, just some errant piece of driftwood. That thought dawned on me, as I struggled just to get down the hall. Compared to the mighty ocean, the *Angie Piper* really was nothing. I also thought about the guts it took for a captain to sail a boat against Mother Nature. As Fred had told me earlier, it took an unlimited amount of courage and an unwavering spirit. It took a blind attitude, with perhaps a sprinkle of insanity. Once more, I questioned my aspirations of owning a boat some day. *Who am I kidding?* I thought to myself.

For all his ugliness, Dave captured everyone's respect on that night. Like the captain, he apparently did not fear certain things. Minutes after helping to save Danny's life, there he went, alone on deck with a flashlight, attempting to diagnose our problem with the hydraulic system.

"Man, we gonna be in bad shape if Dave can't fix that leak," Loni said, guzzling hot coffee.

"He'll fix it," replied Salazar.

"We don't know that for sure, do we?" I asked, looking at Salazar. "What if it's a big-ass leak, or a crack in the line? What if it's a couple of leaks, for that matter?" Salazar didn't reply. He sat in the galley booth, sipping coffee, his face impassive as ever. None of us could possibly know how bad our situation was with the hydraulic system. Yet Salazar seemed to have faith in Dave's ability as an engineer.

We were in dry clothes now, in the galley, warming up before returning to our staterooms for an indeterminable amount of sleep. Coffee in one hand, donut in the other, I considered the unique talents of a ship's engineer. I had known several other deckhands who had run with that title, and in a way, they were all similar to Dave. After talking to them, I came to the conclusion that many engineers had little formal training in their craft, and that they simply acquired their knowledge while satisfying their own natural curiosities. They were the "tinkerers" of this world, quick to take apart radios, drive shafts, and computers, just to see how these things worked. And in the course of these explorations, more questions arose. Nevertheless, as these men picked and pried into the labyrinths of mechanical and electrical constructs, riddles were ultimately solved, encouraging childish laughter and magnanimous comments such as, "I'll be damned!"

The storm was rough. So rough that it made the act of "sitting" in the galley booth difficult. Wave after punishing wave had each of us gripping a corner of the table. More than once, I thought I might be sick. I pictured Dave out on deck, the wind blasting through his raingear, the pitch of night surrounding him like mountainous, slavering jaws, circling swells of murderous ice water, a single-beam flashlight in hand, peering under slick floorboards into the gritty blackness of the *Angie Piper* for a single, small leak. That he expected to find anything seemed absurd. Absently, I gazed into my coffee cup, realizing just why Salazar had so much faith in Dave's ability to diagnose our problem. To find that leak.

"Maybe one of us should go check on him," I said. But just as I said this, we heard the metallic creak of the outside door opening, followed by a howl of wind so fierce, it sent shivers down my spine. "Never mind," I added.

Seconds later, Dave shuffled into the galley. His raingear was off, and his clothes were a sodden mess. He left behind large puddles as he made his way to the fridge. The rest of us looked at each other as if trying to determine who would be given the task of asking that dreaded question: *so what's the status?*

"Well ... did you find it?" Salazar finally asked.

We all looked on, the suspenseful moment hanging dead in the air, while Dave casually explored the contents of the refrigerator. He moved containers to the side then back again, as if deciding what to select. Settling for his usual can of Mountain Dew, he popped the lid and then turned to face us.

"Yeah, I found it," Dave replied, before he kicked back all twelve ounces of the soda. The way he leaned his weight against the counter and guzzled that drink evoked a vision of Dave in his own house, slamming his twelfth beer of the night, his wife and kids tiptoeing down the hall.

"And ...?" Salazar asked.

"It's fixable." That's all Dave said before grabbing another can from the fridge and leaving the room. *Fixable by whom?* I wondered. The mechanics in Kodiak? But such was not the case, and I think we all knew it. Everyone seemed to sigh with relief, the tension in that room melting like grease in a hot skillet. I thought about Dave, the obscurity of his past and the complexities of his personality. The range of his talents. Some things, he made look so easy. Things that no average person could come close to accomplishing. And this baffled me. How—or what—had gone into the making of that man?

Another heavy wave hit our starboard side, sending the *Angie Piper* into a good twenty-degree list to port. Loni and Danny both chuckled, and I heard Dave curse somewhere in the hall. Salazar simply pushed another cigarette between his lips and lit it. He took a deep drag, and then stared right at me. "Told you so," he said, before erupting into a burst of smoke and laughter.

CHAPTER 18

————•————

Most of the crew managed to get a few hours of sleep before the seas settled down. I had second watch duty in the wheelhouse, but after Loni came up to relieve me, I got four solid hours of rest. When I woke, the storm had passed, and the *Angie Piper* was skimming through the ocean at a stable pace. I knew we'd start to turn the gear soon, pulling and dropping pots, which oddly enough struck me as a welcoming notion. After the previous night on deck, it would do everyone good to get back into the rhythm of work.

I climbed out of my rack and got dressed, noticing that Danny wasn't in the room. Laughter erupted from down the hall in the galley, and I suspected he was in there eating a hearty breakfast. The thought of Danny becoming more and more independent as a deckhand put a smile on my face. Knowing that he didn't need me to tell him what to do every minute of the day was a relief. Yet more than that, it supported my decision to introduce Danny to this horrible life.

We still had Dave to contend with, though.

Coffee was my number one objective at that moment, and I smelled it, along with a mouthwatering combo of eggs, bacon, and hash browns. Rounding the corner and entering the galley,

I was hardly surprised to see that I had been the last man to wake.

"Good morning, sunshine!" Loni said. "You get your beauty sleep in, eh?" Everyone sat around the room drinking and eating, except for the captain, who I assumed was up in the wheelhouse.

"You bet I did," I replied, pouring myself a cup of coffee. "I had the craziest dream, though. I dreamt about a terrible storm, with waves crashing over the rail." I turned and smiled. "A crazy pot swung across the deck."

"We dodged a bullet last night, that's for sure," replied Salazar.

The coffee tasted good, and it was the perfect appetizer for the breakfast I piled onto a plate. While scooping up hash browns, I stole a brief peek at Dave, who had been sitting on a barstool, facing the hall. Naturally, I was curious about his current demeanor, and wondered if I should say something regarding the night before. After all, sometimes a crisis will bring men together. Like two sworn enemies who become the best of friends after they duke it out. There was hope, I reasoned.

"Hey, Dave, thanks for everything last night." I said this with as much sincerity as I could muster.

Dave's look verged on total astonishment, as if thanks was the last thing he expected. "Just doing my job, that's all," he said.

"Yeah," I replied, "but with Danny, also."

He shrugged. "Whatever. The last thing we need is another dead man swallowed by this bitch of a sea."

The crew spent a good hour talking about the night before, processing the event. It was our therapy session, I supposed, despite the general awkwardness caused by Dave's lukewarm attitude. Even though he added his own comments and opinions regarding the night, he still managed to convey his contempt at having Danny aboard—this time, without saying a word about it. His expressions were subtle now, an occasional roll of the eyes and ambiguous headshake to punctuate the long stretches of silence. I wondered again what the captain had meant about Dave letting his past go.

Halfway through my breakfast, Fred came down to tell us we would be on the gear soon—nine pots now, excluding the one we had to cut loose, which we conveniently dubbed "Danny's pot."

"And get ready to dump half our gear in about six hours," he added. "Let's just hope the crab hasn't moved by then."

Tanner crab lived in huge populations called biomasses, at the bottom of the ocean, and these masses wandered the sea floor for food. As scavengers, they sometimes stayed in one area, particularly if it was ideal for collecting dead matter, such as a valley, or canyon. But oftentimes the crab moved around. Fishing for them was a gamble that always kept a good captain guessing.

"But what about the hydraulic leak?" I asked.

"Dave patched it while you were getting your beauty sleep," replied Fred. "Now," he continued, "I think I need to remind you guys about general safety on deck." The captain paused, scratched his chin, and then looked at the ceiling. "You boys need to watch your fucking backs!" he suddenly blurted out. "I know that last night was rough, and certain things can't be helped, but dammit—don't go looking for trouble!"

It was obvious to everyone that the last statement was a clear reference to Danny's attempt at manhandling the errant pot.

"Look, boys, this is a deadly job," Fred continued. "It is real dangerous out here, and every year we lose a few fishermen, no matter what. Sometimes they die from happenstance, like accidents, and things that just can't be helped." Fred turned toward Dave. "You remember that blond kid from Detroit, the one who picked a fight with you in town a few years ago?"

Dave nodded.

"Well, that kid got his neck broke falling from a stack of pots—while they were sitting in port. He was killed instantly, from a single slip. But other times," Fred continued, as he paced the galley now, staring holes into downward-turned faces, "men die doing stupid things. They die making bad decisions. For example," and now, the captain stopped and stared directly at Danny, "it is never a good idea to try and handle a swinging pot."

Danny dropped his head, like the rest of us, and looked at the ground, silent as a dead man's whisper.

"And it is never a good idea to lose track of your deck mates!" Fred shouted. "I've never lost a man doing this job. And, as God is my witness, I don't intend to. So from here on out, I want every one of you to keep your fucking eyes glued on each other like you're brothers!" Fred's eyes landed back on Dave. "Is this understood?"

After a moment of deathly silence, Loni squeaked out, "Aye aye, captain."

"Dave and Ed," continued Fred, "as soon as you two are done eating, I want you out on deck testing the hydros. Run a few pots around, make sure that patch holds." With that, the captain left the galley, and us, in a rush that was both a relief and distressing. No one said a word in the vacuum that followed.

As much as I dreaded that next hour working alongside Dave, it wasn't bad. Dave's demeanor was quiet and concentrated as we tested the hydraulic controls, running a few pots across the deck. We also made some general inspections of the boat, considering any damage that might have occurred from the previous storm. And like a wise man, I just listened to Dave's instructions. He was quick to tell me what to do.

I admit it was tolerable, even mildly pleasant, working alone with him for that stretch of time on deck. In fact, the mood was such that I decided to take a stab at having a conversation with the man. Or at the very least, at trying to get to the bottom of why he was so ill-disposed toward Danny.

"Man, you sure found that leak quick enough," I said, easing into it. Presently, we were testing out the dogs against an empty pot. "How'd you do that?"

Dave shrugged, his stare undecided between the devices of the boat and the open sea. "Gut feeling, I guess," he said. Then, more to the point, "Some of the lines—they were getting old."

"You know, Dave, aside from last night. Well ... all in all, Danny's done pretty good out here."

Dave glanced sideways at me, then shook his head.

"I mean ... don't you think?"

"No, I don't think."

"I don't get it," I replied. "It's like you've got something against the guy."

Dave gave me a pointed stare then said, "Can we get done with this, already?"

So I dropped the subject. I just did the work, which wasn't that bad. But then Danny came outside to prepare bait, and Dave's face screwed up and he turned a mood. Damned if an icy blast of wind didn't blow at my back just then, sending shivers right down my spine.

But once more, I was mildly surprised. Despite dreading the next several hours as much as I had dreaded that first hour on deck with Dave, the time that passed proved to be acceptable. In the six hours it took us to get to the fishing grounds, the crew did an excellent job preparing the *Angie Piper* for the upcoming turn of our gear. In the subsequent hours, we launched almost half of our seven-bys into the water without a hitch. Or complaint, for that matter. After a brief soaking, we turned and picked them up. And we found that the crab had definitely moved on. But not even this seemed to discourage us.

Many hours later, an evening sky hovered above our world. The *Angie Piper* was loaded with gear and heading toward another one of Fred's "hunches," while the entire crew settled into the galley. It was time for the feast.

The captain had meticulously prepared us a meal, planned

weeks before, after taking culinary advice from his brother, the chef. As our vessel rode steady through a quaint sea, Fred served us pan-seared duck breast with five spice and balsamic jus, hardboiled eggs with sweet dill dressing and frizzled prosciutto over baby greens, and a pasta and lamb casserole topped with sweet cream butter. No joke. For dessert, we ate red velvet cake.

Collectively, I think we were all amused, and honored— definitely honored. This wasn't the first time Fred had made us a special meal. But after the events of the last two days, every bite of that banquet tasted better than the previous. On that night, we had us a fine supper on board the *Angie Piper*. The meal proved to have a certain symbolism none of us appreciated at the time.

CHAPTER 19

———•———

THE WEATHER WAS supposed to remain mild and steady....
After dinner, the captain announced we could have
several hours of sleep, switching out with watch duty in the
wheelhouse as necessary. As the weather was mild, we were
going to make a slow run north, toward Sitkalidak Island,
then start prospecting for crab. I was scheduled to watch the
helm during fourth shift. My plan was to get as much sleep as
possible, and I had a full belly to help me with that.

Some hours later, I tossed and turned in my bunk, half-
awake and half-aware that things had become rough outside.
That the weather had taken a turn for the worse.

And then ....

"What the fuck!" someone suddenly screamed from down
the hall. I woke completely in midair, falling from my rack into
the darkness. Everything spun. The sounds of metal, wood,
plastic, heavy objects smashing lighter objects, and breaking
glass filled the air.

"Captain!" someone shouted. "Where's the captain?" I'd
landed hard—split my head on something—and my ears rang.
Blood seeped down my face, stinging my eyes, running into my
mouth, flooding my taste buds with rusted iron. My breathing
quickened. I wiped at my face with one hand and reached into

the blackness with the other. I grabbed, pulled, pushed, and struggled with my surroundings in order to find my footing.

I would soon discover that a massive "rogue" wave had hit the boat. These monsters of the sea, once considered a silly sailor myth, were a real threat to even the largest of maritime vessels. They could peak at over one hundred feet, preceding their knockout punch with a trough so deep, a crew would think they were being swallowed by the abyss. Having never before fallen into anything like this "hole in the sea," I had no idea at the time what had hit us. And the not knowing added to the panic.

"Danny!" I screamed. "Where are you? Get up, we're in trouble!"

"I'm over here, Ed," Danny stuttered. "What's happening? I can't move. I don't know what's wrong. Help me."

Tears rushed into my eyes at the sound of Danny's voice.

"I don't know what's happening, Ed," he continued. His voice came from a few feet away, but because of the darkness and the list of the boat, I couldn't tell which part of the stateroom we were in. With no electrical power, another terrifying notion went through my mind: could it be that our rudder was also cut? Were we dead in the water?

"Help me, Ed!" Danny shouted. Then came more screams from a different part of the ship. Focused on the need to help Danny, I reached out and found the corner of a wooden box. I knew it to be the storage container mounted on the floor opposite our racks.

I gripped the corner, spun my legs around, then planted my feet onto the inner bulwark of the ship. I'd figured out my surroundings: the *Angie Piper* was sideways, listing heavily to port.

Legs shaking from fear, I stood. "I'm coming to get you, Danny. Hang tight! I'll be right there."

"I'm over here," he repeated. "It's dark, Ed. I can't see you."

"Just keep talking, buddy."

Reaching into the darkness with both hands, I walked toward Danny's voice, dragging myself against the wall of the ship. Two steps into it and my right hand brushed the edge of our bunk, so I grabbed it, braced my body, and gained some balance. It's amazing how difficult it is to be steady on your feet when you can't see anything, and all that you're familiar with is topsy-turvy.

"I'm coming, Danny," I repeated. "Do you know where you are?"

"I'm on the boat, Ed. I'm on the *Angie Piper*."

"Of course you are, dammit! I mean, where are you?" Quickly, I wiped more blood from my face with a sleeve, then shuffled forward two more steps. The pull of the ocean on the boat had me fighting to stay on my feet. "Never mind, Danny! Just … can you stand up? Are you standing up?"

Before Danny could reply, the boat began an enormous, terrifying drop, like the fall on a roller coaster. My stomach and feet rose as the *Angie Piper* dove into an invisible hollow— the hole in the sea.

I had no illusions on this matter now. We were being taken in by another monstrous wave and had but a few seconds to prepare for it.

"Hold on, Danny!" I hollered. Then I heard more shouting from down the hall, recognizing the voice as Loni's. "Brace yourself, Danny!" I said. "We're going down! We're going down hard!"

I squatted and gripped the rail of the bunk as firmly as I could with both hands. I squeezed my eyes shut, waiting for what seemed like the smash of an ogre's club on the top of my head. I held my breath and whispered a quick prayer—*God, oh God, please!*—and then came the roar.

A great booming sound echoed throughout the cabin, as the *Angie Piper* flipped back up toward her starboard side. The sounds of crashing objects surrounded me, while my body rolled around the stateroom. My ribs were smashed into the storage container, knocking the wind out of me. I heard Danny shouting, as well as Loni from down the hall. I flailed my hands in the air, trying to control myself, for what seemed like several long minutes, until finally, with a sudden jerk, everything just stopped.

"Help me, Ed." This time, Danny was right next to me, shouting into my ear.

"I'm right here," I said, gasping to catch my breath. "Here. Take my hand." We were lying on the floor of the stateroom, our backs against that same wooden trunk that had been next to me seconds before. Although still in total darkness, I understood that the position of our boat was "normal" once again. The wave that had just hit us actually helped to right our vessel. But I wondered how long that would last … and also, what condition the boat was in. Were we taking on water? Too many unanswered questions, and they were scaring the shit out of me.

"Get up, Danny!" I was still in a state of panic. "We've gotta get out of here. We've gotta get up on the bridge to check on things."

"Hooyah," Danny cried, lacking his usual enthusiasm. Then he asked that dreadful question no fisherman wants to hear: "Are we sinking, Ed?"

Hands shaking, I replied, "I don't know, buddy. But we've gotta get out of this room. Let's get up there to find out what's going on."

"Okay," Danny said. Then he gripped me around the waist, lifting me straight up and onto my feet. The action reminded me of Danny's strength, which seemed an odd thought to pop into my head at that moment. Along with it came a dozen shades of doubt as to our chances of survival. I thought about the many stories I had heard, of boats going down, whole crews being swallowed by the relentless ocean. I thought about men floating in survival rafts, deafened by hundred-knot williwaw winds racing down from the north, these same men dying in the end of hypothermia. I thought about the *Polar Betty*, and my friends who had perished in these very waters. And I thought about the friend standing next to me, holding me steady.

"Come on, Danny," I said, "let's get the hell out of here!"

Seconds later, we ran into Loni down the hall. He had a searchlight in his hand, its strong beam cutting a pallid path through the fabric of gloom. "Ed!" he screamed. "Danny! You boys okay?" Then he caught sight of the blood still streaming down my face. "Ooo, boy! Ed-man, you cut badly!"

"I know, Loni. Where's the captain?" My hands still shook and my voice came out rattled and creaky. But I was thankful to be in Loni's company at that moment. "What about the rest of the crew? We gotta find them, Loni."

"I think Captain's upstairs. I heard some noise up there." Loni pulled me closer, holding me steady, shining his light onto my head. "You've got a nasty cut there, Ed. We gotta get that fixed." He turned and made a gesture with his hands toward the stairs. "There's a first-aid kit up in the wheelhouse."

Still surrounded by a blanket of darkness, the boat tossed and jolted up and down with each passing wave. It seemed like every third wave was a killer, smacking our boat with a deafening roar, sending the three of us into a wall. "What happened to the power, Loni?" I shouted. "What happened to the lights?"

Loni ignored me, pushing Danny on the back. "Lead the way, Danny-boy," he said. "Head for the stairs."

"Are the engines dead?" I continued. "Can you hear anything, Loni? Can you hear them down below?" During calm seas, not only could you hear the engines running, you could actually feel their vibrations with your feet. But this sudden storm was so rough and so loud that I could barely hear my own shouting voice.

"Let's just get upstairs," Loni replied. "We'll find out soon enough."

The three of us shuffled down the hall until we met the stairs leading up to the wheelhouse. Then we noticed water trailing down those steps from above.

"Holy shit!" I cried. Loni froze, staring, his body against the wall, while Danny stood next to me, his mouth open. It seemed the three of us were in shock.

Bracing a hand against the wall, I thought I heard a sudden, deep moaning sound and looked up. My heart sank. Was the captain injured? Was he dying, or even dead? I felt nauseous, realizing just how dependent we were on our captain.

"Get us up there, Danny!" This time, Loni's voice screamed with urgency. We were almost at the top, but it seemed as if our own boat was fighting against us. It was painfully difficult climbing those stairs, our bodies smashing into the walls three, four times. Blood rushed down my face, distorting my vision, which revealed little more than a dark hallway, sporadically splashed in white from Loni's searchlight.

But we finally made it. We made it to the top, Danny leading the way. He pushed open that door, and then the three of us stood, awestruck, as we witnessed the aftermath of a rogue wave crashing through the wheelhouse.

Chapter 20

———•———

THE WHEELHOUSE WAS absolute chaos.

"Captain!" Loni shouted.

The three of us, we were completely baffled.

"Hurry! Help him up!" cried Loni.

We were in total shock as we stepped into the center of a raging hollow—a dimly lit wheelhouse that mimicked the maw of a screaming leviathan, with shattered windows for teeth, a blackened night for its gullet, and the howling winds for its breath.

"Help him up, guys!" Loni screamed, running to the captain. "Help him up!"

Driven by the wind, the rain stung my eyes and face like angry hornets. I held my hands across my face for protection and followed Loni's lead, staggering toward the captain, who lay face down behind his chair. Standing behind me, Danny grabbed my arm, holding me steady. Loni and I reached down for the captain. It was a tight squeeze, the three of us behind the captain's chair, but we managed to roll Fred over.

"Pull him over here," said Loni. Dragging Fred's limp body to the center of the wheelhouse, Loni suddenly shoved the searchlight into Danny's hands. "Hurry, Danny. Get the first-aid kit over there," he said, pointing to a wooden cabinet on the opposite end of the wheelhouse.

The flashlight in Danny's hand illuminated our surroundings with a vague, opaque light in the swelling darkness of the night. Even so, I could see enough to get a quick impression of the situation.

"It was a fucking wave," I shouted, stating the obvious as I helped Loni check the captain for injuries. "A wave came through the windows—looks like it fried the electronics. Everything's wet and dead!" I looked back down at Fred, who gave a weak groan.

"Well, he's not dead," replied Loni. He felt behind the captain's neck, then shook his chest. "Captain! Can you hear me?"

More moaning from Fred, as Danny arrived, holding the first-aid kit. "Good job, Danny-boy," said Loni. He looked up, glanced at Danny, then said, "Think you can find the others, Danny? Can you go find Dave and Salazar?"

I shuddered at the thought of Danny heading back down into the ship. For whatever reason, and however ridiculous it seems in retrospect, I felt somewhat "safe" in the wheelhouse. The prospect of heading back down into the darkness, perhaps even out on deck, set off an acute pulse of terror in my head.

"I can do it," Danny replied. "I'll go and find them." Then he handed the searchlight to Loni, who just laughed in return and shook his head.

"You take it, Danny-boy. You gonna need it down there."

Danny turned and stared at me. His face was flushed pink with fear and excitement as he asked, "Are you gonna come with me, Ed?"

I paused, thinking about the situation. I didn't have an answer. Between my own terrors, the captain's moaning body, the clamor from the storm and the waves ....

But then .... I choked on a breath of air as the *Angie Piper* started to fall once again.

"Oh shit!" Loni screamed. The boat swooped down another

slide of water. "Everyone, hold on!" Loni sprawled his body over the captain's, Danny dropped to the floor and I just stood, like an idiot, looking out the broken window.

"Get the fuck down, Ed!" Loni reached up, tugging on my pant legs. "We gonna roll again!"

I couldn't see a damn thing. I looked into the raging sea, searching for that menacing wall of water, and saw nothing but darkness. Our boat rushed to the bottom of the trough, and I heard her hull creak as she came to an abrupt halt. Then came the momentum of her descent, the mounting pressure. It hit me square in the back of the knees like a baseball bat. I collapsed onto Loni, floundering with my hands to hold on to something, anything.

A brief pause in the movement of the sea preceded a silence so distinct, so gripping, I shut my eyes tight in anticipation. "We're gonna die!" I hollered. "We're gonna fucking die!" Then we waited—a few of the longest seconds in our lives. We waited for that wall of water to roll us, smash us, and send us straight to oblivion.

Our surprise came in a rush as the *Angie Piper* broke free from the hole and began a rapid climb up the invisible wave.

"Ahaaa!" Loni laughed, triumphantly. "We still holding together, boys! We gonna make it, you watch and see." He lifted his head, and then pointed at Danny. "Go find them, Danny! Go find Dave and Salazar, and get them up here. Ed's gotta stay with me."

"Hooyah!" Danny replied, lurching toward the stairs. He gave me a brief glance, as if asking permission to leave, and then headed down into the ship. Fear sped through me at that moment, and I cringed, feeling that I would never see my friend again.

"Go get 'em, Danny!" I shouted. "Go find our crew! You can do it! You're a Navy SEAL, dammit!"

Danny disappeared, and that's when I realized just how cold it was. Everything inside the wheelhouse was soaking wet.

Disheartened and miserable, I tried to still my body's violent shivering. Nothing seemed as it should be. The floor was a sopping pad of salt water, inches deep, with rivers of foam floating over the ruined carpet. My chilled hands ached from the cold, and I had completely forgotten about the gash in my head as I surveyed my surroundings once again. Nobody was steering the fucking boat!

I cried out my sudden realization. "Loni! I gotta steer this thing!"

"The captain's coming around," he replied, ignoring my statement. "We gonna get out of this yet."

I stood and lunged for the wheel, my hand stretching toward the jog stick, hesitating. I could see that the engines were left half-open, assuming that they were running at all. But I couldn't see a damn thing out the window. The night was a snapshot of the abyss, and it was anyone's guess as to how fast I should push the Angie Piper into the oncoming waves. Shit, it was anyone's guess as to where those waves were even at. I had to rely solely on the sway of the ship to determine our position against the sea.

"Just keep her steady, Ed!" Loni shouted. "Keep her steady. Captain's gonna wake soon, I know it!"

Holding the wheel firmly, I strained my eyes, looking into the darkness. If only I had some kind of light, any light. I guessed at our position. I tried to keep the Angie Piper quartering the waves so we wouldn't get killed running sideways in the trough. But this was a powerful storm, mean and ferocious, bringing water from all directions. And I couldn't see a damn thing.

"Come on, Fred!" Loni's voice carried the same terror flushing through my veins as he tried desperately to wake the captain. He found a small flashlight in the first-aid kit and turned it on. "We gotta get you up, man. You gotta run this boat." He lifted Fred against the wall, lightly smacking at his cheeks, to no avail. Loni then opened the first aid-kit and dug out a package of ammonia inhalants—smelling salts. I could see both men out of the corner of my eye, and I watched with an anxious mind as Loni cracked open a tube and waved it under the captain's nose. My knuckles had long since faded white over the wheel, but now, the anticipation had me queasy with dread. I felt sick to my stomach, about to hurl, as I waited for a response from the captain, something that would indicate he'd pull through.

"What the hell happened?" Fred suddenly muttered.

"The captain ... he's awake!" shouted Loni.

I smiled with joy, yet was perplexed by my reaction, considering our current predicament. We were but a few men battling for our lives against the blows of Mother Nature, and there I stood, elated at the sound of Fred's voice.

"Oh Lord," Fred said, rising from the floor. Loni's hands were under the captain's armpits, helping him up, and I saw the captain stare at me, then past me, then all around. His eyes were stricken white, gaping at our surroundings, bulging with grave recollection. Then he blinked, and his face flushed with color as he lunged forward, pushing me away from the wheel.

"How long have I been out?" he asked, his hands dancing over controls, flipping switches. He did a double take at my forehead, and then said, "Christ, Ed! Loni ...! Get a rag on this man. He's bleeding everywhere."

Fred's words were like a fist punching through a thin sheet of ice. The cold terror that ran through my veins, causing my hands and legs to shake, was quickly being displaced with a gush of warm adrenaline. *Our captain was alive.* He was alive, barking orders, and because of this, we were going to survive.

Loni grabbed me by the arm, and we both staggered to the floor a few feet away. He squinted against the darkness and then tilted the small flashlight over my gashed forehead, checking my wound.

"Here!" the captain shouted, tossing a bright, SureFire flashlight over to Loni.

Of course, I remembered. In the maddening chaos that had brought us to this moment, I completely forgot about the captain's flashlight he kept in the compartment near the wheel. Or the .38 Special he kept clamped under his chair. Or the flare gun on the wall behind us, the fire extinguisher near the door, the extra survival suits in the bench next to me, and then just outside, below, mounted on the fo'c'sle … the inflatable life raft. Would we need it soon? I choked on the thought, and then pushed it out of my head.

"Where are the others?" the captain asked.

"Danny-boy went looking for them," Loni replied, dressing my wound with antiseptic wash and several gauze pads. "Just left a few minutes ago."

The captain cringed, and then said, "Well, we need Dave up here as soon as possible. I also need a status report from below. The last thing I remember was that fucking wave hitting us. Could've cracked a weld or something—God forbid."

Bilge alarms would help let us know if the *Angie Piper* was taking on water. But in our current situation, nothing could be counted on. We had taken a massive rogue wave, all the electronics were fried, and nobody knew what kind of shape the rest of the boat was in. All this, while we rode up and down fifty-foot swells and hundred-knot gusts of wind screamed through the wheelhouse.

"Cut's not as bad as it looks," Loni said, applying pressure to my head with the gauze. "Should stop bleeding soon. Don't know if you'll need stitches or not." He took my hand and pressed it against the wound, which turned out to be an inch-long cut above my forehead. Head injuries are notorious for looking worse than they are. "Here now," Loni said, "you hold it down. Keep it tight. You gonna be good soon."

Loni stood and stepped behind the captain, looking over his shoulder, while I sat on the floor with my head against the wall. I felt a migraine coming on. Everything around me—the darkened wheelhouse, Loni and Fred, the dials, switches, and radios, the broken windows—everything spun uncontrollably. I closed my eyes, hoping to fight back the nausea welling inside my gut. But the heavy sway of the boat only made things worse. I felt I had to stand and get my eyes focused on something.

"We need to find Dave, Loni!" the captain shouted. "We need that man up here. Right now!"

I grabbed the back of the captain's chair and pulled myself up.

"Might be that Danny-boy will find him!" Loni replied.

Stepping to my right, I wedged myself between the chair and the wheelhouse bridge. A violent wind rushed through the window and across my face, forcing me to shield my eyes in the crotch of my elbow.

"Or .... Might be that he ain't even on the boat anymore," Loni added grimly.

"Well, quit your damn speculating," Fred commanded. "Get down there and find out."

"Aye aye, captain." Flashlight in hand, Loni made a move toward the wheelhouse door, and then stopped abruptly, pausing to look back, as if about to say something. A short stretch of silence passed between us then. A short and eerie stretch. I thought I was imagining it, but the captain seemed to sense it too, looking over his shoulder at Loni, then at me, standing to the right of him.

And then, suddenly ....

The tide of shadow that surrounded us, the ominous night that had chained our weary sight down onto the abyss, our blackened nightmares, our living nightmares, which undoubtedly captivated the whole of each of our minds .... In the blink of one solitary eye, our entire world erupted into a bloom of white light. Suddenly we knew what we were up against.

CHAPTER 21

"**M**OTHER OF GOD!**" The captain's curse said it all. All eyes stared at the boiling sea beyond, illuminated now from the *Angie Piper*'s running lights, allowing us to see how things had changed. Since that first monstrous wave had hit us, the ocean had turned into a raging, screaming bitch, with the fury of a mother grizzly protecting her young. Fifty-foot waves roiled past us in cold anger, pitching our boat into stunning crests and bottomless troughs every other second. We were mere men sailing in a crippled vessel against a storm that cared nothing for our existence.

Losing the battle with my stomach, I turned and retched in a corner. Fear and the tumultuous sea had finally overtaken me. After throwing up, I hunched down behind the captain's chair, frozen in place, unsure what to do. I worried about Danny, somewhere down below searching for Dave and Salazar. I wondered how badly our boat had been damaged. Apparently, all the electronics in the wheelhouse were ruined, which made it impossible to radio an SOS. The question was, did we need to?

"Now we know what we're up against, boys!" the captain hollered, flinching against the rushing wind. "Ed! Get some wood over that!" He pointed to the starboard window. The window was shattered, allowing for a constant stream of wind and rain to badger the captain standing at the helm, steering the boat.

Fred's command rattled me into moving once again. After Loni headed down below, I stood and staggered to the wheelhouse door, then looked down into the brightly lit hall. I remembered the plywood board stored behind my rack, likely for this very purpose but long forgotten, and then made my way down the stairs. Halfway to the bottom, I spotted Loni standing in the hall. Danny was stumbling toward him, Salazar hanging on his shoulder.

"What happened?" shouted Loni.

Salazar winced with each step—or hobble, for that matter—and said, "I think I busted my ankle." His face was frozen in a pale, sour expression, showing his battle with the pain.

"Danny," I said, stepping into a stateroom to let them pass, "what about Dave? Have you seen him?"

"No ... I don't know," Danny replied.

"He might be down below in the engine room," added Salazar. "Or," and here, Salazar chuckled grimly, "he might be in the ocean."

Either scenario was plausible. After the *Angie Piper* had taken a wave of that magnitude—straight through the wheelhouse—and the electricity was lost, Dave would have been anxious to check on things down below. But if he had been outside on deck ....

The fact that we now had partial lighting throughout the boat was a telling sign. Perhaps that was Dave's doing. I wasn't sure, but I suspected it to be the case. At the time, I had little understanding of how the boat worked in terms of mechanical and electrical functions. That was Dave's job.

"Just put me down in there, Danny." Salazar pointed to the rack in a stateroom. "Then go find Dave; hopefully he's down below."

I helped Danny get Salazar settled in a bunk, then reached

back and retrieved the piece of plywood. With a nod, Loni disappeared down the hall and toward the engine room door. "We're gonna find out soon enough," I said, motioning to Danny. "Come help me with this. We gotta cover the window in the wheelhouse."

Salazar stared at me from the bunk, then his face twisted in grim understanding. I didn't have to tell him that the wheelhouse had taken a wave. All the same, he appeared lost and fearful. As Danny and I left once again for the bridge, I realized he had been silently questioning me, asking whether we were going to make it or not.

Danny and I struggled our way up to the wheelhouse and began fixing the board against the window. We used a concoction of tape and sheet-metal screws that we drilled in using a battery-powered drill gun, effectively sealing out the roaring wind. Only, I wasn't sure how long the patch would hold.

"Thanks, guys," said the captain. Immediately, the atmosphere inside the wheelhouse calmed down several notches. The wind only whistled through two windows now, portside. "Has anybody found Dave yet?" Fred added.

Just then the door leading downstairs pushed open, and Dave staggered in, suited up in his raingear. Grease was smeared across his hands and face. From his expression, one could only guess what his thoughts were. He appeared distant and remote, not the least bit alarmed. I couldn't get how anyone could act so calm at a time like this. Shame burned inside me, such that I avoided eye contact with him. Wasting energy on shame was absurd, given our current predicament, but that was how I felt.

"Dave!" the captain shouted, laughing, his eyes sparkling with relief. "Thank God you're here, man!" He reached out and squeezed Dave's shoulder.

"I think we lost a few pots when that wave hit us," Dave replied stoically. "We're gonna need to get out there and take a look. But she's running strong down below—just had a generator flood on us, that's all." He looked over at Danny and me standing near the starboard exit, then at the window we had just covered. "Grab some floorboards from the engine room and cover those other windows," he said. "Then gear up—might need you outside."

I could have stepped right through the starboard door and jumped over the rail. This man was fucking nuts! "Gear up," he'd said. *Why don't we launch a few pots while we're out there?* I thought.

Dave was correct, though. The deck of our boat was a disaster waiting to happen. Loose pots dangling over the side could be enough to bring the *Angie Piper* right over with even the smallest of rogue waves.

My face must have given me away. "That's right, Ed—gear up," Dave said. "But you can leave Danny here. I don't want anything stupid happening out there."

Even now, I thought. My legs shook violently. I stood near the starboard door, tightly grasping the captain's chair. I tasted bile in my mouth, and my ears rang from the mounting pressure of blood pulsing in my head. I wanted nothing, nothing else at all, other than to punch Dave right in his smug face.

Looking back on everything—our fateful voyage, my life growing up with Danny—I know that at that moment, right there in the wheelhouse, I had reached a crossroads. That moment was my "left turn," as I finally began the process of cutting loose from a life of cowardice.

Of course, I didn't know this at the time. I simply kept my mouth shut, hunched my shoulders, and ignored Dave. And I headed back down those fucking stairs. "Come on, Danny," I said, releasing a heavy sigh. "Looks like we're going to the engine room."

We ran across Loni at the engine-room hatch. He was in the ready-room fighting with his raingear, trying to suit up—not easy considering the brutal pitch of the boat.

"Might have some loose pots out there, boys," he said. Then

Loni stumbled with his pants, falling face down onto the floor. Danny and I reached out to help him up, and he laughed, and cursed, and said, "Sure hope I don't fall down out there."

"Don't worry, Loni," I replied. "I'll be out to help, as soon as I cover the porthole on the bridge."

"Where you going, then?" he asked, cinching up his pants.

"Getting floorboards from the engine room. Then I'll suit up and head out. Be sure to save some work for me." I chuckled, albeit vaguely, the breath in my chest gone weak as vapor.

"Oh, you bet for sure, Eddy-boy!" Loni replied. "I gonna save you and Danny all the hard work."

We were struggling men, and we knew it. Loni knew it. I knew it. Probably even Danny knew it. Inside the *Angie Piper*, the sound of the waves crashing against us brought a deafening roar. This storm was the worst any of us had ever seen, and there were too many questions looming. Even though our boat appeared to be running solid, the fear that hung over our heads cast the blackest of shadows. And our voices did little to conceal this fear.

"Danny ain't coming out, though," I said, lifting the hatch door leading down into the engine room.

"Why not?" asked Loni. "We gonna need his strength."

"Dave doesn't want him to," I replied. "Says he might do something stupid."

"Bullshit!" cried Loni. "You put your gear on when you're done, Danny-boy. Understand? Don't go listening to that asshole anymore. He ain't our captain."

Danny climbed down into the engine room after me, but then turned and shouted back up to Loni, "Aye aye, sir!"

As with the rest of the boat, there was stuff everywhere. Tools, buckets, and rags littered the floor of the engine room. The noise was so loud down there, between the engines and the storm outside, that I wanted to cover my ears. But I needed my hands free for balance. Danny and I made our way to the back, where we could find and retrieve some floorboards.

Halfway there I paused. My mouth began to water, and then I turned and puked again, my stomach reeling and lurching.

"You okay?" Danny asked, reaching for my arm.

"I'm fine, Danny," I replied. I threw up one last time, spit, wiped my face with my sleeve, and then stood. "But he's right, buddy. Loni's right. We ain't listening to that asshole anymore."

Chapter 22

———·———

"I THOUGHT I said to keep him here!" Dave rushed down the hall, his features contorted in various knots, from his eyes to his mouth. Even his ears seemed to change appearance. He looked so large and menacing that I thought of a stampeding bull.

Danny and I had just finished battening down the remaining windows in the wheelhouse, leaving Dave with the captain to discuss the damage on the bridge. Then we headed back downstairs. Now, accompanied by Loni, the three of us stood in the ready-room. We had our raingear on and were preparing to open the door to the deck when Dave came screaming at us.

"There's been a change of plans!" I replied. I could hardly believe my own words.

"That's right Dave-man," Loni added. "We gonna do this as a team!"

"Hooyah!" Danny said, summing up our mood.

Apparently Dave didn't feel like arguing, as he just slipped angrily between us without saying a word. Yet for me, it was the smallest of victories in a lifetime of battles against fear. Which brought refreshing relief from all the bitterness hanging in the air.

I grinned, and then I almost fainted when Dave opened the

door. All my thoughts of victory vanished when I saw what loomed over the brightly lit deck of the *Angie Piper*.

Yes, Alaska is a bitch ... and here she was. She screamed her williwaw across the deck like a banshee cursing in the night. The noise was so loud I covered my ears, and then I pressed my body into a corner of the ready-room. The wind nearly flung the door off its hinges. The wind, in fact, was so strong, so powerful, and so vicious that I swear it was a visible entity. You could see it streaking past the rails and the crab pots, which themselves were a dangling nightmare of chaos. Dave had just opened the door to insanity—a laughing, hysterical, hair-pulling insanity.

"Remember ... nothing stupid!" Dave shouted against the wind. Then he lurched out onto the deck, the three of us trailing behind.

A tempest of wind and rain cuffed our bodies, ripping through our raingear. Everyone reached out, grabbing elbows, arms, and sleeves. I splayed my legs wide, trying to stay upright as the boat pitched and rocked and damn near threw me right over the rail. How the hell we were going to accomplish anything in this deadly squall was beyond me.

Pots were hanging from both sides of the ship. A few had already been lost to the sea. But the ones that were still there, hanging haphazardly, banging against the bulwark, were a threat to our survival. Somehow, we had to cut them loose. And depending on the situation, we had to consider cutting loose all our pots—a decision that would cost us almost two hundred thousand dollars. But, this storm being what it was, we were dangerously top-heavy. It had been a miracle that that first rogue wave hadn't ruined us, considering all the gear we had on deck. Perhaps the loss of a few pots had actually helped right the *Angie Piper*. Maybe it was all the crab in our holding tanks. Or the sea had done it on her own.

Looking at the mountain of steel not twenty feet away, I thought about how to deal with the situation. Those pots that hung from the main-stack and over the side were wrapped in coils of twisted chain.

"We're gonna need some bolt-cutters!" I shouted.

"Go get them," Dave replied. "Loni, you fire up the hydros. Let's see if the picking crane works."

Turning back into the ready-room, I shivered intensely, understanding exactly what we had to do now—what we were going to do.

We kept the bolt cutters in a cabinet just inside the ready-room. I grabbed them, steadied myself after the boat pitched hard to port from a massive wave, and then stepped back outside onto a deck suddenly submerged in seawater. A bolt of icy shock rushed up my legs, sucking the breath out of me. I held tight onto the door jam and then watched in helpless horror as several tons of water drained itself right into the belly of the *Angie Piper*.

"Shut that fucking door, goddammit!" Dave screamed.

But I couldn't. The force of the water was too strong. I heard bilge alarms go off, as I fought frantically to close the door with one hand while holding the bolt cutters with the other. Briefly, I pictured the captain's face up in the wheelhouse, his focus sharpening at the sound of those alarms. And I pictured Salazar's face, deathly white as he lay in the bunk nursing his broken ankle. Undoubtedly, they would think the worst: a crack in the hull.

"Shut it, Ed!" Dave repeated. "Shut that damn door already!"

Anger swelled deep inside me, heavy as an anchor. I turned and gave Dave a nasty look, and then threw the bolt cutters at him. "I'm fucking trying!"

Dave caught the bolt cutters in one hand and glared at me.

Out of nowhere, Danny was at my side. With the two of us pulling and yanking, we forced the door shut. It battened with a cold, muffled thump, like the final closing of a casket, and I felt a sickening shiver course through my body.

From behind me came the squeal and moan of the hydros.

Loni had fired up the system and was testing the picking crane. "We've got power on this baby!"

"Great!" replied Dave. "Keep her running—just hold on!" Dave positioned himself next to Loni and stared at the main-stack of pots, apparently studying the situation further. "We're gonna need to cut those ones first," he shouted, pointing to the starboard side. Two pots were lying on end at the corner of the stack, with a third dangling low over the side.

"Maybe we should rig one of us onto the picker?" I suggested, screaming at the top of my lungs to override the horrendous wind. "We could hoist ourselves up over there." I didn't even want to think about climbing around on the main-stack at this point. The job is dangerous enough on its own, never mind in this weather we were up against. That would have been sure suicide.

"Brilliant idea, Einstein!" Dave replied sarcastically. All the same, he tossed the bolt cutters back to me and then gathered some stray line bundled under the rail. With a pocketknife, he cut the rope, then proceeded to make an improvised climbing harness. Stupidly, I realized that my idea was his all along.

Before Dave could finish, there was a sudden shift in the boat. The *Angie Piper* rode high into the seas, climbing the height of another great wave. "Hold on!" Loni shouted. Each of us scrambled for a handhold, anticipating the dreadful descent we all knew was near.

Securing the bolt cutters between my legs, I grabbed a handle near the door with both hands, and waited. But before the *Angie Piper* dropped down into the trough, she dragged heavy along the crest of the wave, and then the entire deck flooded once again.

A waist-deep torrent of frigid seawater whooshed across the deck, knocking my feet out from under me. I clenched the handle with one hand while reaching down to grab the slipping bolt cutters with the other. My entire body was now submerged in the ocean. Icy cords of water rushed through my raingear, my boots, my mouth. I shook violently from the cold.

The *Angie Piper* began her descent into the trough, and I struggled to gain my footing once more and catch my breath. This was a big wave with a long fall and a heavy punch at the end. When we reached bottom, my footing was swiftly torn away again. With all that water, I slipped onto my back and across the deck, heading straight toward the rail. And for a split second, or maybe longer, much longer, my world fell into a pool of darkness.

The bolt cutters washed clean away. I felt a powerful tug on the back of my raincoat. Two feet from going over the rail, Danny saved me. He had his iron grip on me now, while his other hand clung to a piece of steel rigging. He dragged my trembling body midship, then reached under my armpits and hoisted me up onto my feet, all in one quick motion.

Like a dog, I shook water from my head, then reached out and grabbed hold of the picking crane for balance. My raincoat had been torn at the neck and was all but useless, since every inch of my body was now drenched. Yet I was still on the boat. I was alive, and I owed it all to Danny.

"You almost went over, Ed!" Danny shouted. His hands gripped the picking crane next to mine. "Gotta be more careful, remember? And don't you smile; it's known to happen." Danny's eyes twinkled as he repeated the advice I'd given him that first day on the *Angie Piper*.

"Thanks, Danny," I replied. "I guess I owe you one."

"Don't worry, Ed. You don't owe me anything."

A vicious wind howled past the boat, whistling, screaming, moaning through crab pots and rigging. I looked around and spotted Loni pressed up against the superstructure. I saw Dave hunched down near the railing I'd almost gone over. The remaining tons of that hulking wave flushed down through the scuppers and back into the godforsaken sea.

"Nothing stupid!" Dave bellowed, as he stood, lifting the bolt cutters at the level of his head. The tool I'd lost had gotten pinned between the pot launcher and the rail.

Dave stepped forward and handed the bolt cutters my way, but then he pulled them back and scowled. "Shit. Maybe I should give them to the retard instead."

"Fuck you, Dave!" I shouted, snapping at last, for once in my life. "Fuck you! Fuck! Fuck! Fuck you!" I got up in Dave's face. "I'm sick and tired of your shit, you asshole!"

In a screaming rush, Loni was between us. "Whoa, brothers!" he shouted, pushing me to the side. "We gotta keep things cool, man. Or we all gonna die out here."

"Get in my face again, Ed," Dave replied smoothly, "and I'll cut your fucking balls off." He raised the bolt cutters in a threatening manner, opening and closing them.

Something strange happened after that, alarming, yet ultimately exhilarating. It was a moment I had never witnessed but always wondered about. Ever since childhood.

"Hurt my friend, and I'm going to hit you!" Danny's voice seemed louder than the williwaw winds. Both Loni and I glanced at each other, our thoughts likely the same: *did we just hear what we think we heard?*

It seemed as if Mother Nature had heard it also, taking a pause from her tantrum, giving Danny the platform for one brief moment. A calm silence broke over the rail, bringing a refreshing lull from the maddening chaos of the night. During that crucial moment, Danny's words echoed in my head.

Dave was angry—but also hesitant. Glaring at Danny, he said, "Maybe you should just try that, Danny-boy."

Things went sort of white after that. I felt a rage boil through my veins, instantly warming my frigid body. I felt it pound from behind my ears, banging for a way out. I felt it in my hands, as I clenched them into white-hot fists. It seemed I'd had enough.

"Fuck you, Dave," I said, evenly, danger lingering in my tone. I wasn't sure what the man would do then, but I was ready for him, and I think he knew it. Maybe there was also something in my eyes, or perhaps the way I stood on deck.

Dave backed off. "All right," he said, "maybe I had that coming." He grumbled something else as he turned away, and then, awkwardly, the four of us went back into work mode.

"Let's all get back in, check on the captain," Loni said, much to my relief.

Dave nodded, his attention on the bundle of line in his hands. "I'll finish this harness. Then we'll cut those fucking pots loose." He turned and strode toward the door. I was amazed. *So is this how it is when you stand up to someone?* I wondered. I wasn't so sure. It all seemed too easy, sort of anti-climactic. The incident left me energized, but oddly, also depressed.

"Well, how about that," Loni said, as soon as Dave had left. Loni was smiling, and then he added, "Looks like Ed's got him some iron balls!"

Our short break from the storm was over. Mother Nature caterwauled across the rail once again, bringing a torrent of rain, pelting my face with a barrage of needles. I felt Danny at my side. He placed his hand on my shoulder and said, "Thanks, Ed." But I didn't reply. I tried a smile, but I didn't feel like saying anything. Not to him or to Loni. And certainly not to Dave.

Another poop-sweeper crashed over the rail and onto my back, sobering me with an icy push forward. I used this sudden momentum and stumbled toward the door. It seemed as if an eerie coldness had gripped me somewhere deep inside, sharp and malevolent, like a clutch from the hand of Death. I bit my lip and reached for the door handle, knowing that the only thing I felt like doing at that moment was getting the hell inside.

CHAPTER 23

———•———

IT TOOK THIRTY minutes for Dave to make a harness, and in that time I thought I was going to die. At one point, my shivering got so bad, I couldn't stand anymore. I sat in a corner inside the galley and braced my feet against a cabinet for stability.

Danny sat at my side, shivering as well, and he kept glancing at me, a concerned look on his face. "Should we change our clothes, Ed?" he asked.

"We should," I said, my teeth chattering violently, "but it'd be pointless, Danny. We're gonna be out there again pretty soon."

"Maybe we should do some jumping jacks then. That's what the Navy SEALs do when they get cold, Ed. They do jumping jacks on the beach and stay warm, because jumping jacks do that for you. Jumping jacks make you warm."

I laughed, picturing the captain's bemused expression if he came in and saw Danny and me doing jumping jacks in the galley.

"Nah," I replied, "let's just move around some, maybe go upstairs."

Helping each other up, Danny and I left the galley and headed toward the wheelhouse. In the hall, I spotted Dave sitting near the door in the ready-room, adding the final touches to his rope harness. I wondered about that man and our confrontation just minutes prior. There was something about him I couldn't read, something I couldn't quite figure out. As I headed up the stairs to the wheelhouse, I thought about the conversation I'd overheard, days before, between Dave and the captain. Something about Dave's past, about him letting things go. Something about Danny.

We met the rest of the crew once we got to the top of the stairs. Sometime while we were outside, Salazar had hobbled up to the wheelhouse. After coming back in, Loni also made his way up to check on the captain. Now the five of us huddled, pondering our situation.

"If you boys can suitcase those pots," said the captain, "we just might get through this." Fred stood heavily against the steering wheel, his knuckles white in their grip, sweat beading his forehead. He was using manual steering and a manual compass—old-fashioned sailing—and I wondered if the man wasn't actually loving it, despite the mortal danger.

"I figure I'll just keep us heading northeast as much as I can," Fred continued. "That'll get us closer to Kodiak, anyway. And when this bitch of a storm settles, we'll be all right."

"You want us to cut all the pots, Captain?" Loni asked. "Suitcase them all?"

"If you can," the captain replied. "I know it's a lot of money, but we need to lose as much weight as possible."

I thought about how low the *Angie Piper* had sat in the water when that recent wave rolled through us. It seemed as if a hungry leviathan had swelled up from the deep to swallow a minnow. The captain was right, and we all knew it. If we wanted to stay alive, we had to get as many of those pots as possible off the deck.

From below, Dave bellowed, "All right, girls, let's go!"

The captain looked at me, then at Loni. "You guys be careful, you hear? Salazar stays with me, but I want the rest of you back up here once those pots are gone. Got it?" Like a true captain, he was worried sick about his crew. It showed in his eyes. And for a brief moment, I saw half a dozen phantom stares come out of the man's face. I saw my father's and mother's, the day I left home for the first time. I saw Mr. Wilson's, that night he came over to tell my parents that his wife had passed away. I even saw the stare of Mr. Elmsworth, the high school swim coach, as I pictured it on the day when he gave Danny that apologetic "No." And for a brief moment, I might have seen my own stare.

We struggled down the steps once again, cursing under our breaths. Since the rude awakening caused by the fall from my bunk, nothing had let up. Things had only gotten worse outside, which made the inside of the boat a navigational nightmare. It was crowded with obstacles and beveling floors, and anything and everything that could get in our way. I slipped halfway down the stairs, crashing into Danny's legs, bumping my head against the wall. Blood poured out of the gash above my forehead, but I didn't care anymore. As long as I could see, I didn't care.

Danny helped me up, and the three of us eventually met Dave in the ready-room. He had his harness on; it was a simple climber's rig that looped around both thighs, up his back and over each shoulder. Also, he had made a small loop on the rig, at the center of his back, where there dangled a large, steel carabineer. I marveled at the man's ingenuity, and might have complimented him if I didn't feel he would take the words as open sarcasm.

"Hey, weren't we just here?" Loni said, chuckling. Unlike Dave, Loni never ceased to look for the unseen gem in life, wherever it might hide. "Nothing stupid, right Dave?" he added.

"That's fucking right!" Dave replied. "Now listen …." His tone was serious and to the point. "When we get out there, I'm gonna rig this harness to the picker. Loni, I'll need your help. But then, get back to the hydros, understand? And Ed, Danny," he continued with just a hint of contempt, "stay back and keep your eyes and ears open." He handed me the bolt cutters once again, then gave me a queer look. I couldn't tell if he was angry or just serious. I figured he was angry, but Dave confused me by adding, "Whatever happens, don't lose these, Ed. Everyone's counting on you."

Once again, out the door we went, and that damn wind smacked us all the more violently this time around, as if furious that we had escaped her first beating. Mother Nature was in our faces now, bawling us out with a temper that rivaled Poseidon's. And Lord if it wasn't fifty degrees colder ….

"Ooh-wee," Loni began, "let's get this night over with already!"

We stumbled out onto the deck as a group and made our way over to the hydro machine, tucking ourselves up against the superstructure for cover. I brought up the rear, and this time I quickly secured the door into the ready-room before I followed everyone.

Dave and Loni mumbled something to each other, and then they both lunged toward the picking crane, timing their movements with the list of the boat. One error in judgment now, and a person would find himself hurtled into the main-stack of crab pots. Or worse, over the rail and into the sea.

"Hook me up," Dave hollered. His hands gripped the picking crane, while Loni struggled to fasten the carabiner from Dave's back onto the crane cable. Twice, our Polynesian deckhand almost went over the starboard rail after the boat pitched hard against the waves. And twice, Dave grabbed Loni by the shoulder and reeled him back.

"Get this fucking thing hooked already!" Dave said. He looked over at Danny and me, and then shouted, "Get ready with those cutters, Ed!"

"I'm ready!" I hollered back. I looked down at the tool in my hand and thought for a second. "Wait a minute!" I added. "Just hold on!" I made my way back inside the boat and grabbed a length of rope from the ready-room, which I then lashed to the bolt cutters, making an improvised sling. When I returned on deck, Dave was glowering, but his face relaxed when he saw what I had done.

He nodded, taking the bolt cutters after I approached him. "Good thinking, Ed," he said, strapping them across his shoulder. "You're full of surprises tonight."

Thinking about Dave's words, the way he said them, brought to mind my actions of the past, and how I had at one time treated Danny. I thought about my own motives, as well as my ever-present confusion, which seemed to be the catalyst for all my grief. In the past, I had let this confusion turn me into the same man I was now staring at, and that was the toughest realization ever. On that night at McCrawley's, Dave had given me a look, a knowing look that I was just now beginning to understand.

The wind tore through my raingear, bringing me back to the present and chilling my bones into an aching misery. I stepped back against the superstructure, next to Danny, and braced myself. We watched as Dave and Loni proceeded with the plan to cut loose the pots.

"Okay, Loni, get me up there!" Dave's bellowing voice ripped through the howling cacophony of the night. "Starboard side. Let's cut those fuckers loose!"

Slowly, Loni worked the levers of the hydraulic system, and then I focused intently on Dave's feet. A sliver of separation turned into a half-inch gap, which turned into a good foot off the deck, and then Dave's body began to swing like the pendulum of a grandfather clock.

"Hurry the fuck up!" Dave shouted. If Loni lost control of the crane's "cargo," Dave's body would succumb to the will of the ocean and the sway of the boat. He would likely turn into a bloody pulp after slamming against the picking crane, the main-stack, and then the superstructure. "Get me up there!"

Loni was frantic, working the levers faster now. Dave rose

ten feet off the deck, across the starboard rail, and over the churning waves of the icy sea. I imagined the horror of a cable snapping at that moment. Would we even bother trying to save the man, if he fell right then? Could we? In seconds, the deluge of swirling water would gulp his body down and suck him under the *Angie Piper*, spitting him out no less than a minute later, and somewhere into the darkness fifty yards away. Dave would be gone forever.

Almost as bad for us, our vessel tipped hard to port when a large wave rumbled over deck. In no time, we were waist deep in the frigid sea once again, while Dave's body now swung midship, out of control, dangerously close to the main-stack. I clung to my handhold, afraid of being washed over the rail. Then I watched as Dave's knee clipped the corner of a crab pot, causing him to recoil in obvious pain.

"This is fucking crazy, Loni!" I hollered.

Loni didn't respond. His body straddled the hydraulic controls, eyes staring a direct path to Dave. He was attempting to regain control of the situation. His hands worked furiously over the levers, never mind that we all stood in a river of icy water. Loni cursed and spat into the wind, yet thirty seconds later his skills prevailed. He had Dave suspended off the starboard rail once again, and with a deliberate pace, inched the man toward the outside edge of the main-stack.

Most of the water cleared our deck in less than a minute, and now Dave was two feet from the first dangling pot. He reached for the corner of the main-stack, pulled himself closer, and then wriggled his feet into the sides of the stacked pots, finding footholds in the netting.

"How the hell are we gonna cut all these pots loose?" I shouted.

"One at a time, sailor-boy!" Loni replied, keeping his stare on Dave while his face broke into a crazy grin. "We gonna cut 'em one at a time."

Dave jerked down on the bolt cutters just then—one, two,

three solid times in a row. The sagging pot, which had been banging violently against the ship, plunged down along the bulwark and into the hungry waves, gone.

"I still think this is fucking crazy!" I shouted.

Two more pots hung near the rear of the main-stack, starboard side. Dangling haphazardly on edge, they were the next target as Dave vigorously motioned with his hand. He might have been yelling at us, but thirty feet through the wind, his was a dead man's voice. A squall of white foam and snow hurried over the deck, briefly erasing Dave from sight. Concerned, I looked down at Loni's hands and saw that they had gone motionless at the controls.

"One at a time, right?" I hollered.

"You bet," Loni replied. The Polynesian was a basalt statue, focused at the hydro station, his eyes on Dave, completely indifferent to the raging storm around us. "Just gotta get him down to those other pots."

Danny had been standing behind me against the superstructure, silently watching, until he stepped forward and tapped my shoulder. "Maybe we should climb up there to help him, Ed."

"No way, Danny," I replied. Our boat advanced into the trough of a large wave, and Danny and I fell back against the superstructure. "This shit is crazy enough as it is. We shouldn't even be out here."

The wall of white passed, and then Danny pointed at Dave, still perched on top of the main-stack. We watched Loni let out slack with the picking crane's cable, allowing Dave to shuffle down to the other pots. It was visual torture just standing there. I felt a sudden urge to run forward and climb up the tower of steel, as Danny had suggested. But I knew that in seconds I would get thrown off the boat and into the water. The *Angie Piper* was swaggering through the seas in complete disorder, like an angry drunk, making the act of standing on deck hard enough. Climbing up and around the main-stack without being attached to the picking crane would be plain suicide.

It took several long minutes for Dave to scramble across the top. Twice, he lost his grip and tumbled, but the crane cable kept him from going too far. When he finally reached the other loose pots, he was close to the rear of the main-stack, portside. His body sagged against a hundred-knot wind rushing past with fierce determination.

"Come on, Dave," Loni hollered, "cut them boys!"

There was no way Dave could have heard Loni, but strangely, it seemed as if he had. He shook his head, hunched forward with his body, extended the bolt cutters, and gave a sharp "jerk" against the chain. Then he changed his position slightly, and clamped down on another section of chain. About half a dozen times and five minutes later, there came a deep boom from above, as the pots fell in unison, clashing against the bulwark and right over the edge.

Those of us on deck cheered, but our enthusiasm died quickly. Dave was now frantically motioning with his hands to bring him down. He looked desperately tired, slumped down on the main-stack. Loni worked the controls to lift Dave's body, and then lowered him straight toward the deck. Danny and I lunged forward and stabilized Dave as if he were a crab pot.

A cold sensation of hopelessness went through my mind when I looked at Dave. His face looked like aged granite: gray with fatigue, ragged, and dusted with flakes of snow. He wasted no time at all draping his limp arms over Danny and me. I unclipped him from the picking crane, and we helped him over to the superstructure, immediately sitting him down.

"What a bitch," he muttered, shaking his head. "That wind is a bitch."

"You wanna get inside, Dave?" Loni asked.

"Fuck that! We've got the rest of these pots to deal with. Just give me a second to catch my breath."

"How's your knee?" I asked. Twice, I observed Dave reach

down and rub the knee he'd smacked into the corner of a pot.

"Hurts like hell. But I'll survive."

"You think we can climb up there now?" Loni asked. He pulled in the remaining slack from the picking crane, then hunched down with the rest of us. "Just untie, and pull the bastards down, eh?"

Dave nodded, and then paused, as if in thought. "I think so. As long as we're quick. Gonna have to take turns doing it, though." He stood and leaned against the superstructure, the color coming back to his face, while it surely drained from mine. The thought of having to climb the main-stack sent surges of arctic fear throughout my body.

"It'll be suicide climbing up there," I argued, pointing to the main-stack.

"It'll be suicide if we don't," Dave replied.

"He's right," Loni added. "Using the crane takes too long, and we gotta get them pots down. We can take turns, one at a time, bring 'em down to the deck." He looked at Danny, grinning. "And Danny-boy can help set 'em in the launcher."

I trembled inside. We would run the pots down onto deck as if we were going to bait and launch them. It was the quickest method to dump all our pots. Taking turns, we'd climb up the main-stack, un-secure chain and rope, and then secure the picking crane. Our only saving grace was that we would pull from the front of the stack, unlike Dave, who had been toward the rear. But still ... we'd have to get up there into that ghastly wind without being tied down.

"Hold on!" Loni shouted suddenly, as the *Angie Piper* pitched high into the sea, and another body of water rushed over the rail, flooding us waist-deep in misery. I grabbed Danny by his elbow and we braced ourselves against the superstructure. Every passing minute, every gust of wind, and every enormous wave brought with it a more bitter coldness than before. I clenched my teeth in pain and waited for the water to recede off deck.

"Let's get this shit over with, then!" Loni hollered, as soon as the deck had cleared. "Dave, you run the hydros. I'm going up!"

"Here you go," Dave replied, handing Loni the bolt cutters. "Take these. Don't fuck around with the chains. Just cut 'em." He stepped over to the hydro station, and then looked back at Loni. "You got a knife?"

Reaching to his belt, Loni gave a quick nod.

"Cut the rope, also," Dave said. "Hell ... just cut everything!"

Ten seconds later Loni was halfway up the tower of caged steel, the picking crane hook trailing close behind. Near the top, his speed slowed dramatically. His raingear flapped violently against the wind, and he clutched at the steel girding of the crab pots. When he finally made it, he craned his neck backward to look for the picking hook. I had never seen Loni move with such slow deliberation. A chill rattled my bones. It would soon be me climbing up there.

With his hands now buried deep into steel and mesh, as if operating on a monstrous robot, Loni effectively disconnected the first pot. He pulled the picking crane over and hooked it, then scrambled to the side.

"Get ready, Danny!" I shouted.

Dave waited for no one. He had that pot lifted out of the main-stack and lowered toward the deck as soon as Loni was out of the way.

"Careful, Danny," I said, "it could start swinging crazy any second now. Don't try to grab it if it does!"

Just before steel met the wooden planks of the deck, I rushed in and grabbed the cage. I felt the fierce power of Mother Nature surge beneath my grip, tugging at the crab pot through the list of the boat and the churn of the violent sea. With a stab of fear, I knew that in seconds my strength would fail against the sudden jolt of a passing wave, and that box of steel would go berserk. But then I felt Danny take hold of the pot. He had listened to the warning: stay ready and move quickly. He pulled the thousand-pound cage over to the launcher. Dave lowered it into position. I unhooked the picking crane, then stepped back. The launcher squealed. Over the rail the cage went.

"Hooyah!" Danny shouted, as the ocean swallowed the pot.

"Hooyah!" I replied, smiling briefly, despite my growing terror of having to climb the main-stack, the ungodly storm, and the fact that we were men fighting for our lives.

"Fucking, Hooyah!" With this last holler, coming from none other than Dave himself, I almost burst into elated laughter. His hostile attitude was forgotten. Here was the point I had desperately longed for since that first altercation with the man, back in Kodiak. It seemed that Dave was finally coming around.

No time to think about any of that just then. We had a hundred and seventy more pots to get rid of.

Loni yelled down at us, at Dave, signaling for the picking crane; he had already cut loose the second pot.

Dave operated the hydro controls, while Danny and I waited. In less than a minute, we had the second pot at the launcher. Danny set it, I un-hooked it, and *bam*. Over the rail she went—*hooyah!* The speed with which we dumped those two pots gifted us with hope for mercy. I saw it in Dave's eyes, as well as Danny's. I sensed it myself, and it had me feeling warm again—until five pots later, when Loni climbed down.

Loni's weariness was as clear as a naked sky. His cheeks were flaccid, his arms trembling, legs wobbling. "Whoa, boy ..." was all he got out through his rattling teeth. We helped him to the superstructure, where he collapsed into a seated position. I was vaguely perplexed, wondering just how bad it was up there on top of the main-stack.

"It's your turn, Ed," Loni stammered, handing me the bolt cutters. "Have fun."

With bile rising from the depths of my stomach, I clenched my teeth and faced the main-stack. Another large wave belched over the rail. My quivering body was doused with water once again, benumbing and icy, clouded with salty foam. It brought with it nothing remotely vague or perplexing. The water brought with it clear and certain pain.

Chapter 24

———•———

My battle came more from the *Angie Piper* than it did the wind. It was tough getting up that main-stack in the face of a furious williwaw, its breath thrashing through my raingear, peeling at my face, my eyes, ripping at my skin as if to uncover my weakened spirit beneath. But this was nothing compared to holding on for dear life. Against fifty-foot waves, gale-force winds, and billowing currents, the *Angie Piper* had little trouble convincing me of her own conflict while I held on, high above the deck.

Every fiber of muscle went into anchoring my body, keeping it from catapulting into the sea. The crab pot I aimed for was three feet away, top of the main-stack. I kept myself pressed into the tower of steel, inching my way up like an insect, trying to move with the pitch of the boat, not against it. I imagined having Danny's strength every time the boat angled acutely toward the frothing waves, threatening to toss me in. And I had to be quick. When the moment was right, I had to get up and over the highest pot in haste, knowing that my time clinging to the side of the main-stack was limited.

That moment came when the *Angie Piper* suddenly careened low into her stern, attempting, as it seemed, to pitch me toward the back of the boat. Like a swift insect, I scrambled onto the top of the last pot, exposing myself to the winds that screamed past. Then, for the briefest of moments, lying at the highest point of the planet for miles around, I took in the scenery—the limited, confining scenery. I took in the desolate blackness of the eternal sea, its bleak shadows, its haunting forecast, its taunting bellows spewing from a mouth of unhinged sanity. And I pictured this scenery embossed with icy fingers of death, fingers that reached up and forward, toward the *Angie Piper*, toward us, toward me.

I shuddered, shook my head, and searched for the picking crane hook. Dave had tracked my path up the main-stack within inches. The hook was less than an arm's length away. I reached for it and managed to grab hold of it first try.

Hooking the pot was simple. Un-securing the pot was a nightmare. I retrieved the knife clipped to my belt and cut the mesh surrounding the pot, providing ease of access to the bindings I needed to remove. Then I pulled the bolt cutters loose from my body, a challenge in and of itself. I turned on my side and wriggled the rope tied to the cutters up and over my head, nearly rolling off the main-stack in the process. Afterward, I dug my feet into the ribs of an adjacent crab pot for stability. Reaching with the cutters and my knife, I plucked away at both chain and rope, cutting everything as Dave had suggested.

Chain links popped loose and tumbled toward the deck. I inched from one corner to the next, cutting and slicing. The less than five minutes it took to un-secure that crab pot felt like a lifetime. The fear alone was exhausting. I caught an acrid, foul-smelling odor wafting upwards from the crab pots. Like death, it was thick enough to taste and robbed me of energy. I shuddered once again.

When I finished with the pot, I rolled away so that Dave could lift it. But I shifted my weight incorrectly and fell with the pitch of the boat. The ferocious wind pushed me across the top of the main-stack as if I were a helpless bundle of rags, rolling and tumbling for the edge, careening toward the hungry sea below.

I clawed for netting and kicked for steel girding, trying to catch or brace myself. I heard my own voice mutter, "Oh no!" I grabbed hold of a piece of steel, just before plunging over the edge, angering the williwaw all the more, it seemed. That bitch of a wind barreled across my chest with such violence, she ripped holes in my raingear. I tucked my chin and rolled forward, catching a glimpse of my deck-mates scurrying about, pointing at me, shouting silently into the wind. Then I reached with my other hand and wove it into the netting of a crab pot. I found my footing upon steel girders, exhaled a deep breath, and buried my face between my splayed arms. Knowing how close I had come to going over the edge, I felt my limbs buckle with fear, yet also surge with an adrenaline that brought with it unimaginable strength. I briefly asked myself, who was I at that moment? But more importantly, who was I about to become?

I'd always suspected that what I wanted most in life would come at a price, a dear price—one measured in pain, perhaps even death. And now, it might be the time to pay the piper. But these inner thoughts fled almost as quickly as the wind presently rushing past. There were crab pots to unload.

Several minutes later, I was cutting away more netting with my knife. Thankfully, I still had the bolt cutters, and I tried using them. Dave hoisted away another crab pot. I moved forward then, in slow, tedious inches. Timing the boat's movement against the current's relentless pull kept me from losing my balance. The storm still weltered around the *Angie Piper*. The winds still raged. And the waves still washed over the rail, splashing hard onto raingear and wooden planks. But I pressed onward, finding a raw bundle of energy accompanying the strength that kept me on top of that main-stack.

I managed to stay up there for ten pots. I'd found a rhythm. Dave, Loni, and Danny were relentless maniacs, as every thousand-pound cage that landed on the deck found itself in a quick transaction over the rail and toward a rusty doom. Those ten pots had pushed me beyond my limit. I wasn't sure how I could keep moving up there. How we, as a crew, could keep up our fight against that dreadful storm. I only knew that I needed to get back down on deck, out of the wind and away from the constant threat to my life.

No sooner had I reached the main deck and stepped away from the stack that a wave no smaller than a school bus crashed down from the portside of the wheelhouse. The wall of water collapsed onto Danny's back and my chest, sending both of us sprawling across the deck. I felt the immediate onset of bruises on both of my elbows, and then the back of my head, which had bounced against the hard, wooden deck planks. That was followed by darkness.

"Hey! Quit sleeping on the job, Ed!" I opened my eyes to the sight of Loni, kneeling before me. The wave had knocked me clean out. "But nice work on them pots, eh? You ready to get back up there for some more?" He motioned to the top of the main-stack.

"Fuck that," I replied. An unremitting, intense throbbing drummed in the back of my skull, like the cadence of a loud and terrible song.

"Come on, then," Loni said, his voice less jovial and more sincere. He helped me up and over to the superstructure. Danny was at my side also, and I remember seeing rivers and creeks and full waterfalls trailing off his sodden raingear. To my right I spotted Dave near the hydros, securing the rope attached to the bolt cutters around his neck and shoulder. He looked at me and grinned before giving me a thumbs-up.

"How long have I been out?" I asked, sitting against the superstructure.

"Only a minute or two," replied Loni. "Not bleeding, not dead …. You're still in the game, Eddy-boy."

I smiled in spite of the pain and mounting worry. Ten, fifteen, seventeen pots—over a hundred or so left, and my mind and body felt like they had both endured seventy-nine lashings from a cat o' nine tails. But at least there was Loni—thank God for that.

"All right, Loni!" Dave shouted, ready to make his climb. "You girls can kiss later!"

Loni patted my shoulder and said, "Catch your breath, Ed. We gonna have another pot down here soon, so be ready." He stood and staggered over to the hydros, signaling with his hand for Dave to go on up.

"It's about time," Dave said, shaking his head.

My whole body was in pain, but I stood nonetheless. Danny leaned into me and gave me a side hug, supporting my sagging weight with his strong arm. His eyes beamed with hope.

"Thanks, Ed," he said, graciously. "You almost fell off. It was scary. But you stayed up there a long time. You got down a lot of pots for us."

I barely heard Danny's words. I wiped my face with both hands vigorously, attempting with friction to stave off the bitter cold.

"Do you think we can do it, Ed?" Danny continued. "Do you think we can get them all off the boat?"

"We sure as hell better," I replied.

"But are we going to sink if we don't?"

"I hope not, Danny." I turned and looked at him. "Don't you worry about that, okay? Trust me, we'll be fine. Besides, do you think I would've brought you out here, fishing for crab, if I didn't know we'd make it back?"

Danny's swollen, pomegranate face creased. He looked down, sideways, not at me. I had the uneasy feeling that he doubted my words. It was unsettling, in fact, for Danny had always trusted me. Until high school, perhaps, when things had literally changed overnight, and over one incident. Until then, I'd always had Danny's unwavering confidence.

That brief, painful moment there on deck, with that look in Danny's eyes, reminded me of our younger years, of the awful mistake I had made, and it felt then like a piece of cold steel was slowly driving through my heart. "You can trust me, Danny," I said, almost muttering the words.

"Ten pots, Dave-man!" Loni's sudden holler hammered against the wind. "Nothing less than ten pots!" He wrapped his hands over the hydraulic controls and ran the crane forward, chasing after Dave's thick body, which slowly scrambled up the main-stack. "Nothing less than ten, or you're a worthless son of a bitch!"

Twenty minutes later, Dave lurched back onto the deck, smiling grudgingly. "Ten pots, Loni-boy!" he said, imitating Loni's Polynesian accent. He passed the bolt cutters over to Loni, and then took over at the hydros.

"Yeah, man … but you still a son of a bitch!" Loni replied. Both men laughed, before Loni headed for the main-stack. He threw a glance at me on his way, and winked. "More pots coming down, boys. Be ready." There was that usual tone of enthusiasm in his voice, but I could see on Loni's face just how tired he was. Like the rest of us, he was running on the fumes of his spirit.

In the time it took for Dave and Loni to switch up, Danny and I had taken a seat against the superstructure to catch our breaths. Exhaustion was a close companion by now, and I simply gave up thinking about it. I gave up thinking about the cold, and the wind, about my weary muscles and aching bones. All that was on my mind were more crab pots that needed to get off our boat. More pots, and then hopefully, afterward, we'd get some rest. We'd get back inside, at least, and eat some food. Drink coffee.

I looked at Danny sitting next to me and realized that we were probably thinking the same thing at that moment. "We'll be done soon, buddy. A few more hours at this rate … as long as things hold up."

"I'm hungry, Ed," Danny replied. His eyes seemed fixed on

his gloves, but then he looked up, wiggling his fingers absently. "Do you always throw pots away, Ed?"

"No, Danny .... But yeah, a little bit, I guess. In a way. It gets nasty is all, the weather and the waves. But we've never had to dump all the gear. And I've never seen a wave crash through the wheelhouse, either."

"Well, do you think Dave is right about me? Maybe I'm a ... superstition.

"Bullshit, Danny! You're no superstition, so get that out of your head. We're gonna be fine."

After a few minutes, Loni gave Dave the signal to start lifting. Danny and I stood, our backs against the superstructure, ready to manhandle the oncoming pot. I wondered about my friend, standing next to me, his shoulders slumped and sullen. It wasn't like him to dwell on the future, or to ponder the many "what-ifs" that often plagued other people. I hadn't realized he had that kind of imagination. Yet I knew he must be dead tired, like me, and tiredness has a way of stretching a man mighty thin. With a weak punch to his arm, I said, "Cheer up, Navy SEAL. We'll get through this yet."

As time crept by, more pots came down, more went over the rails, and more weight came off the *Angie Piper*. We could see the difference we had made as our decks gradually took on less water. Our vessel was riding higher in the seas, which lifted our spirits. With about half as many pots left, we started un-securing them as a team, scrambling over the lower ones like rats. Even Danny joined in. *We'll get through this yet*, I thought. Those words abated my own fears, and the fervor of hope surged through my veins. Ragged, cold, raingear torn beyond repair, the wind and the waves still punching us like a bully from a nightmare, and all I could think about was hot food, and hot coffee, and some much-needed rest. And it was all just a few measly hours away, if that.

Curiously, I watched as Dave suddenly stepped away from the hydraulic controls. He stumbled over to the main-stack, shielding his eyes against the wind, and appeared to study the crab pot attached to the picking crane. Much to my dismay, I saw that this pot had somehow snagged on the corner of another one. Then, suddenly, there came a dull, snapping sound, and a low-pitched twang, followed by a faint screeching above us. I looked over and saw the picking crane's cable flog the air, like a thin willow branch thrashing in the wind. Then I saw the crab pot attached to that cable come crashing down—a terrible monster of the night. It moved slowly enough to punch a hole of fear in my gut, but too fast for some of us to get out of the way.

CHAPTER 25

—————◦—————

THE POT WALLOPED into the side of what was left of the main-stack, clanging against steel and deck-board before pitching itself into an ugly, terrifying lurch midship. It stopped with a dead thud, lying broadside—yet curiously uneven, angled.

Dave's scream was a jagged fissure in the fabric of night.

"Oh fuck!" I shouted. "Loni! Loni, get down here!" I dropped to my knees and looked under the crab pot. Dave lay beneath it on his side. His sickening howl faded into a deep groan as the weight of the entire pot pressed down on him, crushing him into the deck.

"Help me, Danny!" I gripped the corner of the pot and pushed with all my strength. I might as well have tried to move a bulldozer. The thing wouldn't budge. I grabbed at it from beneath, lifting with my legs. The pot inched away from Dave's body. I heard the man gasp for air, but then I panicked. The weight was too much for me. My back felt ready to give out, and my knees bulged from the weight, threatening to blow. And then there was the fear, the fear of letting go—the crab pot would crush Dave even more. "Help!" I stuttered, my body shaking as a whole. "Danny, help me!"

Danny curled his fingers under the lip of the crab pot, same as mine. He gave a great heave, his arms and legs pushing away from the deck. Sure as shit that pot came straight up to Danny's chest. Not stopping there, he switched his grip and began to push the thousand-pound cage across the deck, stepping over Dave's body, crashing the lethal steel box into a corner near the rail. My God, I was amazed.

Loni was down on deck, crouching near Dave, taking cool control of the situation. He gently rolled the man onto his back. "Can you hear me, Dave?" he said, lifting one of Dave's closed eyelids.

Dave moaned in response.

"We gotta get him inside," Loni said. "Gotta get him in a bunk."

Danny reached under Dave's shoulders from behind, and lifted the man into a seated position. Blood trickled out of Dave's mouth, he groaned again, and then Loni and I tried in vain to lift him up. But Danny blocked us with his body, smoothly curled under Dave, and put him right onto his own shoulders. It was a perfect fireman's carry—and why wasn't I surprised? When Danny had learned that was how a man carries a wounded comrade off the battlefield, he had his dad teach him the maneuver, and then he practiced it on me every chance he got, until he owned it.

"All right, then," I said, leading the way off deck.

Moments later, I slammed the door tight against the furious night, only to meet a similar commotion within the *Angie Piper*. Loni dashed down the hall and up the stairs, straight for the wheelhouse. "Get him on the floor, guys!" he hollered, before disappearing from sight. I rode Danny's heels until we reached a stateroom, and then I stepped past him, kicking and throwing duffel bags, clothing, random items out of the way, until I had cleared a spot on the floor.

"We need to get this raingear off," I said, helping Danny set Dave down.

Loni rushed in at that moment, holding a first-aid kit, but

was pushed aside by Fred. The captain's stare was straight and focused, his face pale. Loni had obviously told him what had happened during his mad rush into the wheelhouse.

The captain ripped open Dave's raingear and pressed his hands against his chest, ribs, and then stomach.

"He fell on his side," I stuttered, shivering deeply from the cold.

"He could've busted something inside," Fred replied, almost to himself.

Dave gave a low moan and blinked several times, looking around in a daze.

"Hey, buddy," said the captain, "wake up now! Time to wake up, Dave."

He moaned some more, before he managed to fix his stare onto the captain.

"That's right, you big fool."

But then Dave howled again, painfully, disturbingly. "My fucking leg!" he stammered, his eyes jamming shut. "Oh … son of a bitch!"

We wasted no time getting the rest of his raingear off. With a pocketknife the captain swiftly cut away the suit, slick as gutting a fish. Then I had to blink my own eyes, swallow hard, and tell myself that he wasn't gutting a fish after all, upon witnessing the amount of blood and twisted gore sticking out through Dave's pant leg. Dave's left leg, what remained of it, was a mangled coil of bone and grisly flesh. From the knee down, it was a complete mess. Blood pooled around the floor near our feet. My stomach lurched. I had to look away.

"Oh, shit!" the captain said, the panic in his voice as disturbing as the sound of the bilge alarms. "Right now— somebody get me some rags! Danny," he added, casting a stern look at my friend, "make sure he doesn't move. You got that? Keep him steady, Danny, pin him down if you have to."

Danny responded by pinning Dave's shoulders to the floor, while the captain cut away the remaining raingear and then the pant leg. Loni was out the door and back again before I knew it, holding a bundle of clean rags from the galley. He stooped down near the captain, and the two of them swabbed away some of the blood around Dave's leg. I felt helpless, unsure of what to do. We had the whole crew crammed in this stateroom, except for Salazar, who was upstairs steering the boat. The air was getting hot and clammy. My knees felt brittle, my breathing shallow. Dave's moaning did not hide the horror. His mashed leg, the fractured bone with all that blood—he was on the verge of passing out. I hoped for his sake he would do it soon.

"I'm gonna need a tourniquet," Fred declared, shaking his head, his voice bleak and hollow. "Ed ... go get me some line."

Finally, something to do. I dashed out of the room and down the hall. Finding a large coil of rope in the ready-room, I cut off a four-foot piece and headed back.

"Good enough," said the captain, taking the rope from me. "Now get in the galley and heat up some water ... a big pot," he added, on my way out.

For almost fifteen minutes I braced myself in the galley, holding the pot of water steady on the stove. What a hell of a night. And when the hell would it ever end? Once I had a boil, I handled the pot with rags and carefully made my way back to the stateroom. It was slow going, to say the least, as I had to slide the pot on the floor to keep from losing it against the pitch of the boat.

"Bring it here," said the captain, once I made it back.

Dave was lying in a bunk now, Fred squatting beside him. I hoisted the pot up to him. Fred dunked a handful of clean rags into it, and then gave me a look. The situation wasn't pretty, and his face said as much. He didn't have to tell me that Dave would likely lose his leg. But he did tell me to clean the man up as best I could.

The captain stood and exhaled deeply. "I think it's time to set off the EPIRB, guys."

The Emergency Position Indicating Radio Beacon, otherwise known as an EPIRB, is a commercial fisherman's last ditch effort for survival. Mounted on the bridge, it looks like an oversized walkie-talkie. Most EPIRBs will automatically activate once submerged below ten meters of water, in the event of a sinking. However, they can also be activated manually. Either way, activation results in a digital transmission sent to orbiting satellites, which are monitored worldwide. The information is passed on to local search and rescue units—in our case, the United States Coast Guard. It contains details such as vessel identity codes and approximate location. It also contains the assumed message, "Someone please get the hell over here, we're in trouble!"

No one argued with the captain. No one even said a word. I think the idea of alerting the Coast Guard to our predicament sat well with everyone.

"It'll be some hours before they show up," said the captain, rubbing a hand through his hair. "Loni, take Danny with you outside and do a good sweep of the deck. Get it all secured— the picking crane, whatever else that needs to be tied down. But make it quick." Then he turned to me and said, "Stay here and keep an eye on Dave. Try to clean up his leg, but keep him covered. There's a good chance he might go into shock. And loosen up that tourniquet every twenty minutes."

Fred hesitated for a moment before he left the room. I heard him climb the stairs up to the wheelhouse, and in my mind's eye, I pictured him walking over to the EPIRB to activate it. Finally I let out a deep sigh myself. A sigh of relief, knowing that the Coast Guard would be alerted to our situation.

"Okay, Danny-boy. Let's buckle things up." Loni slapped Danny's shoulder and made for the door. He gave me a wink, and said, "You let the captain know if Dave gets worse. If he starts spitting up more blood or blabbering like a mad man. Understand?"

"Sure thing," I replied. And then Loni slapped my shoulder

too and gave me that wonderful, warm smile of his, which said that everything was going to be all right. I smiled in return, watching him leave the room. I smiled, but I felt a sudden, dim current of sadness ebb within me. I wondered if everything really was going to be all right. And what exactly was the definition of "all right"? We had a badly injured man, our ship was failing fast, we'd lost half our gear .... Fleeting yet powerful, the emotion left me confused and worried. "Be careful out there, guys," I said.

A minute later, I knelt down next to Dave. Deep in thought, I stared at the man's face, which looked tense and strained, his eyes shut tight. "I suppose I should clean you up, some," I mumbled. I took a rag from the pot of water and wrung it out. Then I lifted the blanket covering his legs. *Grim*, I thought. His broken leg was lying on a bloody rag, which I replaced with a clean, dry one. Then I took the wet rag and made an attempt at gently cleaning away some of the blood on his leg, fearful that I'd hurt him more and send him into another howling fit. I spent a good ten minutes at the job, making little progress, it seemed. The bleeding had mostly stopped, but my thoughts still clung to the image of Dave's mangled leg.

After I finished cleaning the leg, I wrapped it in bandages and covered it with the blanket. Then I sat on the floor. I got to thinking. The Coast Guard would be here in a few hours, hopefully, and at least then they'd know about the kind of shit we were riding through. More than likely, they would take Dave away, fly him to a hospital. But the rest of us, we'd stay aboard the *Angie Piper* and try to get her to port. Without a doubt, we'd get us some radios, maybe from the Coast Guard, or perhaps a nearby vessel. As I sat there thinking, a few other things dawned on me. The storm had decreased quite dramatically over the last few hours. There were still big waves, and big wind, and lots of rain, but it was manageable. I realized that I was cold, hungry, and dying of thirst.

Dave was asleep, so I stood and walked into my stateroom

across the hall. I changed into some dry clothes, which felt so good I almost wanted to get wet all over again, just to relive the comfort replacing them provided. But I felt guilty, also. I was the driest person on the boat, and that just seemed wrong.

In the galley, I took a plastic bag and filled it with candy bars and Mountain Dew. This would satisfy me for a few hours. Then I went back to keep an eye on Dave.

I had about thirty minutes of quiet thinking as I ate and drank while sitting on the floor next to Dave's bunk. Then I looked up to the sound of the man coughing. He was awake. His face seemed more relaxed but showed intermittent signs of stress: a wince here or there, probably from a stabbing pain in his leg brought on by his coughing. Or worse.

"You gonna just sit there and stare at me all night?" Dave's comment startled me out of my thoughts. "Make yourself useful, Ed. Get me a fucking beer already."

"Huh? Oh, sure," I replied, staggering up and out of the room. Down the hall and into the galley, I thought about what I was doing—getting Dave a beer. Alcoholic or not, that man never drank while aboard the *Angie Piper*. Never. But to my knowledge, he had never been crushed by a crab pot, either. In light of that, I brought him four beers.

"You probably shouldn't be drinking, you know," I said, sitting on the floor, popping the lid on a Budweiser.

"Shut up, and hand it over," he replied.

I gave him the beer then helped him with a pillow. "Captain set off the EPIRB," I said, shoving a second pillow under his leg to keep it raised above his head.

Dave nodded, unsurprised. "Yeah ... I figured as much."

"Just think," I said with a smile, "in a few hours you'll be in a warm bed in Kodiak."

Dave sneered and gave me a sidelong glance. "Just think," he replied, "in a few hours I might be losing my leg." He lifted the covers and strained forward, taking a peek, then closed his eyes and sat back. I searched for something positive to say, something "chipper," but then changed my mind, realizing that I should just keep quiet.

After a long pause, Dave said, "So, was our greenhorn the one who got that pot off of me?"

"Yeah," I replied. "Pretty much."

Dave chuckled. "Pretty much," he echoed with sarcasm. He drained his beer, tossed the can to the side, and reached for another.

"I'm serious, Dave. This isn't a good time to get drunk and all."

"Four beers aren't gonna make me drunk, kid." He flexed his hand open and closed, gesturing for another. I popped the lid and passed it over. "Who are you anyways, my fucking mother?"

I shrugged my shoulders. "Nah, I'm just saying."

A few awkward minutes passed, and then Dave laughed again. "Pretty much," he repeated, still sardonic. "I bet. That little fucker probably threw it right over the rail." He looked at me with a sour expression on his face, his eyes tight and narrow. "Okay, Ed," he continued, "you win, you son of a bitch."

"What do you mean, I win?" I asked. "Win what?"

"You're gonna make me say it, aren't you?" Dave paused, and kicked back another long swallow of beer. "Fine, then. I guess Danny ain't that bad after all. There you go. Happy now?"

I might have smiled at that moment, feeling a bloom of warmth radiate throughout my core. I shivered, throwing off the last of a cold night while Dave turned away and rubbed his face with his hand. And then there was more awkwardness, as time stretched out between us.

"Forget about it, Dave," I offered, absently opening one of those beers for myself.

"Nah," replied the man. I could see the strain in his face, and that he was struggling with what I presumed was a tough moment for him. "I, ah … I shouldn't have been so hard on you guys."

I kept quiet, letting his words sink in. Then, humorously, Dave added, "You were about ready to kick my ass out there." We both laughed, loosening the tension on the invisible tug of war we'd been waging ever since Danny came aboard. "I guess you should have." He sighed, glancing at his leg. "Knock some sense into my thick skull. Then maybe I wouldn't have fucked things up with that pot."

After a long gulp from my own can, I figured it was time to venture forth with the nagging question that had been lingering in my mind. "So Dave ... why were you so hard on Danny, anyways?" My thoughts were running circles around the obscurity of Dave's history, and what he and the captain had argued about a few days prior.

Dave considered my words in silence, staring at the beer in his hand for a few minutes, scratching at the label. The need to change the subject pressed down on me like a thousand-pound crab pot. "I wonder how long it'll take for the Coast Guard—"

"I had a brother like him, Ed," Dave interrupted, his eyes swimming across the blanket covering him. I noticed his hands were trembling, and then he gripped the can a little tighter and took another drink before continuing, "That's right. I had a brother just like Danny. His name was Paul. Fucking Paul. We never got along, him and I. The little bastard got all the attention, and I hated him for it. He was spoiled rotten, fucking cried every time he couldn't get his way. Cried every time he couldn't eat what he wanted, or play with his toys—or my toys. And that fucker cried every time our parents said so much as a word to me." Dave took another swallow, and then ran the back of his hand across his lips. "I hated that asshole, Ed. He got all the attention. I used to call him Downy Dick, you know. I called him lots of names, but that one was my favorite." Dave paused, shaking his head. "He'd always give me a weird look, troubled like, and then he'd reply with, 'My dick doesn't have Down syndrome. I do.' "

Dave laughed, but then he grimaced and closed his eyes. I

could see the pain from his crushed leg writhe through the wrinkles of his face. "Just take it easy," I said. "Try not to move." And then I thought about the words he had just spoken. I guess it didn't surprise me much, him having a brother like Danny. It seemed a reasonable enough explanation for his resentment.

Several minutes passed before Dave opened his eyes again. He drained his second beer, and then I opened the last one for him. "Thanks," he said, accepting it.

"You know," I said, cautiously, "I've seen kids like your brother. At school, in Danny's classes …. There were always a few rotten kids, I remember."

Dave shook his head. "That's not the point I'm trying to make, Ed." He turned, then looked me square in the eye. His jaw clamped firmly shut. "I used to beat the shit out of him, Ed." And this, this moment here, was when I did become surprised. "Every chance I got," Dave continued. "I tortured my brother. In the backyard, I would rub his face in dog shit, then make him eat it. And he would cry. And before he could go tell our parents what I did, I'd buddy up to him real quick-like. He was a stupid fuck, so it worked every time."

I closed my eyes, swallowing the lump in my throat. "I don't think I need to hear this, Dave."

"The hell you don't." Dave pierced me with his eyes. "You don't fool me, Ed. You never have."

I shook my head. "I don't know what you're talking about."

Dave paused, as if searching for the right thing to say. "We're too much alike … you and me."

I felt a cold, dull ache bleed in the bottom of my gut, and it made me shiver.

"You wanted to know my history, right?"

Avoiding his eyes, I remained silent.

In response, Dave nodded, turned away, and said, "Yeah, I thought so. So anyways … Paul Jenkins, my stupid brother with Down syndrome, was strong as a fucking bull when he put his mind to it—just like Danny. Makes a kid jealous sometimes, don't it? Jealous enough to give a little payback, eh?" I caught Dave's sidelong glance in my direction.

"I'm not sure what you're getting at, Dave," I replied.

Dave chuckled, and then said, "Yeah, I bet you aren't. Like I said, Ed, we're too much alike, you and me."

"Dude, I'm not anything like you." A surge of heat ran up and down my neck. "I don't drink and pick on people like you do. And I'm no bully, either."

"Relax, kid. Don't get your panties in a bind. I never said we're *exactly* alike." And then he gave me another suspicious, sidelong glance that just about made my blood boil. "But someday, perhaps, because here's the thing, Ed: there isn't a bully alive who isn't a fucking coward."

"So what is your point, Dave?"

He sighed, and then clenched his teeth and eyes shut, the pain ripping across his face like a strong tide. "Oh … what *is* my point?" he said, letting another minute of silence pass. A long minute, before he unloaded on me.

"I almost killed my brother, Ed. When I was seventeen. Our parents were gone for the night—Saturday night—and I had to stay home and watch the asshole. I was so mad. I played football, and we'd won our game the night before. A bunch of the guys from the team were having a party on Saturday, and there I was, at home, with Paul. Anyways, I got into my dad's liquor cabinet and just let loose. I got so hammered, I didn't care about anything anymore. I sure as hell didn't care about watching Paul. And when he started bugging me to play checkers with him, I just …. Well, I fucking snapped. I wanted to kill him so bad, Ed. But I didn't. Instead, I just beat him silly. I blew up on him with all my rage, punching and slapping, kicking. He didn't fight back, as usual, so I gave it to him good. I remember screaming at him, and cursing. I said terrible things, told him I wished he were dead. And I saw it in his eyes, all the pain and suffering I'd caused him, which only made things worse, somehow. I beat him within an inch of his life, which was pretty damn far, 'cause some of these Downy kids are fucking tough as nails. But I beat him, Ed. I almost killed him before I went outside and passed out on the porch."

My mouth went dry and my body trembled. I felt a storm of emotions. I was angry with Dave. I was disgusted. But also, I felt desperate and helpless. Surprised. Even hopeless. His words had taken hold of me. Black as the storm outside, they haunted my mind. *We're too much alike, Ed, you and me.*

He looked at me then, a river of tears running down his cheeks. Dave was crying, almost bawling. He said, "My point, Ed, is that I've never forgiven myself for what I did to my brother."

CHAPTER 26

———•———

W HAT WAS THERE to say, at that moment, when the awkwardness hung in the air between us, thick and grotesque, like a massive rusted ship run ashore?

Dave's hand shaded his eyes and then he looked out from under his fingers. "So there you go. There's my history, Ed." He guzzled the last of his beer and then slowly crushed the can. "Maybe that's the reason I'm such a fucking asshole."

I cast about in my mind for something to say. "I, ah … I'm not sure what, um …." The door to outside opened just then. The wind was whistling across the deck, echoing down the hall. I heard Danny mumble something, incoherent, gibberish, thinking out loud as he was wont to do. I heaved a sigh. "I'll go check on him," I said, rather lamely.

When I rounded the corner, I saw Danny bending over, fidgeting with the cuff around his rain boot. And beyond him I saw the deck, still half-laden with crab pots, the colors of brown and black washed white from suspended lights and shaded like ash from the fading night.

Looking at Danny, seeing him there in the hall, I felt the pang of guilt tear at the old wound. "How's it going, buddy?" I asked.

He stood erect, his hands working against themselves,

peeling off gloves. "I gotta go to the bathroom, Ed," he replied.

My laugh was nervous, thin and shallow. "Sure thing, buddy. How's Loni doing?"

Danny nodded. "Good. We're almost done now, I think." He closed the door then walked toward me, his mouth gaping, his face drained. My friend looked tired.

"You doing okay?" I asked, patting Danny on the back as he passed on his way to the head.

"Hooyah," he replied, without much conviction.

I watched my friend walk down the hall. I inhaled real deep, taking in a chest full of air. I was close to tears. Conflicting emotions were roiling in my stomach and giving my legs the shakes. Like a father, or an older brother, I felt proud. Proud of that kid, that young man, who played his dealt hand with the kind of courage few could ever hope to muster. But the guilt …. It thrashed in my core like a chained demon, awoken by Dave's history. The fucking asshole was dead on, I realized. About everything he'd said—the inner turmoil, the jealousy, and how, deep down, every bully is a coward. That's what Dave had been telling me this whole time—that he and I were too much alike. Our propensity for fear, and the pressures resulting from that emotion. And our capacity to react accordingly. Even the dreadful account of him beating the crap out of his brother … those words were like the low toll of a bell ringing from inside my gut.

It could have been the same night, the same incident, for that matter. Danny, he never understood the politics of teenagers. Impressing popular girls, fitting in with social cliques, establishing a reputation—none of these machinations were on Danny's radar, and sometimes this infuriated me. I took him to a party one night, a mistake in itself, and then he got on my case for drinking beer. Some of the other kids were smoking pot, and I wanted to try that as well, but Danny stood his ground. He became Sitting Bull, loudly told me, "No," and grabbed me by the crook of my elbow. The pain from his grip shot up my arm like forty-thousand volts. I snapped. I reacted. I punched Danny in the face. He let go of my arm and went to the floor, in a seated position, his hand pressed against his cheek. His eyes accosted me, filling me with guilt and shame. Betrayal. I could have stopped there, but I didn't—someone had laughed. I jumped on top of Danny and started banging my fists into him, punching head, ears, and nose, afflicting him worse still with profanities. He curled into a ball, after which I stood and began to kick him in the ribs. A few seconds of that and Danny gave up. He stretched out on his back, flat and catatonic, staring at the ceiling, a remorseful sinner accepting his due punishment. And that ended it. Not anything spurred within me. No sudden thickening of guilt. No brave intervention of some poor, sympathetic soul from the crowd. No, it was simply Danny. His unwavering, dog-like loyalty doused the flame of my anger.

Too much alike, Ed ... you and me.

While these memories of the past haunted me, the awareness of my surroundings within the *Angie Piper* suddenly heightened, as if my senses had grown more acute. Dark pockets of shadow, various surfaces, and previously unnoticed ordinary "things" surrounding me—all stood out as if under a spotlight. I felt gooseflesh crawl up my legs and body, releasing a shiver. I walked back to check on Dave, observing that the air in the stateroom smelled earthy and sour, and tasted like brine. And then, I heard something in the far distance, something barely audible.

"Hey," I said, as I stepped farther into the room. Eyes closed, Dave acknowledged my presence with a grunt. My ears locked onto the sound he made and followed it as it passed me, and the ship, and then beyond, into the clouded void of night and sea, where it changed.

The sound was now a distant rumble. A rumble that was active, and perhaps contriving. Working, and proceeding. A rumble that grew.

I looked at Dave, whose eyes flew open. Panic hung heavy in the air. My hands clenched into fists, I heard the captain holler something from above. Another rogue wave was on its way.

It struck the *Angie Piper* portside.

"Ahh!" someone shrieked. Dave's bunk swept up and over my head. The floor lurched out from under my feet. My body slammed into the wall and then the ceiling, and then the opposite wall, the floor, and the wall again. I heard glass explode and a low rush of sound reverberate from the wheelhouse, bringing with it a great flood of icy water. Lights flickered, the *Angie Piper* continued to roll, and my body was slammed once again into the hard steel, the jagged corners, the unforgiving features of the stateroom.

At last she settled. Capsized, swaying, the sounds of straining steel were unabating in the background. Someone hollered again. And the lights continued to flicker sporadically, ominously. I saw Dave lying in front of me, on the ceiling, his hands reaching out toward me, his mouth forming words that failed to register anything remotely intelligible within my brain. The one thing I could focus on at that moment was the twisted absurdity of our environment, the unforgiving shock, the release of sanity. And lastly, taken as whole: our seemingly inevitable death from these things that should not be.

Another flush of cold water dumped onto my head, jolting me back to reality. "Ed!" Dave shouted, his hands still reaching out. He caught hold of my jacket lapel, pulled hard, and then I reacted by crawling forward. "Ed! We gotta get out of here!" The lights dimmed. "She ain't gonna make it!" I thought I heard bilge alarms ringing, but my focus tunneled onto Dave. I blinked rapidly, concentrating, as the fierce instinct to remain alive finally prevailed.

"Okay!" I replied, frantically looking around. My thoughts were on the survival suits contained in the chest above us. "Hold on," I shouted, struggling to stand up.

"She ain't gonna make it!" Dave repeated. "She's going down, Ed ... we gotta hurry!"

I ignored him and reached for the door clasp on the chest. I got a hand on it, but then slipped, crashing down onto Dave.

"Oh!" he hollered. He reached for his broken leg, moaning, pain searing across his face. "Oh, shit!"

"Sorry, Dave!" I replied, hands stretching, hoping to comfort him in some way.

"Forget about it! Just get up there and get those suits. We don't have much time."

I struggled to find my footing, grabbed at corners and ledges that were unrecognizable. Confusion surrounded me, with this upturned version of reality. It was even difficult to think straight. I wrapped an arm around the top of the bunk, pulling myself up, at last gaining control of my balance and my perception to a passable degree. Inching my way farther up, I got a hand on the chest once more, reaching for the clasp. My fingers were numb from the cold, making surfaces feel vaguely formless. The sharp metal corner of the clasp felt like a smooth rubber ball, but I gripped it nonetheless.

The *Angie Piper* swung hard to port, but not before I yanked down. The door dropped open, raining its contents on top of us—an assortment of flashlights, gloves, batteries, matches, and survival suits.

"Get in one!" I shouted. "Get yourself in a suit, Dave!" I heard more screaming, only this time from below us, it seemed. It was hard to tell. My mind still struggled for clarity. I struggled to comprehend the state of having my whole world flipped literally upside down.

Dave fumbled for a suit, his face flinching—undoubtedly from the excruciating pain of his broken leg. I pushed aside all the gear and began to separate the suits. "Here," I said, handing him one. I made a move to help him into it.

"No, no!" He pushed me away. "Get yourself in one first. I'll be all right."

The water, killing cold, bit at my skin, and it rapidly leeched away my breath and energy. Quickly, I reached for a suit and searched for the open end.

"Hurry and get in, Ed!" Dave repeated. He knew the gravity of our situation. Not just that we were going down, but how little time we had left. "Hurry the fuck up, kid!"

As if his words were a syringe injecting fresh adrenaline into my body, I scrambled. I forgot about Dave, the upturned ship, and the cold, cold water. Eyes sharpened on orange fabric with its zippers and sleeves, and my hands moved swiftly and accurately. My training took over as I went through the motions of donning my survival suit. I heard the words of so many captains and deckhands over the years: *less than one minute!* I watched myself splay the suit open. I watched as my feet rushed in and down. I wriggled like a worm in the mud, on my back, up to my waist, pulling and yanking and tugging. Then I thrust my left hand in, my weak hand, leaving my strong hand to affix the hood and pull the main zipper. I did those last steps with seconds to spare, vaguely aware that the boat seemed listless and dead.

I looked at Dave, his suit barely on. He was struggling to get his broken leg into it, the pain writhing across his face, tormenting and dreadful, sending his body into sporadic jerks. "Oh, shit," he murmured.

"Hold on!" I shouted, rolling onto my side. "Let me help you." I shimmied along on my stomach, then got up on one knee. I looked up at Dave, stretching a hand toward him. "I'll help you get in."

But then—and for the last time—the lights went out.

"Mother of God," Dave gasped, a hopeless chill ringing in his voice.

"Here, Dave, here!" I shouted. "I'm right here!" I pulled up next to him, hands scrambling over his body. I found his busted leg and blindly tried to work it into the survival suit. He let out another heavy moan, and then a shriek.

"Forget about it, kid." He tried to push me away. "Just get out of here. Leave me. I'll catch up, don't worry."

I looked around in the darkness, my thoughts now on Danny.

Was he still in the bathroom across the hall? I screamed at the top of my lungs, "Danny! Danny, where are you? Get in a suit, buddy! Get in a suit, and get outside!" My breathing was out of control, rapid and short. My entire body shook from the cold and the ungodly fear. The obscuring blackness surrounding me was a brutal, taunting whisper from Death itself.

"Go on, Ed," Dave said.

"Fuck you, Dave. I'm not leaving you here." I remembered the glow stick attached to the front of my suit. I snapped it, releasing a flood of green light, shoving back a smidgen of darkness and fear. Looking down, I worked my hands into the pant leg of Dave's survival suit, and then squeezed, making fists, pushing against the fabric and his tortured leg. "Now get your fucking leg in there!" I shouted.

Dave grabbed me with both hands, wailing as he pushed, until finally his leg sunk into the suit. "Motherfucker!" he cried, his body jerking in pain.

"Get in!" I repeated, pulling his suit up toward his waist. The muscles in my body protested, already fatigued from moving within my own suit. "Get your ass in here, Dave, right now!"

We got Dave's suit up to his waist, the eye of Hope now shining down on us, when suddenly the *Angie Piper* rolled again. The room churned like a washing machine. Everything flopped, whirled, and crashed against the walls. "Oh shit!" I hollered. Dave howled. I saw his arms swimming in pockets of shadow and green haze from my glow stick.

"We gotta get out of here!" he repeated.

The *Angie Piper* settled once again, a lolling mass of groaning steel. Frantically, I looked around. "How's she sitting?" I hollered. I spotted the door nearby. It seemed "normal."

"She's upright!" replied Dave. "Come on! Let's move!" He started crawling toward me, his suit half on, dragging behind. I put a hand out, caught his, and pulled. Like a rat, my mind still gnawed furiously over Danny, but there was nothing I could do at the moment.

We pulled ourselves up and out of the stateroom, into the hall. The floor pitched downward to our right, a path of darkness leading to the door outside. I wondered how far the *Angie Piper* sat below the surface. Would that door open to a flood of ice water and death? To our left, the wheelhouse loomed like a mountaintop. Wet stairs climbed up into a black hollow, their surfaces slick and steep, demanding skills certainly beyond a man with a broken leg.

"How far down is she?" I asked.

"I don't know!" Dave replied. He motioned forward. "Guess we'll find out."

On bellies, hands and knees, we slithered "down" the hall. I shuddered, picturing how our beloved *Angie Piper* now sat: her bow raised high above the waves, dripping water, her keel exposed to the hideous laughter of the wind, and her stern … submerged into the freezing mouth of the Gulf of Alaska—one step closer to the grave.

"Ed!"

I swiveled around, hearing Danny's voice. He had just crawled out of the stateroom near the bathroom, survival suit on. Tears of joy welled in my eyes. *Thank the Heavens*, I thought.

"Danny! Good job, buddy!" I slapped him on the shoulder. "Come on, let's get the hell out of here!"

The three of us crawled down the hall and into the ready-room. There was a knee-high pool of water near the door leading to outside. "Let's get the rest of your suit on, Dave," I said. "Help me out, Danny." Dave's face grimaced as we finished suiting him up. And when we were done, I turned toward the door, reaching out with a hand.

"What about the captain?" Danny suddenly asked. "What about Salazar, and Loni?"

I stared at my friend. "We don't have enough time, Danny. The boat is sinking." I looked back toward the wheelhouse, thinking about Fred, and Salazar, and the probability of rescuing them. "Captain!" I shouted. "Can you hear me? Captain! Salazar!" And then I thought of Loni—standing out on deck when the wave hit. I dropped my head, the cold sting of reality running a dagger straight through my heart.

"We gotta save them," Danny said.

Dave dropped to the floor, moaning and exhausted. As if echoing in response, the *Angie Piper* let out a deep groan— the strain of steel—followed by a metallic crack so loud, it resonated throughout my body. "No, Danny!" I replied. "We gotta get the fuck out of here!"

"But the captain," he responded, seemingly unperturbed, "and Salazar." Danny turned and looked toward the stairs, then back at me. "Never leave a man behind, Ed," he said. "The SEALs never leave a man behind."

"Christ, Danny!" I hollered. "We're not fucking SEALs! We're just men. And we're gonna be dead men if we don't get off this boat. Now come on!"

Danny ignored me and turned again toward the wheelhouse. He stood and began stumbling back up the hall. My eyes focused on the bull's-eye on his back, the one he had taped onto his survival suit that first day onboard. "You goddamn Sitting Bull," I muttered, shaking my head. "Fine then. I'll be right back, Danny. I'm gonna get Dave out first!" I grabbed Dave by the arm and pulled him up. "Come on, let's go," I said.

With Dave behind me, I braced myself for what waited beyond, and then I opened the door. I flinched, expecting a rush of icy water. But we were greeted by only a cold blast of wind.

Stepping out onto the deck, I hesitated, unsure of what to do. The *Angie Piper*'s stern sat low in the water, but not as deep as I had expected. Beyond her rails, the sky was a slate of midnight blue, infused with veins of orange fire. It seemed that the black night was slowly giving way to the grip of dawn.

Dave slumped to the deck, his back against the superstructure, eyes closed. His face looked sallow and withered.

"Dave," I shouted, shaking his shoulder, "you wait here, okay? I'm gonna go and help Danny!" He nodded in reply, and I turned to go back inside, but then I heard a sudden roar of thunder coming from beyond the starboard rail.

There was no time to react. Out of the darkness, a massive wave punched the deck. It swept me clean over the rail, and far, far away from the *Angie Piper*.

CHAPTER 27

———•———

THE RAGE OF black foam and black water tumbled me off the boat and beyond. It pulled me down below the surface. Fingers of ice greedily plunged through the seams of my suit and onto my skin. It was the coldest I'd ever been in my life. I gagged as bands of saltwater rushed into my mouth. I flailed, arms swinging madly to gain stability, to swim through the maelstrom. I choked and retched and rolled aimlessly through a bitter draft of mind-numbing cold. Not a damn thing was in my control. I was a helpless rag in the sea.

When the wave finally released me, I lay face up on the great belly of the ocean, eyes to the sky. Thin trails of dawn spread across the heavens, but the darkness of night still reigned. Where was the *Angie Piper*? I struggled, paddling through the water, rousing myself to look around. My lips were numb, my breathing short and tight, and my eyes stung. Where was she?

A passing swell lifted me high, and then I spotted her shadowed bow roughly thirty yards away. I swam toward her, fighting against the current and waves. Eventually I rolled over and attempted the backstroke, which I had heard to be the more practical approach to swimming while in a survival suit. My shoulders burned, and my breathing raced, but the *Angie*

Piper never seemed to grow any larger. It seemed I wasn't getting any closer.

"Danny!" I shouted into the night. I looked around for Loni, hoping that he might be floating near me. The chances were dismal, knowing that he had taken that colossal wave sometime before. With only raingear on, he couldn't have survived long.

I cut through the water frantically, stroke after desperate stroke, fighting with all my heart to get back to the boat. There was an inflatable life raft mounted on the fo'c'sle. It should still be accessible, if I could only get there. The current was strong, but it wasn't running completely against the direction I needed to swim. Yet the water was choppy. Six-foot swells undulated from every direction, as if the sea couldn't make up her mind where she wanted to go. I threw every ounce of energy in the direction of the *Angie Piper*, my thoughts focused on that life raft. And I thought about Danny, and the surviving crew— whoever they might be. I threw every muscle into getting back on that boat, and I felt those muscles burn, warming my body. Seeing that I was finally getting closer, I felt a bloom of hope grow inside my gut.

"Danny!" I shouted again, battering the waves with my hands. "Anyone! Over here!"

I judged that with enough time, I could make it back before she went down, and then I'd inflate that raft. I'd get Danny, Fred, and Salazar, and pile everyone in, safe and secure. And with a slice of astounding luck, perhaps I'd even find Loni, floating somewhere nearby, his fingers gripping tight onto the final thread of his life ….

My hand thudded against a solid object. I heard a low moan, grabbed, and pulled. It was a body in a survival suit.

"Dave!" I cried out, recognizing him. I pulled him closer. He was limp, offering no resistance, lying on his back and barely conscious. "Dave!" I shouted again, believing that the man might have thought he was on his way out and was now simply letting death take over.

He gave another moan. I saw the features of his face under the green haze of my glow stick. Everything about him looked so heavy. Every wrinkle and pock-ridden inch of his skin seemed grossly cumbersome, pressed together from the hood of his suit. His whole face was swollen, with blood racing to fight off the bitter cold. His eyelids were sandbags, and he raised them in an apparent struggle to come back to life.

"Come on, Dave, wake up!" I looked at the *Angie Piper*, still believing I could reach her. Somehow, I'd have to pull Dave along. "Wake up, already!"

Dave moaned again and began to move his arms. Lightly, I smacked him on the cheek. Then I grabbed his face and directed his gaze toward me. "Dave! Look at me! We gotta get the raft!" He groaned and blinked. "We gotta swim, Dave. You gotta wake up and help me!"

Our suits kept us buoyant, but the waves were a persistent nuisance. We rode a high swell that rolled over our heads, sloshing water across our faces, and then Dave choked. I gripped him tight as he rasped, his body coiling forward with each hack. When he was finished, he flung his eyes open, swinging his head left to right.

"What the hell happened?" he said. He worked his arms to raise his body, and then looked around. "Where's the boat?"

I felt a surge of relief. "We got washed off! But she's over there," I said, pointing. "We might be able to get the raft!"

Dave turned to face me, the small ember glowing in his eyes almost extinguished by misery. He shivered. "I can't feel my legs, Ed. It's fucking cold …. I'm cold." Then he looked back toward the boat. "Come on," he said, giving the most sluggish, debilitated attempt at a swim. "Let's do it."

Again, I threw everything I had into reaching the *Angie Piper*. My arms were heavy, like solid lengths of iron. I cut water with my legs, scissoring through what felt like an ocean of molasses.

"Grab my leg," I shouted. "I'll pull you." Dave's hand clamped down on the fabric of my suit, at the ankle. He went limp again, heaving and coughing. I heard his breathing over my own. "Hang on, Dave!" I cried, swimming toward the *Angie Piper*. It seemed the boat had shrunk a little. Not that she was farther out, but that there was less of her riding above the waves. Through the dim shadows, I noticed the wave line splashing up against the superstructure, and the door to the inside. My chest stung and my gut hurt.

Exhaustion mounted with each passing minute. We had made little gain against the sea, but I told myself to keep going, to forget the cold and the pain, and to just get back to her. Get back to the boat, before it was too late. My thoughts simmered on Danny and the life raft. It was still possible, I reasoned. Perhaps Danny would be the one to retrieve the raft, and he would be waiting for us when we finally got there.

Dave started coughing again. I felt his hand slip away from my ankle. I stopped swimming and turned toward him. He was flailing, trying to keep his head above the water, retching and groaning. His face was contorted with distress. I grabbed his arms and steadied him, hoping to ease the panic I'd seen flickering in his eyes. He let out a sickening hurl, deep and long, a real gut-buster, followed by a raspy suck of air.

"I can't do it, Ed," he moaned. "Just go on without me."

"No, Dave," I replied. "Come on! Don't give up!"

"Forget it kid." He rolled onto his back. "I, ah ... I ain't gonna make it."

"Yes you are, dammit!" I looked at the *Angie Piper*, getting smaller by the minute. But the reality that made me cringe at that moment was Dave. I grabbed him from under his arm and started to swim a sidestroke, pulling him with me. "I'm not letting you give up," I said. His body went slack, but I kept dragging him through the sea. I swam for our *Angie Piper*, knowing this was our last chance. I pulled and kicked feverishly, my arms and legs aching with a hot pain. I cramped up, felt a sharp snap down my ribcage. Dave's breathing quickened and he began to cough again, but I kept swimming, not once letting up, and slowly the gap to the *Angie Piper* grew smaller.

But then a wave hit us from the side. A white-capped roller sent us tumbling through the sea, and once again we were pushed away from the boat. The distance I'd gained had been lost, with yards to spare. I recovered from the wave, heard Dave coughing just a few feet away, and saw the *Angie Piper.* Her end was near. I reached out and grabbed Dave. I pulled him closer, knowing there was no way I could make it to the boat with him. I'd have to leave him behind.

He turned and looked me in the eye. "Get the raft, Ed. Go on. Go get it." Then he nudged his head toward the boat, coughed some more, and passed out.

The sudden need to make a decision came over me. I thought about my situation, thought real hard. I wanted to leave Dave, leave him and his cruelty behind. I wanted to bail out and swim back to the boat, which now looked so far away. I wanted so bad to swim back and find Danny, my friend. He was there somewhere, maybe still looking for the crew and trying to rescue them. But the *Angie Piper* was pulling farther away from me, pulling down. The sight of her sinking into the black ocean evoked fear and panic. Our beloved *Angie Piper* was heading for the bottom, possibly with Danny inside, and certainly with the captain and Salazar, and there was nothing I could do about it. At that moment, it seemed as if the darkness of the night, in its entirety, had just laid a finger onto my head and pushed me down.

Maybe, at that moment, I was just too tired to keep going. Maybe I was ready to give up. It was so damn cold. Every inch of my body ached with a dull pain that did nothing but incite misery and sap the life out of me. *So this is how it's gonna end,* I thought to myself.

I looked around, determined to take in the last of this world. The *Angie Piper* was a black dagger buried in the belly of the great ocean, her bow now raised straight and high. Trails of dawn continued to streak the sky above, like red fire blazing a warm path across the night. But my lips were cold and numb. My breathing was thin and fading fast. My eyes were stinging at the sight of that golem of steel, as she methodically drove herself into a sea that would willingly swallow her whole. Sadly, I knew that there would be nothing to show for all the effort put forth on this day. No scar left behind, announcing to the world that for one small measure of time, something, or someone, had put up a fight.

I closed my eyes and lowered my head, and Dave and I rode the waves like a fat, orange bobber. I felt horribly sorry for myself. My mind, now certain that the end was near, toured the burdens I'd slung over my shoulder for those short years of my life—the regrets I'd kept, the pain I'd stowed away. The burden that one man, presently in my arms and almost dead, had so cleverly observed weighing me down like an anchor. Our familiar burden.

"What have I done?" I whispered into the night, my voice lost against the heavy wind and the roaring waves. Once again, I'd let Danny down, and now he was left to struggle on his own. This was not what I had promised him or myself. As if in response to my whisper, Dave let out a moan, but then he went silent again. He was slipping in and out of consciousness. I gripped his survival suit and looked at the sea. Nothing would be left behind, not even me. Soon, it would only be the wind and the water. The *Angie Piper* was a thin black nail now. Thirty feet of bow brooding over the brim of a vanishing wheelhouse, she was on her last breath of air. I couldn't take my eyes off her. I would not. I had decided that as one of the last remaining crewmembers, I was duty-bound to catch that final glimpse of our vessel before she went down forever.

But then I gasped. A shadow climbed above the window of the wheelhouse from the darkness below. An orange body, someone in a survival suit, lifting up and out of the sinking vessel. The body turned—its back now facing me—and I caught sight of a distinctive outline traced with reflective yellow tape.

The bull's-eye.

CHAPTER 28

———•———

I SHOUTED AT the top of my lungs, "Danny! I'm over here!" I waved frantically. "Come on, buddy! Over here!"

My heart suddenly burned with a livid pain. I realized that this was my one and final chance. I had never told my friend how I felt about him—that I'd felt so damn sorry for the guy when he cried. That I felt terrible for never sticking up for him back in high school.

Yet there he was now ….

"Danny!"

I had never told him how I thought he was the funniest man alive, or that his work ethic inspired everyone around him. And Danny had never heard my apology for that terrible night back in high school. I just let it go, buried it deep under a thick blanket of lies. Danny had never said a word about that night. Then years had passed, and that night was filed away like an indelible chapter in the book of life.

"I'm over here, buddy!"

I panicked. Danny jumped into the water and began to swim away from me. The wind, the waves, and the numbing cold made for an impenetrable shell of distance. There went my friend, Danny Wilson, headstrong, right into them.

Dave stirred, coughed. I was suddenly reminded of how he

had never forgiven himself for his wrongful actions toward his brother—how they had wrecked his life and ultimately tore a hole in him so big that not even love could fill it up.

"No, Danny! No! No! Come back, Danny!"

I choked on a mouthful of sea water and fell still. Danny couldn't hear me above the raging of the sea. He would have certainly turned back if he had. Instead, he just swam into the appalling black horizon with a dumb courage that even your best Navy SEAL could only pray to possess, while I floated there and thought about myself. I floated in my cold saltwater grave and watched Danny Wilson head off alone to battle the forces of the greatest bully of all: Mother Nature.

Then I wondered, just why am I staying here? Why aren't I following my friend? We were doomed men, all of us. On my own, I might catch up to Danny. I could tell him I was sorry, and then we'd perish together.

My eyes fell on Dave: the irony of the situation. Him, me, our differences … and similarities. I was riding the passing swells of ice-cold water while clinging to a man who throughout his life seemed to be just as cold and bitter. A man who'd allowed his tragic past to dictate his actions. A man who'd passed his judgment on to others through pints of liquor and gallons of abuse. *So this really was how it would end. The coldest I'd ever been in my life.*

Still, hope lingered inside me, like the frayed corner of a distant dream, insisting it wasn't too late. Something about the type of man I wanted to become in this life, never mind how short that life might be.

I pulled Dave closer to me. "I can't leave you."

"No," he said, suddenly awake and conscious. "Leave me."

Tears welling in my eyes, I shook my head. "Not leaving a man behind."

"Bullshit! Go get that raft, Ed." Dave pushed at me, but he was too weak to break my grip. I saw him glance past my shoulder, toward the boat, and then his face went thin and flaccid. His eyelids became sandbags once again. He knew we were too late.

"I'm gonna die," he whispered.

"And I'm not letting you die alone."

Several seconds passed, and then Dave said, still sarcastic despite his loss of hope, "Never leave a man behind, eh?"

"You're damn right," I replied.

"Shit, Ed." Dave's hand squeezed my wrist. "I've never been a man. Never in all my life."

"It doesn't matter, Dave." That's not the answer I wanted to give him. It wasn't what I meant to say. I wanted to tell him that we were all men—him, me, the whole lot of us, even Danny. Especially Danny. We were all men, and that's how we were going to die.

I felt Dave's grip loosen, and his eyes suddenly wrenched open. He looked up into the sky. "It's kind of funny, Ed. I'm not so cold anymore." He turned his head toward me. "How 'bout that?" he said, with a laugh. "All the fucking cold is gone."

"Yeah, it sure is, isn't it?"

Dave's smile melted, and he gripped my wrist once again. "Promise me something, kid," he said. "If you survive this shit, promise me you'll come out different." His jaws chattered violently, and he began to slur his words. "Don't end up like me."

I nodded solemnly. I knew what he meant.

"Promise me, Ed."

Shamefully, I nodded again. Then I dropped my head. I didn't say a word, not until it was too late. I felt Dave's grip go loose for the last time. I lifted my head and looked upon the man. His eyelids were wide open, sandbags no more, a stare firing up into the heavens. His lips were parted, his body was cold and limp, and nothing about him seemed heavy anymore.

"I promise!" I shouted, in case he could hear me somehow.

Then it was like the closing of eternity. Danny was gone— he had disappeared somewhere beyond the shadows and the waves. The *Angie Piper* was submerged at last, slipping forever below this world. I lowered my head for the last time, ready to die. Cataleptic darkness swept in and took me away, yet not before I said in a final whisper …

"Please forgive me, Danny."

CHAPTER 29

————◆————

CAPTAIN FRED MOONEY saved my life. Not long after he activated the *Angie Piper*'s EPIRB, the Coast Guard base in Kodiak sent out their search and rescue team. I felt as much as heard the rhythmic *whop-whop-whop* of rotor blades over my head when they found me. I remember looking up and seeing a helicopter hovering under a purple sky, its lights shining bright like bug eyes. Then the rescue swimmer jumped out, splashing into the water not twenty feet away from me.

I was in a state of numbing fear, delirious from my ordeal and barely conscious when Petty Officer First Class Les Sherman swam over to me.

"You gotta let go!" the man cried, attempting to pry my hands off Dave's body. My grip was the only thing I had left. In my delirium I was not letting go of Dave. "Let go, already!" he kept shouting, his words mixed with the sounds from the helicopter and the choppy water. Then I passed out.

There was nothing after that. I was lifted out of the water by the rescue litter, then sent back to Kodiak Medical Center via helicopter—none of which I recall. I only remember waking up in a soft bed, confused yet indescribably grateful for the warmth that surrounded me. The lights of my hospital room shone with a dull, almost polite brightness. The smells of clean sheets and bleach, and a sterile, medicinal odor lingered in the air. There was a muted television sitting high in one corner of the room, and on the table below, a vase of flowers. It all seemed surreal.

For those first several minutes of consciousness, I kept still, savoring the heavenly touch of cotton and wool against my face. I wiggled all my fingers and toes, thankful that I still had them. I mentally surveyed the many cuts and bruises spread across my body, then took several deep breaths of air. Each exhale carried a long sigh of relief, liberating me from residual tension. I embraced the warmth, and I relished the absence of that bone-chilling cold. For those first several minutes, I did nothing but "catch my breath," so to speak.

A shuffling sound passed the door to my room and I caught a glimpse of a janitor pushing a cart down the hall. He looked like Danny, and I was immediately reminded of my friend, the *Angie Piper*, the nightmare, everything. Half a ton of concrete collapsed onto my chest just then, bringing with it too damn much to think about.

I imagined a possible headline for the Kodiak newspaper: JAMES EDWARD THURMAN: SOLE SURVIVOR. The thought was damning, despite all that I'd been through.

And, like other sole survivors, I faced the painful guilt that came with the situation. I felt guilty for being the only crewmember to survive the sinking of the *Angie Piper*. I felt guilty for coaxing my best friend into taking a job that would eventually kill him. The guilt just went on and on.

Continuing with this newspaper theme in my imagination, I went through the obituaries. Danny was certainly the first one who came to mind, but I pushed him out of my thoughts briefly. I guess I wanted to save him for last.

I saw Fred's face on the day he first welcomed me aboard the *Angie Piper*: a jovial smile preceding a strong handshake. He called me "son" and gave me the tour, and gradually I learned that I could have taken everything about that man at face value. There was nothing complicated about Fred Mooney—that's why he was such a damn good captain. Our last supper—duck breast, pasta and lamb, red velvet cake—would make his brother proud. I made a silent vow to track that man down and tell him about our feast.

Perhaps Salazar's cat, Georgina, could be permanently adopted by the woman who had been caring for it. I would try to arrange that somehow when I let her know. If she asked for details, I'd simply tell her the truth: Salazar went down with the ship.

The cold lingered with me in that hospital room. I shivered when my mind suddenly flooded with several dozen images of Loni's trademark smile.

What a man that Poly was. A bright man, in every sense of the word. A man who, although small for a Samoan, was as big in heart and strong in soul as all seventy of his cousins. An exaggeration, I supposed, but I knew there would easily be four times that many people at Loni's funeral. His heart and soul were all that would represent my fellow crewmember on that day. In the end, Loni's body would never be found. Nor Fred's, nor Salazar's.

I thought about Dave. They had his body, and I felt grateful for that much. The fairness of this particular outcome never weighed heavily on my mind. I was beyond stewing over the fact that better men should have been spared such bleak fates as becoming "lost at sea." Dave wasn't the worst of men. I like to think that he did the best he could with his life, given his circumstances. But more importantly, he was one of us. They had his body, so there would be closure for his family. When I saw those people, I would tell them how much of a hero Dave had been.

Danny Wilson. I turned over on my side and began to cry, not able to stop, not even trying; I just let it all out. I couldn't get that last image of him out of my mind—alone, swimming into the dark horizon, swimming toward the abyss. I wondered if Danny had been afraid, and if he had felt miserable and burdened with despair, the same as me. It was my hope that he hadn't—that the salvation from wretchedness could be found somewhere in his simple mind, and that Danny suffered little before he succumbed to the will of the sea. Better yet, perhaps he imagined himself in the midst of a SEAL mission, loaded down with gear, leading the way, his teammates trailing behind him. He would've liked that, I'm sure—a dream come true. My friend—he was worthy of that esteemed title, and he'd been proving it to me his whole life. All the way up until the end, Danny was the man I needed to be.

What would I tell Danny's father? He'd arrive at the hospital soon enough, along with my own family and other families. There would be a mess of tears, an unlimited number of questions.

The notion of explaining my ordeal to others got me thinking real hard, pushing a few hours fast ahead. I thought about myself, of life, and of my eternal quest. I wanted so badly to own the title of someone who would never hesitate to do exactly the right thing, at exactly the right moment. Looking back on my recent tribulation, a part of me doubted myself. There were too many what-ifs, should-haves, and could-haves plaguing my thoughts. It became painful to think about "the man in me."

Dave certainly had me pegged. Knew my face in perfect detail, as if looking straight into a mirror. He knew what kind of man I was. But also, he knew what kind of man I could become. In Dave's final words, I had heard a note of optimism: *don't end up like me.* There was hope. And since I was still alive, I had a promise to keep, the one I'd made to Dave.

A vague sliver of relief crept out of me by way of a deep sigh. Had Danny been lying at my side just then, I think he would have been proud. I never left Dave behind, so there was hope for me yet.

Then I remembered Dave's words about never forgiving

himself over what he had done to his brother, and once again my heart was filled with despair. It was too late to apologize to Danny. And the very notion of this "lateness" summoned a terrible regret, deep inside my gut. As for forgiving myself—well, I wasn't so sure how a person went about doing that.

I closed my eyes and rolled back over, exhausted, mentally spent, physically beaten. I fell asleep for a few hours, eventually waking to a nurse checking in on me. She told me that I had a few "eager" visitors, and she asked if I was up for company. I nodded, then closed my eyes once again, my mind racing. Only this time, I began to consider something much deeper than the slippery surface of defining my character.

I thought about the life a person gets in this world—never a significant amount of time, no matter how long we live. Remorseless, this life sweeps by like a southern updraft, stirring nothing more than a few whitecaps on the boundless sea of the Universe.

Swallowing hard, I heaved a deep sigh.

Then I cocked my head up at the white ceiling panels of my room. It suddenly occurred to me: how much time does a person need, after all? How many years does it take to be a rare human being, to observe Life as the single most challenge yet, and to tackle its obstacles with insurmountable courage? How long until a person learns to accept and then reject the notion that we all have our own form of disability? I wondered: how much time does it take to be like my friend, Danny Wilson?

I left it at that. I wasn't ready to die anymore. I was ready to live. I was ready to laugh, and to cry, and to tell my story. And maybe one day I'd be able to forgive myself.

CHAPTER 30

———•———

THE NEXT DAY they found Danny. I was still at the Kodiak Medical Center when Les Sherman walked in to give me the news. There had been a stir of voices down the hall minutes before. I was surrounded by my family as well as Danny's, and we all looked at one another, curious. Then, as Les entered the room and I saw his face, my heart sank into my chest.

He told me where they'd found my friend—on the eastern point of Sitkalidak Island. I remember looking away from Les just then, staring into the folds and creases of the sheets I lay under, thinking about how Danny must have looked when they found him. And also worrying if Danny had been overcome by terror while in the grip of what must have been the coldest and loneliest of all deaths.

Les's voice trailed off into the background. I barely heard him when he told me that they didn't find Danny on the beach, tangled up in seaweed. Nor did they find him facedown, snagged between a few rocks with that yellow bull's-eye beaming skyward.

"Our helicopter came around a rocky outcrop," Les began, "and that's when I saw the orange spot on the shoreline. I knew it was a survival suit." I gulped, as Les continued with the news. "I was pretty tired. We'd been searching all night. But as we got closer, I realized that no, I wasn't hallucinating after all." Les' face suddenly broke into a wide grin.

"What the hell are you saying?" I asked.

"I'm saying that when we flew down on that island, our pilot froze with shock and almost crashed our ride. Danny Wilson was doing jumping jacks on the goddamned beach!"

Danny had been found, all right, and he was very much alive. He slept for twenty-four hours after they picked him up, but later the next day, he and I were reunited amid a crowd of reporters, our families, a bunch of nameless fishermen, and just about the entire population of Kodiak Island. It was one of the greatest moments of my life.

They tried to push me over to Danny's room in a wheelchair, but I refused. I wanted to walk. I turned a corner then saw my friend down the hall, walking toward me as well, surrounded by people. He was wrapped in a blanket and looked ragged as hell—until we made eye contact. Then Danny's entire face beamed with life, and we ran to each other.

I ran to Danny, knowing that I would get another chance to tell him everything he deserved to hear. I ran to him, feeling pure and whole in my own mind, knowing that I would never again leave him alone to endure the brunt of some bully, or to battle Mother Nature. I ran to my brother, Danny Wilson, happy to be a man, ready to ask him for the forgiveness that I should have begged for years ago.

Our bodies crashed together into a huge hug of sobs and laughter.

"You made it, buddy!" I said, crying with astounding relief. "You made it!"

From under our embrace, and amongst his own stream of joyful tears, Danny shouted in return, "Hooyah, master chief!"

Epilogue

---•---

IN THE WINTER of 1980, crab fisherman Rick Laws survived the longest stretch of time adrift in the Gulf of Alaska, wearing nothing but a survival suit. He rode the waves for twenty-seven hours before a fishing vessel picked him up—at which point, Rick was barely clinging to life.

Danny Wilson missed Laws' record by an estimated thirty-eight minutes. Although no one is certain exactly how long Danny was in the water, including Danny himself, a study taken by a team of scientists pinpointed the time to twenty-six hours and twenty-two minutes.

The measured data began with the approximate time Danny had jumped into the water, as taken from my account of the subsequent events that occurred after Fred had set off the EPIRB, and it ended with the time Danny had staggered ashore, based on his best estimate as to how long he was there before his rescue—he told them how many jumping jacks he'd performed.

The *Angie Piper* sank roughly seven miles east of Sitkalidak Island. Prevailing winds, currents, and the tide were factored in as well—Danny's body mass and buoyancy were provided from the survival suit. The missing link, of course, was Danny himself. Or more accurately, his will to survive. This unknown factor was mathematically represented by the letter X, and when matched against the combined data, it ultimately accounted for six hours of time—the time he made up with his swimming.

Regardless of how long Danny was in the water, he became an overnight superstar. It's not every day that a person swims to shore from a sinking vessel in the Gulf of Alaska, and in the dead of winter—let alone a person with Down syndrome. The press loved it, and they ate Danny up. Like the tide, he was swept off Alaska's shoreline to tour across the Lower 48. Bedazzled with glitter and flashing lights, my friend made the cover of several magazines before he finally realized the significance of his miraculous feat.

Danny rarely went on about his achievement, though. Or his sudden stardom. And that's because what mattered most to him, since the day of his rescue, was the day his dream had come true.

Four and half months after Danny staggered onto the shores of Sitkalidak Island, he stood at attention on another island. On a weathered blacktop in Coronado, California, Danny was surrounded by people once again—the media, family, friends, and military personnel. As the embodiment of courage— lauded as having an unmatched, tenacious will to never surrender—Danny Wilson was made an honorary Navy SEAL.

When they pinned that SEAL Trident onto his chest, Danny never even smiled. I think he was so overcome with pride that it was all he could do to stand there and hold it together. Quite frankly, it might have been the toughest day of his life.

That was the moment when things changed for me, seeing Danny there on that blacktop, representing to the whole world the purest form of honor, as crafted from triumphant glory and staggering fear. Ironic as it seems, I discovered on that day a much deeper bond to my friend. Before, Danny had already been a superhero in my mind. A creature in the wrestling booth who sipped soda and chewed peanuts while he tore men down. A kid who shrugged bullies off his back like they were nothing but mild chills. A man who conquered the sea. To my greatest surprise, I realized that Danny was nothing like how I'd pictured him. Now ... well, he was just like me—a simple human being.

In time, something about this newfound perspective changed my attitude about people, and I suppose about life. Eventually I saw Danny not only as a person capable of accomplishing his dreams, but more importantly, as a man capable of taking care of himself. And capable of fear. I finally observed the human qualities that we shared, and because of this, I developed the deepest respect for my friend. Seeing the full weight of his character, there on that blacktop, with its strengths and weaknesses ... I guess it helped validate my own self-worth.

As for now, many years later—well, I no longer worry about some of the things I used to. My thoughts are almost never interrupted from all the shit I think about day to day. Such is the good life of being a captain of my own fishing vessel. I still live in Alaska, though, and she's more of a bitch than she ever was—but she's a beautiful bitch. When I fish for king crab in the Bering Sea, I never take for granted the serenity cast in her silver horizon. It is an endless yawn that pulls at the bow of my ship as well as my heart, and it acts as the leader to my soul. When I haul opilio crab near the Aleutian Islands, I often catch myself staring at a distant, snow-capped volcano—just one massive link in a rising chain of land. And every time I run gear in the Gulf of Alaska, there's a certain route I take on my way back to Kodiak. A certain island I pass, and a certain spot a few miles away where my crew and I pay our respects to our fallen brothers—and where I hold myself accountable for a promise I made long ago.

I run a crew of six hardworking deckhands, most of them permanent members. There's the occasional drifter, yet most of my guys know a good job when they see it. But I will never have an opening for a greenhorn, as my bait-boy is the best damn worker Alaska has ever laid claim to. He wears a ball cap embroidered with the SEAL logo, and he sets the pace down on deck like nobody's business. His name is Danny Wilson, and he's a brother who will always have a place at my side.

My home is a one-hundred-and-thirty-foot twin-screw commercial crabbing vessel. The wheelhouse is located at the stern, so I have a good view of my crew when we're hauling gear. During the off season, I occasionally tender for salmon runs, but most of the time I hole up in Kodiak to catch my breath. Standing outside McCrawley's, that's where a person is likely to spot my vessel, my home, moored in the harbor. She's the blue-on-black beauty, rightfully named the *Master Chief*.

CHRIS RILEY LIVES near Sacramento, California, vowing one day to move back to the Pacific Northwest. In the meantime, he teaches special education, writes awesome stories, and hides from the blasting heat for six months out of the year. He has had dozens of short stories published in various magazines and anthologies, and across various genres. *The Sinking of the Angie Piper* is his first novel.

For more information, go to www.chrisrileyauthor.com.

From Coffeetown Press and Chris Riley

THANK YOU FOR reading *The Sinking of the Angie Piper*. We are so grateful for you, our readers. If you enjoyed this book, here are some steps you can take that could help contribute to its success:

- Post a review on Amazon, BN.com, GoodReads, bookstore websites, and/or library websites.
- Check out Chris' website or blog and send a comment or ask to be put on his mailing list.
- Spread the word on social media, especially Facebook, Twitter, and Pinterest.
- Like Chris' Facebook author page and our publisher page.
- Follow Chris and Coffeetown Press on Twitter.
- Ask for this book at your local library or request it on their online portal.

Good books and authors from small presses are often overlooked. Your comments and reviews can make an enormous difference.

Questions for Book Clubs

1. How do the characters, both major and minor, reinforce Ed's misconceptions as to the measurement of a person's strength? How does perception of strength, both physical and psychological, color men's attitudes toward their friends and colleagues? Can you think of examples in this story or in your own life?

2. Does Ed ever live up to his own self-expectations? If so, when does this happen? And how?

3. How are the bonds of humanity and love expressed throughout the story?

4. How does a situation such as the one these men find themselves in bring out the best and worst in people and these men in particular?

5. What does the *Angie Piper* symbolize with regard to Ed's character? What does the fishing vessel's fate represent?

6. How does the author foreshadow Danny's final battle with Mother Nature?

7. How do Dave and Danny each represent Ed's greatest fear and his greatest ambition?

8. "Forgiveness" is a major theme in the story. How does Ed, or anyone, go about forgiving themselves? Do you think Ed ever forgives himself for what he's done to Danny?

9. Alaska is renowned for being both destructive and beautiful. Do you think the author convincingly depicted these elements?

10. *The Sinking of the Angie Piper* is a tale about persistence, forgiveness, and compassion. What lessons does it offer us in our own lives?

CPSIA information can be obtained
at www.ICGtesting.com
Printed in the USA
FSOW01n2134200517
34296FS

9 781603 813891